"This is Mega-Metals... PLANT 2 at once. F... will result in serious...

Lando keyed his m... 'serious consequences' might those be? What will you do? Nudge me to death with a tug? Give it a rest, Orbital Control. I'll get back to you in ten or fifteen minutes."

There was a squawk of outrage, but Lando keyed the comset off. Angel loomed large below. A luminous ball surrounded by a skirt of silver. The view was spectacular, but Lando had little time to enjoy it.

The smuggler's fingers fairly flew over the keyboard as he gave the NAVCOMP control of the ship, pulled the data cube out of his pocket, and dropped it into a player.

"What are you doing?" Wendy demanded angrily. "Land this ship immediately!"

"In a few minutes," Lando answered grimly. "After we buy ourselves some insurance."

DRIFTER

WILLIAM C. DIETZ

ACE BOOKS, NEW YORK

This book is an Ace original edition,
and has never been previously published.

DRIFTER

An Ace Book / published by arrangement with
the author

PRINTING HISTORY
Ace edition / September 1991

ISBN: 0-441-16813-2

Ace Books are published by The Berkley Publishing Group,
200 Madison Avenue, New York, New York 10016.
The name "ACE" and "A" logo
are trademarks belonging to Charter Communications, Inc.

PRINTED IN THE UNITED STATES OF AMERICA

10 9 8 7 6 5 4 3 2 1

For my dearest Marjorie. Thanks
for the adventure, the companionship,
and the laughs. Remember, we'll know
it when we see it.

I would like to thank Dr. Sheridan Simon for his design of the planet Angel, for his unending patience, and for his good-humored advice. The "good science" is his, and the "bad science" (if any) belongs entirely to me.

1

Pik Lando felt *The Tink's* landing jacks touch duracrete and cut power to the ship's repellors. The freighter groaned loudly and slumped to port. The control compartment tilted with her.

Lando touched a switch and a green indicator light came on. Good. Number 3 lubricant began to drip from a special tank located under the port wing. As each drop hit the repellor-warmed landing pad it hissed for a moment and turned to steam.

Any maintenance tech in the empire would take one look, shake his or her head, and proclaim sadly, "Sorry, Captain, but your port-side landing jack hydraulics are shot. This is gonna cost you but good."

Lando grinned. Of course it wouldn't cost him "but good," since there was nothing wrong with the ship's landing gear, or any other part of the vessel for that matter.

The truth was that in spite of all appearances to the contrary *The Tinker's Damn* was in excellent shape. The ship's frame and skin had been welded together thirty years before Lando was born, but her electronics, life support, and weapons systems were only five years old. And her drives, well, they were practically new, and capable of pushing *The Tink* through space faster than anything short of a speedster.

"Speed," his father liked to say, "is a smuggler's best friend. You can forget all the fancy weapons systems and leather upholstery. It's speed that'll save your ass every time."

Lando knew it was true, as were most of the things his father had told him, which explained why *The Tink* looked like salvage but really wasn't.

With speed born of long practice Lando's fingers danced across the control board, shutting most of the systems down, and placing the rest on standby.

It was night outside. All four of his external vid screens showed Lando different angles of the same thing. The dark, partially lit shapes of other ships, a scattering of greenish float lights, and beyond them the low, blocky shape of HiHo's main terminal building. Most of the control center was sensibly underground, safely removed from the possibility of a drive explosion or similar accident.

Or as his father liked to say, "If bureaucrats value anything, it's what they sit on."

There was a soft chime from the ship's comset. A female voice flooded the cabin. "Ground control to newly arrived vessel FTC six-niner-two. Welcome to HiHo. Please stand by for a customs inspection."

Lando swore softly under his breath. Why so efficient? He'd hoped for some additional time.

Lando touched a key on the deceptively grimy control board. "Ground control, this is FTC six-niner-two. That's a roger . . . am standing by."

Lando's leathers creaked slightly as he stood and looked around. He compensated for the tilt through force of habit. The control compartment was a total mess. Empty coffee bulbs sat here and there, almost invisible under piles of old cargo manifests, and stray items of clothing. Lando was playing a role, the part of a surly, somewhat eccentric one-man freighter crew, and everything must support that image.

"You can't just *play* at it," his father had told him over the years, "you've got to *be* it."

An empty meal pak crunched under Lando's boot as he turned and made his way out of the cockpit. A light came on as he stepped into the tiny head.

Like everything else aboard *The Tinker's Damn*, the mirror was filthy. Lando's face rippled when he moved. The three-day growth of beard and the bloodshot eyes made him seem older than his twenty-six years. It had been a long run and he was tired.

Lando activated the tap, let some water flow into his cupped hands, and slapped it against his face. It felt good.

Wait a minute. Lando looked at his hands. They were clean. Completely clean. That would never do!

Lando touched a panel and it hissed open. He grabbed a jar labeled SKINSOFT, and opened the lid. Rather than the white cream the jar had originally contained, it was half full of Number 6 grease.

Lando took a dab of the black stuff and rubbed it into both hands. He was careful to get some of the grease under his nails. The result was a pair of grimy-looking paws that could belong to any engineer in the empire.

Now, should he pull one last check on the cargo? Or head for the lock instead?

Lando decided in favor of the lock. The cargo would be as he'd left it, and customs inspectors didn't like to wait, especially for the likes of tramp-freighter captains.

The smuggler walked down the narrow corridor, past the tiny cabins, through the circular lounge, and stopped by the main lock. He was just in time. There was a loud *bong* followed by a hoarse voice. "Inspector Critzer here . . . open up."

Lando palmed a dirt-blackened control panel and felt something heavy hit the bottom of his stomach. There were all kinds of customs inspectors. Good ones, bad ones, honest ones, and corrupt ones. Now for the fifty-thousand credit question: Was Critzer honest or corrupt? Of the two, corrupt was better. Honest inspectors are notoriously unreliable, while corrupt inspectors do what they're supposed to.

An indicator light went from red to green, indicating that the outer hatch was closed. Lando touched a button, and as the inner hatch started to open, video appeared on the small screen located just under the lock controls. The smuggler didn't like what he saw.

The customs inspector had short salt-and-pepper hair, a small nose, and large sensual lips. The lower one protruded slightly, giving him a pugnacious air.

Lando saw that Critzer was about six feet tall. The custom inspector's once muscular body was now turning to fat. His blue uniform was neat enough, but a huge gut hung out over his police-style gun belt, and bounced slightly as its owner turned towards the inner hatch. Honest or corrupt? There was no way to tell.

The smuggler slid into the surly but slightly oily persona that went with his appearance, and waited for the hatch to cycle open.

Critzer stepped out, gave Lando an insulting once-over, and looked around. "This ship is absolutely filthy. Don't you ever clean the damned thing?"

Lando shrugged and smiled weakly. "Yes, sir, but I'm runnin' kinda short-handed, and it's hard ta find the time."

Critzer activated his portacomp and looked officious. "So, you're master of this wretched scow?"

Lando nodded eagerly. "Yes, sir. Patrick Dever's the name, sir."

Critzer looked bored. "Okay, Dever, let's take a look at your registry and cargo manifest."

Lando unzipped a breast pocket, reached inside, and withdrew a small, carefully doctored data cube. Though entirely bogus, the cube was a nice piece of forgery, and had cost Lando more than two thousand credits. Money well spent if it worked, a ticket to the rock pile if it didn't.

One side of the cube had been smeared with filling from the fruit bar in Lando's pocket. The smuggler wiped at it with his sleeve, grinned apologetically, and handed the cube to Critzer.

The customs inspector accepted the cube with obvious distaste, dropped it into the receptacle on his portacomp, and touched a key. Data flooded his screen. He read aloud.

"Ship, *The Tinker's Damn*, registered on New Britain, to one Patrick Dever."

"That's me," Lando said proudly, and threw in a silly grin for good measure.

Critzer looked up from the screen and scowled. "Shut up, Dever. If I want to hear from you, I'll ask. Now, where was I? Oh, yes. Most recent port of call, the Dallas industrial-agroplex on Terra, where you loaded five thousand pounds of animal protein."

Critzer raised an eyebrow. "Animal protein? What the hell for? We've got plenty of meat."

Lando did his best to smile ingratiatingly. "Not just *any* animal protein, sir. These are one hundred percent genuine Terran steaks, the best in the empire. Each one is perfectly marbled, hand-trimmed, and flash-frozen ta preserve that wonderful flavor. All ya gotta do is take one of these babies, defrost it, and pop it on an open grill. Before long, ya start ta hear that fat sizzlin' 'n' poppin'. Then ya flip it a coupla times ta seal those juices in, and bango, ya slice it up. It fair ta melts in your mouth, sir . . . and I'm thinkin' they'll sell real quick."

Critzer ran his tongue over thick, fleshy lips. Lando's description had set his stomach to growling and he could almost taste the Terran steak. He cleared his throat.

"Maybe, and maybe not. It's true that Terran cattle don't do well on HiHo, but we've got some pretty good variants, and I don't hear anybody complaining. Still, I suppose there might be a market, *if* you're willing to pay the duty."

"Oh yes, sir," Lando answered eagerly. "Of course I'll pay. I run an honest ship, I do."

"I'm glad to hear that," Critzer replied sanctimoniously. "There's far too much smuggling these days. Hang the bastards, that's what I say. That'll slow 'em down."

"Yes, sir," Lando agreed soberly. "That'd do it, sir."

"Well, enough of this chitchat," Critzer said, motioning towards the bow of the ship. "Let's see what's aboard."

Critzer began his inspection in the control room and worked his way back towards the stern. Whatever else he might be, Critzer was no fool, and the ensuing inspection was one of the most thorough that Lando had ever seen.

The portly inspector looked under, over, beneath, behind, and around everything. At Critzer's insistence, Lando was forced to open crawl spaces, to take up deck panels, to remove equipment facings and prove there were electronics inside.

Scared to begin with, Lando became increasingly frightened as the customs man proceeded to find many of the little hidey-holes he'd used successfully before but were presently empty.

Lando came to dread the moment when Critzer would inspect the hold. Would the inspector see right through the scam, laugh, and arrest him on the spot? What were HiHo's jails like, anyway? Could you buy your way out?

These questions and more filled Lando's mind, and added weight to the rock in his gut until his hands were shaking and his mouth was desert-dry.

Finally, after what seemed like an eternity, the two men passed from the engineering space into the hold itself. It was half empty. Here one could see *The Tink's* ancient ribs, still strong under layers of dirt, curving down to meet a heavily scarred deck.

The freezer module sat at the very center of the otherwise empty hold, illuminated by a single cargo light and strapped to sturdy rings set into the deck. A small break in the container's seal allowed a thin tendril of vapor to drift up and away from the lid.

The module had its own power supply, but was connected to the ship's as well. A thick black cable squirmed across the deck and disappeared into darkness.

Lando swallowed as Critzer ignored the tool boxes, storage cabinets, and other paraphernalia that lined the bulkheads, and went straight for the freezer. It was large, with four different lids set into its top surface, and a deactivated power pallet underneath.

"So, here they are," Critzer said patting the module's smooth surface. "Those famous steaks. Open this baby up and let's have a look."

Lando managed to hide the fact that his hand was shaking, by inserting his entire body between the freezer module and the customs inspector. Lando placed his thumb on the print lock and heard a faint click. He stepped aside and waved towards the lid. "There ya go, sir . . . a load o' prime beef."

Critzer grabbed the lid, lifted, and felt a wave of cold air rush past his face. Vapor swirled and dribbled over the sides. A light came on and revealed rank after rank of closely packed plastic bags. Each contained a single piece of meat.

Lando held his breath. This was the critical moment. Could Critzer tell the difference between frozen steaks and lab-grown human kidneys? Not just *any* kidneys, but high-quality blanks? Each organ requiring only hours of chemical conditioning prior to use? The next few seconds would tell. The government of HiHo had placed heavy taxes on replacement organs, thereby creating a rather healthy black market for spares. A market that Lando hoped to exploit.

Critzer turned. There was a frown on his face. His eyes glittered from black caves. "So tell me something, Dever, how do I know this protein is what you say it is? This might be monster meat from the planet Swamp for all I know."

Lando found it easy to look concerned. "The proof is right on the cargo manifest, sir. Take a look and you'll see certification from the processor, the proper Terran exit codes, and a sign-off from my insurance company."

Critzer hooked the portacomp to his belt, leaned back on the freezer module, and folded his arms.

"So what? Every one of those things can be faked by someone who knows what they're doing. Nope, the answer's a full array of lab tests. You don't have a thing to worry about, assuming that the cargo's legit, and if it isn't, well, the government has rock quarries for the likes of you. It takes a lot of granite to build a brand new capitol, and we're going at it full bore."

Lando forced himself to stay calm. There was one last chance. He produced what he hoped was a noncommittal shrug. "If that's the way it has ta be, then that's the way it has ta be. Still, there might be a shorter, easier way ta get the job done."

Critzer raised a skeptical eyebrow. "Oh really? And what would that be?"

Lando grinned. "Well, I don't know about you, sir, but I'm kinda hungry, and that bein' the case, I wondered if you'd join me for dinner? I'm in the mood for some nice juicy steak."

Critzer's face lit up, but turned to a frown. "Dever, are you trying to bribe me? Because if you are, you'll be swinging a sledge by sundown tomorrow."

Lando held up a hand in protest. "Never, sir! It's just that you seem a reasonable sort, and one bite o' Terran beef's worth all the lab tests in the world."

Critzer allowed his expression to soften. The very thought of a juicy steak filled his mouth with saliva. He swallowed. "Well, since you put it that way, I accept. After all, why incur the expense of lab tests if we can settle the matter right here?"

"Exactly," Lando agreed. "Now, if you'll allow me ta select the best o' the best, we'll fire up the galley and get dinner under way!"

Lando stepped up to the freezer, reached inside, and grabbed two of the plastic bags. The cold stung his fingers. Unlike those which contained kidneys, these bags were marked with tiny pieces of black tape, and had Lando needed them, there were four more as well.

The freezer lid closed with a solid thump as Lando held the steaks up for Critzer's inspection. They weren't Terran, but they *were* from New Britain, and almost as good.

"Pick your steak, sir . . . I guarantee you'll be pleased."

Critzer pointed a blunt finger at the larger of the two pieces of meat and Lando nodded his agreement.

"An excellent choice, sir. If you'll follow me to the galley, we'll throw these on the broiler, and prepare the way with a beer."

Critzer grunted his approval, and Lando began to celebrate. Even after all his overhead, and the stiff duty he'd be forced to pay on the Terran "steaks," he'd be fifty thousand credits richer. Crime not only paid, it paid very well indeed.

2

Wendy Wendeen brought her fist down hard. She felt the old man's sternum give slightly. Wendy positioned her hands for cardiac compression and leaned forward.

She pushed down and released. One . . . Two . . . Three . . . Eighty compressions per minute—sixty if she got help with the mouth-to-mouth—and a short pause after every five compressions.

The man had been standing only ten feet away when he collapsed. A quick check had confirmed her first diagnosis. No pulse, no respiration, and bluish lips. A heart attack.

Wendy looked around. A crowd had gathered. Most just stared, but one, a boy in his teens, looked as if he wanted to help. All he needed was someone's permission. Wendy caught his eye.

"Hey, you! Yes, you! Can you perform mouth-to-mouth?"

The boy nodded silently and fell to his knees. Wendy watched the teenager check the old man's airway, pinch his nose shut, and blow air into his lungs. One breath for every five compressions. Good. The kid knew what he was doing.

. . . Four . . . Five . . . Pause. A woman was fanning air towards the old man as if that might help him breathe. She had sun-damaged skin, a beat-up electro-implant where her right eye had been, and the look of a rimmer. Wendy nodded in her direction.

"Ma'am? Would you do me a favor? There's an emergency comset mounted on the far bulkhead. Pick up the handset, and tell whoever answers that we've got a medical emergency on D deck. We need a crash cart, cardiac monitor, and resuscitator. Got that?"

The woman nodded and disappeared into the crowd. She was back moments later.

"They won't come." The woman said it levelly. A statement of fact, nothing more.

Wendy pushed. One . . . Two . . . Three . . . "What do you mean 'they won't come'? This man is dying! Did you tell them that?"

The woman nodded. "I told 'em, miss. They said I should read my ticket. Something about medical services being available on C deck or above."

Wendy swore. Damn them! She'd known about the restrictions on a D-deck ticket but hadn't taken them seriously. Surely a fellow doctor would place more value on a passenger's life than the words printed on a ticket? Apparently not.

Wendy checked the man's pulse. Nothing. She looked at the boy. He shook his head. No pulse and no respiration.

Wendy considered the contents of her medical bag. She did have some epinephrine cartridges for her injector, but even if the drug worked, the old man would still need intensive care and she had no way to provide it. Not without use of the ship's medical facilities.

The boy caught her eye. Wendy shook her head. Both of them stood up. She looked around. The crowd had started to thin out. Death was nothing new to these people. Rimmers mostly, fresh from planets where life was hard, and death came young.

But the onlookers didn't go very far. D deck was too small for that. Being the globe ship's lowest passenger deck, "D" was located right above the hold, and was rather small in circumference.

That hadn't stopped the shipping company from packing them in, though, and Wendy was reasonably sure that there were more passengers on D deck than on A and B combined.

The result was a crowded maze of curtained-off double-tiered bunks, lights that burned around the clock, the smell of food cooked over portable burners, air so thick you could cut it with a knife, and noise that never stopped. Talking, laughing, yelling, and crying. It went on around the clock.

It made Wendy yearn for Angel's wide open spaces, for the clean wind that whipped across the open plain to chill her skin, and the privacy of her own room.

A newborn baby cried somewhere behind her and Wendy looked down. The old man's cheap blue ship suit seemed to billow up around him as if filled with air instead of flesh.

The old man's features were enlarged with age. He had a large beak of a nose, ears that stood almost straight out from the side of his head, and a long thin mouth which curved up at the corners as if amused by what had happened.

Wendy felt someone brush her arm, and turned. The woman with the electro-implant smiled hesitantly. "His name was Wilf. He had the bunk over mine."

Wendy smiled. "Did he have friends or relatives aboard?"

The rimmer shook her head. "No, miss, none that I know of."

Wendy nodded. "Well, we can't leave Wilf here. Let's carry him over to the lift tube. The crew will take it from there."

The woman made no move to help. "They won't say anything for him, will they?"

Wendy imagined a couple of bored crew members, laughing and joking as they loaded the body into an ejection tube.

"No, I don't suppose they will."

The rimmer pointed to the brooch pinned over the pocket of Wendy's jacket. It was a triangle surrounded by a circle of gold. "You're Chosen, aren't you?"

"I'm a member of the Church of Free Choice, yes. Only our enemies refer to us as The Chosen. They use those particular words to makes us seem arrogant and self-centered."

The woman gave an apologetic shrug. Light reflected off her electro-implant. "I meant no offense."

"And none was taken."

"It's just that I'm not very good with words, not that kind anyway, and I wondered if you'd say something for Wilf. You know, something about God and so on."

Wendy nodded solemnly. "I'd be proud to say something for Wilf."

And so it was that three strangers said goodbye to a man none of them knew, while their fellow passengers looked on, and a costume ball took place two decks above.

Later, after they'd carried Wilf's body over to the lift tubes and notified the ship's crew, Wendy had retreated to the comparative privacy of her own bunk. The curtains were thin but better than nothing at all. A pair of newlyweds were busy making love right below her, but Wendy tuned them out.

She discarded the distractions around her one by one until she was all alone inside a cocoon of warmth and peace. It was there that she examined Wilf's death and the circumstances that surrounded it.

She felt no sorrow, for Wendy believed that Wilf's essence lived on, but the manner of his passing troubled her greatly. Why had the ship's medical personnel denied him treatment? How could the vast majority of her fellow passengers be so callous? What could she have done to make things better?

They were difficult questions, and Wendy failed to find any easy answers. But the episode did prove the elder's wisdom. There is little room for good where people are packed too closely together and machines hold sway. The sooner she reached HiHo and discharged her responsibility, the better.

Two more cycles passed before the liner reached the correct nav beacon and made the transition from hyper to normal space. Like most of the passengers on D deck, Wendy knew very little about the physics involved and was forced to trust the machinery around her.

Part of Wendy, the part that had grown up on a farm where even robo-tillers were regarded as necessary evils, was troubled by this dependency on technology.

Another part, the part that had attended and graduated from the Imperial School of Medicine on Avalon, trusted machines and what they could do.

Both parts felt the momentary nausea that goes with a hyperspace jump and gave thanks that the first half of the journey was nearly over.

But it still took the better part of a full cycle for the ship to work its way in from the nav beacon and enter orbit around HiHo.

After that it was semiorganized chaos as everyone pushed and shoved, hoping to get aboard the first shuttle dirtside. They were soon disappointed, however, as passengers from A, B, and C decks were taken off first.

Hours passed. Children cried, people argued, and the air grew thick with tension. The pressure of it, the feeling of being confined within such a small space, gave Wendy a splitting headache. She popped two pain tabs and washed them down with some of the ship's bitter water.

And then, when all the upper decks had been cleared, and the D-deck passengers were clumping their way aboard a pair of clapped-out contract shuttles, Wendy forced herself to go last. It was a form of self-discipline, a self-imposed penance, a punishment for her own lack of inner tranquility.

Finally, after she had passed through the liner's huge passenger lock, and boarded the reentry-scarred shuttle, she got to look out a viewport. This, and only this, was the part of spaceflight that she loved.

Wendy saw nothing of the spacecraft's bolt-down seats, the bare metal bulkheads, or the trash-littered decks beneath her feet. Her eyes were completely taken with the huge brownish-orange orb below, a one-in-a-billion miracle of physics, geology, biology, and chemistry that could support human life. A creation so wondrous, so perfect, that it could single-handedly prove the existence of God.

Not some white-haired tyrant in a mythical realm, but a natural order, which had expressed itself in a multitude of ways, including the planet below.

These were fourth-class passengers, and the pilot had her orders, so she chose the shortest and most economical path down.

The trip was smooth at first, but the shuttle started to jerk and shudder when it hit the atmosphere. Adults swore, children cried, and the hull groaned in protest.

Wendy shut it out, kept her eyes on the planet below, and held onto the armrests with all her strength.

Eventually, after what seemed like an eternity but was something a good deal less, the shuttle glided in over HiHo's principal spaceport, and lowered itself onto a blast-burned landing pad.

The other passengers released their seat belts within seconds of touchdown, and stood in the aisles.

Once again Wendy forced herself to wait, rising from her seat only as the last few people were exiting the main hatch, and following behind them.

It was early afternoon and Wendy blinked as she stepped out into bright sunlight. Her boots made a clanking sound as she made her way down the metal roll-up stairs to the duracrete below.

It was warm and she took a moment to strip off her jacket

and stash it in her backpack. That, and the molded duraplast med kit, was her only luggage. Somewhere behind Wendy a destroyer escort fought clear of its pad, engaged drives, and screamed towards space.

It was a long walk from the economy-class pad to the low-lying terminal, but Wendy enjoyed it, glorying in the opportunity to stretch her legs under the vast sweep of HiHo's blue sky.

She had been to HiHo twice before, so she found her way through the crowded terminal with little difficulty, and stepped out onto a congested street. There was garbage everywhere. It smelled, and the heat made it worse.

All sorts of transportation was available, ranging from long black limos to beat-up hover cabs.

Wendy disliked both options, and looked for something simpler, closer to bone and muscle. There were no animal-drawn carriages in sight, but she did see a dilapidated pedicab, and waved it over.

The vehicle's operator was an ancient Tillarian, so wrinkled and burned by the sun that he looked like a raisin from which all moisture had been drawn.

Like all of his basically humanoid race, the Tillarian had a crested skull and a pair of very round eyes. He wore a sweatband with an advertisement on it, a pair of baggy shorts, and some sturdy sandals.

As Wendy climbed into the pedicab's passenger seat, she wondered what whim of fate or personal decision had brought the Tillarian to HiHo and left him stranded like a piece of sentient driftwood.

Unlike many of the alien races that man had encountered among the stars, the Tillarians were antisocial almost to the point of paranoia, and rarely ventured beyond the limits of their native system.

Wendy provided the Tillarian with an address, and he placed his feet the worn black pedals. Pumping hard, he pulled out in front of a hover cab, ignored the blaring horn, and slid into the flow of traffic.

Five cars back, the woman with one eye swore as her limo driver rear-ended a delivery truck and Wendy disappeared into traffic.

The pedicab's hard rubber tires hummed over hot pavement.

Since the three-wheeled vehicle had very little in the way of suspension, Wendy could feel each little bump in the road. But she liked the slow, steady pace at which the scenery moved by, the pressure of the warm, thick air against her face, and the feeling of connectedness that the ride gave her. A few bumps were a small price to pay for such important pleasures.

Like many of the cities that grow up around spaceports, Zenith had evolved along the path of least resistance, until a certain level of success had been achieved and the second generation followed the first.

At that point a sense of civic pride had bubbled up from some unseen source, and with it, the desire to impose order on chaos, a process that involved master plans and zoning laws.

Wendy watched as the jumble of run-down bars, sex shops, and cheap hotels gave way to clean, orderly streets and carefully constructed stores.

Both areas, old and new alike, struck Wendy as crowded, confining, and ultimately deadening. She couldn't understand it. Given the fact that they had an entire planet to work with, why did they choose to live in each other's laps? Was it something in their genetic codes? A thousand years of conditioning? Or just plain stupidity?

Wendy was still considering various answers when the pedicab coasted to a stop in front of a well-cared-for building at the edge of town. The site had been carefully chosen so that it was backed up against the edge of a dry wash where no one else could build.

Behind and beyond the building there were miles of semiarid land, dotted here and there with low-lying vegetation shimmering in the afternoon heat. And there, halfway to the brown horizon, mountains formed a jagged line between land and sky.

Wendy paid the Tillarian, tipped him handsomely, and made her way up a short walk to the blindingly white building. The front door was made of durasteel and strong enough to stop high-velocity bullets.

A brass plaque announced the name of INTERSTAR IMPORT-EXPORT and a gold-plated knocker invited Wendy to make her presence known. Like her brooch, it featured a circle with a triangle mounted within. She lifted the knocker and let it fall. The result was surprisingly loud.

A minute passed before a woman opened the door. She had black hair streaked with gray, a kindly face, and bright blue eyes. She wore one of the loose white tunics that many locals favored at home. Her expression was polite. "Yes?"

Wendy smiled. "Aunt Margaret?"

Aunt Margaret's face lit up with happiness. "Wendy? Is that you? You're all grown-up! Well, don't just stand there. Come on in! Here, let me take that case."

The inside of the building was just as Wendy remembered it. Cool and dark, part warehouse and part home. About half the structure was given over to the import-export business and the rest served as her aunt and uncle's home.

Wendy had been about sixteen years old during her last visit to HiHo, and the building had been brand new. It was the smells that Wendy remembered the best. A heady mix of preservatives, alien leather, and exotic spices. She'd enjoyed her time with her aunt and uncle and wished that this visit could be as carefree as the others had been.

Wendy followed Aunt Margaret down a long hallway and into a large room. It fronted on the dry wash and the desert beyond. Though forced to live in Zenith for economic reasons, her aunt and uncle had done everything they could to make their home seem as if it stood alone on a windswept plain.

"Sydney! Look who's here! It's Wendy!"

The room was just as Wendy remembered it. A large sunlit chamber full of the old-fashioned books that her uncle liked to collect, and the bright splashy canvases that Aunt Margaret painted when she had time.

Wendy's uncle sat in his favorite recliner, pipe in hand, a cloud of smoke hovering over his head. A computer sat on his lap, and his right leg was in a cast.

As Uncle Syd raised his head, Wendy found herself looking at a male version of her mother, and a lump formed in her throat. He had the same even features, the same high cheekbones, and the same brown eyes. Those eyes were filled with excitement as he tried to rise.

Wendy dropped her backpack and rushed to his side. "Don't you dare! What did you do to yourself?"

Uncle Syd gave Wendy an awkward hug and kissed her on the cheek. "What did I *do* to myself? And you call yourself a doctor? What's the matter? Never seen a broken leg before?

Never mind. Let's have a look at you."

He made a show of looking Wendy over. She had short black hair, large luminous brown eyes, a nice straight nose, and full red lips. They curved upward in a smile. "Well?"

"Gorgeous," Uncle Syd answered solemnly. "Absolutely gorgeous. A terrible temptation to men everywhere."

"Oh, really?" Wendy asked lightly, "Then, why am I unmarried?"

"A very good question," Aunt Margaret put in sternly. "We receive letters, you know, and your father tells us that a number of young men have asked, and that you say 'no.' "

"My father exaggerates, and should mind his own business," Wendy replied primly. "Now, Uncle Syd, tell me about your leg. What happened?"

During the next couple of hours Wendy heard about the packing crate that had fallen on Uncle Syd's leg, the stiff competition they faced in the import-export business, and how hatred for the Church made matters even worse.

The hatred was nothing knew. It had started hundreds of years ago, when a small group of people had committed themselves to what they called "a life of free choice, guided by the voice within."

Unlike most religious groups, they had no ministers or priests, no written credo, no enforced rules. But they did share some common values. Included was a belief that life should be simple, nonviolent, and productive.

In order to pursue that kind of a life they avoided cities, built homes in rural communities, and did their best to avoid conflict.

But cities had a way of expanding, eating up more and more farmland with each succeeding year, until the life they'd sought to avoid surrounded and crushed their farms.

Avaricious land developers labeled them "anti-progressive"; other religions made fun of their self-directed ways, and planetary governments used their taxes to wage war.

So they moved from city to country, from planet to planet, but it was always the same. No matter how isolated they were, no matter where they went, others would come and take control. Unable to live under those conditions, the members would be forced to leave their homes, often selling farms and other property at a fraction of their true worth, or losing them altogether. It was a pattern that had occurred over and over again.

In an effort to resolve this problem, a huge meeting was held. Representatives came from a dozen planets. Discussions went on day after day. And finally, after each voice had been heard, a decision was made. A world would be purchased, a planet where the membership could live life as they chose, and enjoy the fruits of their own hard work.

It was a bold plan, but more realistic than it might seem, since Imperial Survey ships discovered a couple of inhabitable planets each year, and most were offered for sale or colonization.

So a team of scientists was assembled and funds were pledged. Many years passed, during which a number of planets were considered but none was purchased. Some were too hot, some were too cold, but most were simply too expensive. The most desirable worlds, those with potential as pleasure planets, were bid up by the powerful mega-corporations.

But eventually, in what could only be viewed as a massive compromise, half of a planet was finally obtained. It was largely barren, and they'd be forced to share it with a mining operation, but something was better than nothing.

The planet was named Angel, and with the exception of the time she'd spent in med school, Wendy had lived there all her life.

So Wendy understood the stories her aunt and uncle told. Tales of planetary import licenses that went to members of more accepted religions, accounts of business deals lost because they refused to deal in arms, and stories of mega-corps that conspired to underprice them.

And for their part, the couple were hungry for news of the progress on Angel, since it was their dream to sell the import-export business and retire there some day.

How much land had been cleared? What crops grew best? And was the mining company causing problems?

Wendy's aunt and uncle asked those questions, and more, until the sun had set beyond the mountains and darkness had claimed the desert.

It was then, over one of Aunt Margaret's wonderful vegetarian dinners, that the conversation turned to the reason behind Wendy's visit.

Uncle Syd took a sip of wine, savored it for a moment, then let it slide down his throat. "So, enough of our silly questions. You came to HiHo for a reason."

Wendy smiled. "So don't keep me in suspense. . . . Have you got it?"

Her uncle nodded soberly. "It took the better part of three months to find exactly what the elders asked for, and a great deal of money, but yes, there are ten tons of concentrate waiting on Weller's World."

Wendy put her glass down and clapped her hands. "That's wonderful! The fertilizer will make a tremendous difference! We could be self-sufficient by early next year."

Uncle Syd held up a restraining hand. "Aren't you forgetting something? Weller's World is a long way from Angel. Not only that, but from what your father says in his letters, the company may try to stop you. How will you move it?"

Wendy took a bite of bread and chewed thoughtfully. "We anticipated that. I'll hire a freighter."

"Not a regular one, you won't," Aunt Margaret countered. "It wouldn't be worth it. They'd charge double the going rate to carry such a small cargo."

"If they're willing to do it at all," Uncle Syd added. "Angel is way off the main shipping lanes and there'd be small chance of a return cargo."

Wendy shrugged. "Okay, I'll hire a smuggler. If everything goes according to plan, we'll need one anyway."

Husband and wife looked at each other. There was truth in what Wendy said. They'd be forced to deal with a smuggler eventually, like it or not. Uncle Syd nodded.

"Granted. But we must choose carefully. Most smugglers are little more than common criminals."

"Jonathan Troon could give us some advice there," Aunt Margaret said.

"Yes," Uncle Syd agreed, waving his fork in Wendy's direction. "Jonathan's our shipping agent. I'll contact him in the morning. If anyone could put you in touch with a reliable smuggler, Jonathan could."

"If there is such a thing as a 'reliable smuggler,' " Aunt Margaret said doubtfully. "Most of them traffic in arms and drugs."

Wendy smiled. "The Lord works in mysterious ways."

3

The woman screamed as the man in black leather brought the whip down across her naked back. Even though Wendy knew it was a holo, and even though the woman was okay, she still jerked in sympathetic response. Wendy had nothing against eroticism per se, or pornography for that matter, but couldn't stand to see violence used as a sexual stimulant.

She looked around. No one else was watching. The holo was nothing more than a backdrop for other activities. The background noise came close to obliterating the woman's screams.

The bar was packed, full of spacers mostly, with a scattering of enlisted types from the Imperial destroyer that had touched down earlier in the day. They moved back and forth, a living tapestry of ship suits, uniforms, and body armor. She saw very few aliens, and assumed they spent most of their time in other, more cosmopolitan establishments.

The air was so thick with smoke that it made Wendy's throat sore. She hated the noise, the smell of sour alcohol, and the feel of bodies pressing in around her.

She looked across a pair of untouched beers to Jonathan Troon. She hoped that he'd notice her distress and take her somewhere else. No such luck. Troon was watching the crowd.

Wendy tried to guess what Troon was thinking, but the shipping agent was a cyborg, with a face of rigid plastic. Some cyborgs were too poor to pay for a lifelike plastiflesh face, but not Troon. Judging from his brand new ground car, and his expensive clothes, the cyborg could buy anything he wanted.

No, for reasons known only to the cyborg himself, Troon wore an expression of eternal happiness.

Wendy considered it. What if she was limited to a single expression? Would she choose happiness? Sadness? Something in between?

The cyborg turned in her direction and interrupted Wendy's thoughts. He wore a high-collared evening cloak, matching skin-tight breeches, and a pair of knee-high boots. "Is everything okay? Would you care for another beer?"

Wendy indicated the full glass in front of her. "No, thanks." She gestured towards the rest of the room. "Are you sure this visit is necessary?"

Troon shrugged. He made the gesture seem elegant. "It's like my mother used to say. If you want to swim with the fish, then jump in the ocean."

Wendy raised an eyebrow. "And if you drown?"

Troon laughed. "Mother was an optimist. You have nothing to fear, however. I guarantee your safety."

Wendy wanted to say that her desire to leave the bar had nothing to do with her personal safety, but that would seem ungracious. Troon was trying to help. The least she could do was wait the process out. Wendy hoisted her beer and forced a smile.

"Here's to the fish."

Pik Lando entered the bar and looked around. As Lando's eyes drifted over the crowd, he saw things that others might have missed. There were roid rats, rimmers, smugglers, bounty hunters, merchant marine, mercenaries, and more.

Bounty hunters sat in corners with their backs to the wall, constantly scanning the crowd for fugitives. Mercenaries drank the same way they fought, taking possession of entire tables and defending them against all comers. And, with a few exceptions, roid rats drank alone, as suspicious of each other as they were of everyone else, glowering at people who came too close.

Under normal circumstances Lando favored the bar, where he could watch the room in the large mirror, and leave quickly if the heat arrived.

But tonight was different. Lando was hungry and they didn't serve food at the bar. The smuggler wound his way through the tables, chose one next to a group of reasonably sober engineering types, and activated the tabletop menu. Burning blue letters appeared under the table's plastic surface.

Scanning through the menu, Lando saw steak, nearly rejected it due to the cost, but thought, *What the hell, I'm fifty thousand to the good, and I haven't had a good piece of meat since my dinner with Inspector Critzer. God bless his greedy soul.*

Lando grinned and touched the word "steak," followed by "medium," and "coffee, Terran."

He had just settled back, and was about to do a little woman-watching, when he saw one rise from her seat and turn his way. She was different. Not a spacer, not a bounty hunter, something else.

The short hair would look terrible on some, but was perfect for her. It served to emphasize the soft symmetry of her face. A face that looked, well, determined somehow, as if on some sort of important errand.

And then there was her body—a very nice body, which in spite of some shapeless clothes, managed to make itself known in all the right places. She wore a pin of some sort. A circle with a triangle mounted within. He'd seen that design before but couldn't remember where.

Yes, the woman had both potential *and* an escort in the form of an upscale cyborg. A borg with a plastic smile, a rather obvious blaster tucked away under his left armpit, and something else. An attitude that said, "Screw with me and you could wind up seriously dead."

What the hell? The unlikely pair were heading straight for his table. Heat? Competition? Clients? Lando had settled on the last possibility by the time they reached his table.

"Good evening," the cyborg said smoothly. "My name's Jonathan Troon, and this is Dr. Wendy Wendeen. Could we join you for a drink? Or some dinner perhaps?"

Lando made no attempt to rise. Troon, Troon. The name was familiar but he couldn't quite place it.

The cyborg spoke as if reading Lando's mind. "Your father might have mentioned my name. We worked together many years ago."

Jonathan Troon! Of course! Lando's father loved to tell the story of how he and a cyborg named Troon . . . had smuggled a quarter-million credits worth of black market biochips onto Terra by making it appear that they were part of the borg's motor control subprocessor.

Lando smiled and got to his feet. His slug gun slithered into its holster. The smuggler held out his hand. "I'm pleased to me you, Citizen Troon. My father has mentioned you many times."

"And I him," Troon replied politely. "Tell him that since our little adventure I've moved into a safer line of work."

"Consider it done," Lando replied, turning his attention to the woman.

The cyborg nodded, acknowledging Lando's comment and Wendy's presence at the same time. "Dr. Wendeen, and the people that she represents, have need of your services."

Lando took the woman's hand, noting the short, utilitarian nails, and the firm grip. "It's a pleasure to meet you, Dr. Wendeen. Citizen Troon glossed over the matter of my name, but it's Pik Lando, and friends call me Pik."

Suddenly aware that the handshake should have ended some time ago, Wendy released Lando's hand. He smiled.

Wendy felt flustered. Outside of the ugly-looking gun, the smuggler was nothing like the slimy underworld type she'd imagined. Just the opposite in fact.

Lando had shiny black hair pulled back into a ponytail, quick brown eyes, and a slightly hooked nose. The nose gave him a slightly predatory air, which Wendy found both exciting and alarming at the same time.

"Please call me Wendy. *Doctor* Wendeen is off duty."

Lando nodded and gestured towards his table. "Please . . . I ordered some food. Would you care to join me?"

Wendy selected a vegetarian dinner, and Troon ordered a fruit salad. Lando wondered if he'd eat it. Some cyborgs ate, and some didn't, depending on how they were put together.

Once the others had finished making their selections, Lando smiled and looked from Wendy to Troon. "So here we are. You mentioned a business proposition."

The cyborg nodded. "Yes. Wendy's aunt and uncle are friends of mine. And when they told me Wendy had a rather special cargo to move, I thought of you."

Lando looked from Troon to Wendy and back again. Was this for real? Or part of a scam? They seemed sincere, but as dear old Dad liked to say, "Appearances can be deceiving."

"No offense, Jonathan, but how did you know that I was on HiHo? And why me?"

Troon shrugged. "I'm a shipping agent. I ship most of my cargo via legitimate hulls. But not all of it. Some of my clients have shipments that require special handling. I make it my business to know who can help them, where they are, and what it will cost. Information, like everything else in this universe, is for sale. I buy it, mark it up, and sell it. As for you, well, your entire family has a good reputation."

Lando nodded. It made sense. The Landos were pretty well known in smuggling circles.

A shiny robo-waiter brought dinner to their table, paused while they took their food, and whirred off towards another table. Lando waited until everyone had been served, took a bite of steak, and caught Wendy's eye.

"So, tell me what you want to move, where the cargo is now, and where it's supposed to go."

Wendy looked at Troon, saw his nod of approval, and turned towards Lando.

"The cargo consists of fertilizer concentrate. It's stored on Weller's World. I want it delivered to a planet called Angel."

Lando raised an eyebrow, checked to make sure she was serious, and broke into laughter. "Fertilizer? Weller's World? Angel? You've got to be kidding!"

Wendy was annoyed. What was so funny? She frowned. "I enjoy a good joke, Citizen Lando . . . but I fail to see any humor in what I said."

Lando struggled to get the smile off his face. "I'm sorry, Wendy. I meant no offense. Your comments took me by surprise, that's all. It's the first time that anyone's asked me to smuggle fertilizer. Precious metals, body parts, and electronics, yes, but not fertilizer."

Wendy relaxed slightly and took a sip of her tea. Looking at the request from Lando's point of view, it *did* seem sort of funny. She smiled.

"I see what you mean. But your words serve to illustrate our situation. On Angel, fertilizer *is* as precious as gold, to us at least, and that's why we need your help."

Lando looked thoughtful. "If fertilizer's as precious as gold, then Angel must be made out of solid rock."

Wendy smiled grimly. "Angel isn't quite that bad . . . but it comes pretty close. Up until roughly one hundred thousand years ago, Angel was a perfectly ordinary Earth-type planet similar to HiHo, but wetter. Then a nickel-iron asteroid came along, hit the planet, and bounced into space.

"Our scientists say that the asteroid was about fifty miles across, weighed in at a couple of quadrillion tons, and was moving at roughly thirty miles a second when it hit. You can still see the scar along Angel's equator. It's two hundred miles wide and a thousand miles long.

"Needless to say, the collision threw a tremendous amount of matter into the atmosphere. Enough to drastically reduce the amount of sunlight that reached the planet's surface, kill off most of the vegetation, and the animals that fed on it.

"In the meantime the impact triggered major volcanic eruptions, creating even *more* dust and smoke, not to mention rivers of molten lava."

Wendy put down her fork. "There wasn't much left by the time the whole thing was over."

Lando tried to imagine what it would look like as an asteroid hit a planet, caromed off, and disappeared into space. The scale was so huge, so awesome, that he couldn't quite grasp it.

"So what's Angel like now?"

Wendy's eyes lit up. "It's beautiful, not in the ordinary sense perhaps, but beautiful nonetheless.

"The impact scar filled with lava soon after the collision, and with water after that. From space it looks like a long, narrow canal. We call it the Finger of God, because for reasons known only to her, that's where she touched our planet. There's no life in it, due to the sulfur compounds which bubble up from below. It's beautiful, though. The water is always warm, and the beaches are made of black sand. . . ."

Wendy paused for a moment, as if remembering something long past. She was back a few seconds later.

"I should also mention that there's some primitive plant life in the oceans that cover about eighty percent of Angel's surface. That, along with some pre-collision ground cover that managed to survive the long twilight, provides us with plenty of oxygen. Our volcanos outgas enough CO_2 to keep the biosphere in balance.

"The continents are rugged, extremely mountainous, and largely barren. There's very little soil along the ridge tops, or on the slopes for that matter, because wind and rain push most of it downhill. That's where we live, in the valleys, or on small plateaus."

Wendy pushed her plate away and took another sip of tea. "What soil we have tends to be dry and sterile. We want to bring in Earth-type plants, but that requires chemicals, and bacteria."

"Which brings us back to the fertilizer," Lando said thoughtfully. "You need fertilizer to grow crops. So what's the problem? Since when does fertilizer qualify as a 'controlled substance'? And why hire me? A tramp freighter would cost a lot less."

Troon cleared his throat. Lando noticed that his salad was still untouched.

"First you must understand that the settlers own fifty percent of Angel. The rest belongs to a corporation called Mega-Metals."

"That's right," Wendy put in. "The elders couldn't afford to purchase the entire planet. So when Angel came on the market, they bought half of it, hoping to raise the rest of the money before another buyer came along."

Troon shrugged. "But time went by, the colonists were unable to raise the money, and Mega-Metals bought the other half. Angel has some good iron and nickel deposits, which when combined with mineral-rich asteroidal debris, makes the planet well worth mining."

"Not just *any* mines," Wendy said heatedly, "but *open pit* mines, huge ugly things that look like skin ulcers."

"Yes," Troon agreed evenly. "And because those mines are rather profitable . . . the company offered to buy the rest of the planet from the colonists."

"An offer that we refused," Wendy said indignantly. "It's *our* world and we plan to stay."

"Unless they're forced out," Troon continued smoothly. "In which case Mega-Metals could acquire the rest of the planet at a bargain basement price.

"And, given the fact that the Emperor has seen fit to grant the corporation quasi-governmental powers where Angel's concerned, they have the means to make things quite uncomfortable. Like placing enormous duties on fertilizer for example. A substance the colonists need in order to be self-sufficient.

"The company claims the duties are 'just compensation for the expense of protecting and administering the planet,' but that's little more than a legal fiction. Mega-Metals doesn't do anything on and around Angel that it wouldn't do anyway."

"And there's something else," Wendy added, fingering the pin at her throat. "Have you heard of the Church of Free Choice?"

Now Lando remembered where he'd seen Wendy's brooch. It was a symbol used by The Chosen, much like the Christian cross, or the Star of David.

Like some other controversial religious groups, The Chosen had been featured on countless vid casts, and gradually acquired a reputation for quiet intransigence.

On Lando's home planet of Ithro, The Chosen had refused to pay that portion of their taxes which went to defense, and many had been jailed as a result.

Lando's father had referred to the situation as "damned foolishness," and Lando had been inclined to agree. As long as there were pirate raids, and the possibility of war with the alien Il Ronn, weapons were a necessary evil.

But like most smugglers, Lando was anti-authoritarian to the core, and not very fond of the Establishment. Strange though The Chosen might be, Lando found that his sympathies lay with them rather than the corporation. He smiled.

"Yes, of course. Your Church gets a good deal of publicity."

Wendy's laugh was a pleasant surprise. "We get publicity all right . . . especially when our membership refuses to pay taxes. So you can imagine what sort of hearing we'd get at the Imperial Court on Terra. I can see the headlines now: 'The Chosen refuse taxes, but demand justice.' "

There was silence for a moment as Lando sipped his coffee. "Okay, I think I've got the picture. But you failed to mention the most important thing."

"What's that?" Wendy asked innocently.

"Money," Troon answered smoothly. "Pik wants to know how you plan to pay him."

"Oh that," Wendy said, as if money were nothing more than an unimportant detail. "Well, our supply of cash is somewhat limited, but we wondered if you'd considered a trade."

Lando groaned internally. What could The Chosen possibly have that would interest him? He tried to look intrigued. "Oh? And what did you have in mind?"

Wendy fumbled with an inside pocket and withdrew a holo cube. She handed it over. "This is what we have in mind— well, not the cube, but what it shows."

Lando gave it a squeeze and the holo cube came to life. It showed a large industrial-type scale with something sitting on it. A rock or a boulder.

Lando squeezed again. The previous shot dissolved to a close-up. The color was unmistakable. Gold . . . and a lot of it. He looked at Wendy. "Is that thing real?"

Wendy nodded. "All sixty-nine pounds of it. Elder Perez found it while clearing his fields."

Lando opened his mouth to ask a question but Wendy held up her hand. "No, we looked, and didn't find any more. But Lord help us if Mega-Metals finds out. They'll peel Angel like an orange."

Lando did some mental arithmetic. At 650 Imperials per ounce, or 10,400 Imperials to the pound, the gigantic nugget would net around 717,600 Imperials. Assume some impurities, plus the costs involved in refining the stuff, and add normal overhead.

He'd still clear a cool half million, and maybe more. Enough to buy a better ship with change left over. Assuming the nugget was real.

Lando handed the cube to Wendy. "I'm tempted, but how do I know the nugget's real?"

It was Troon who answered. "It's real, but I don't blame you for being cautious. I think this will put your fears at rest."

So saying, the shipping agent handed Lando a notarized permadoc. It was a surety bond in the amount of 700,000 Imperials. If Lando delivered an unspecified cargo and The Chosen were unable to pay, Troon would make it good.

Lando looked at the cyborg's face and wondered what went on behind the smiling plastic. Why was Troon willing to risk 700,000 Imperials of his own money on The Chosen? He wasn't a member himself. The blaster proved that. So why?

Judging from the expression on Wendy's face, she was wondering the same thing. Sensing their unasked questions, Troon shrugged. "It's good for business. I'll get a percentage of everything that goes off-planet if the colony succeeds."

Troon was smooth, and quick enough to be credible, but Lando didn't believe it. The colony wasn't even self-sufficient. A percentage of nothing is nothing. But, so what? The cyborg's motives were none of his business. Lando stood and held out his hand. "Doctor, you've got a deal. Weller's World to Angel orbit. When do we lift?"

Wendy shook the smuggler's hand, careful to withdraw this time. "Say 0900 tomorrow?"

Lando nodded and held out his hand to Troon. The cyborg's hand was cool but firm. "Thanks, Jonathan. I enjoyed meeting you."

"Likewise," the cyborg replied warmly. "The concentrate has been paid for. Wendy has the necessary documents. Please give your father my best."

Lando smiled. "I certainly will. Jonathan, good night, and Wendy, I'll see you in the morning."

Wendy watched the smuggler wind his way towards the main entrance, then turned her attention to Troon. The cyborg was retrieving a credit card from a slot in the tabletop. "Well, he *seems* trustworthy."

The cyborg nodded. "Yes, unusually so. A man of honor in his own way. Come . . . I'll take you home."

Wendy shook her head. "No, Jonathan, you've been far too kind already. I'll catch an autocab."

"As you wish," Troon replied. "But I'll see you to the cab."

A single eye followed the two of them out of the bar. The other one had been destroyed on a planet half an empire away, and replaced with an electro-implant. The woman looked better now. Healthier, stronger, and very well-dressed. So well-dressed that Wendy would not have recognized her.

The woman said something to one of her male companions, and the three of them headed towards the rear of the bar.

It took three minutes for Troon and Wendy to make their way outside the bar and hail an autocab. It whirred to the curb and Wendy got in. She waved through the open window. "Take care, Jonathan. And thanks."

Troon waved in reply and watched until the autocab had passed from sight. He liked Wendy and hoped that she would have a safe trip.

Turning, the cyborg walked around the side of the bar and towards the parking lot. He felt the cool night air flow over his plastic skin. Row after row of vehicles gleamed under the widely spaced lights. Troon made his way down the second row and approached his ground car. He'd just pulled the electro-key from his pocket, when something hard poked him in the side.

"Hold it, borg . . . put your hands on top of your head." The voice was male and sounded mean. Troon did as he was told. A hand reached to grab his blaster.

"What the hell?" It was another male voice this time, deeper, and sort of hoarse. "Look at this . . . the blaster's a fake . . . a goddamned toy!"

Troon felt an emptiness where his stomach should be. For more than twenty years the bluff had worked. The cyborg prepared himself.

A woman stepped into the space between Troon and his car. She was nicely dressed and had one good eye. The other was an implant and glittered with reflected light. "How cute! A toy blaster. You know what I think, borg? I think you're one of them. I think you're an arrogant, self-important, religious zealot."

Troon remained silent.

Hard shadows played across the woman's face. "I want the Wendeen woman. Where is she?"

Troon said nothing.

The woman nodded. "Have it your way. Okay, boys, make him hurt."

The blows came hard and fast, some connecting with plastic, some with flesh. Things snapped and broke. Troon grunted and fell.

The woman bent over and grabbed his plastic nose. She used it to turn his head. One of Troon's eyes was broken and the other had begun to fade. "The Wendeen bitch, and the spacer you had dinner with, tell me where they're headed. Tell me and live."

The cyborg started to pray. "Yea, though I walk through the valley of the shadow of death, I will fear no evil: for thou art with me . . ."

The woman spat disgustedly and turned to a man in beat-up space armor. "The cyborg wants to die. Grant his wish."

4

The sun was well over the distant mountains and still climbing when Lando left the ship's lock. His boots clanged on the metal steps. The spaceport was relatively quiet, with only an occasional ship landing or taking off, and the cool morning air felt good against his skin.

Though not a trained engineer, Lando was more knowledgeable about his ship's systems than most pilots were, and liked to perform his own preflight maintenance checks. It was one of the many lessons his father had drummed into him from an early age.

"Son, there are three things you should never do. *Never* allow someone else to tend your money, your woman, or your ship."

Lando smiled at the memory, and started his maintenance check. He began at the bow and worked his way towards the stern. He examined the landing jacks, sensor housings, weapons blisters, access panels, repulsor jets, and hull plates, looking for signs of damage or excessive wear.

And, outside of the intentional lube leak, and the tricked-up landing jack, everything was fine. As well it *should* be, given the number of credits Lando had poured into *The Tink* over the last year.

Which raised an interesting question. Once Lando had delivered the fertilizer, and sold the gold, should he keep *The Tink*? Or put everything into a new speedster? The more successful smugglers owned a variety of ships, using each according to need, or hiring people to make runs for them.

His father opposed this practice, pointing out that "the bigger you get the more you feel the heat," but Lando wasn't so sure. Why settle for second- or third-best, when you could be top dog?

Lando's thoughts were interrupted as a robo-jitney squealed to a stop near the bow of the ship, discharged a single passenger, and rolled away. It was Dr. Wendy Wendeen.

She looked even better than she had the night before. Although her clothes were extremely practical, Lando couldn't help but notice how well she filled the khaki-colored T-shirt and matching utility pants. He smiled. Dad was right. Work *can* be fun.

Lando wiped his hands on an oily rag as he walked over to greet her. "Good morning. Here, let me take that case."

Wendy smiled bleakly as she looked up at the ship. She pointed at the port wing where it slumped towards the ground. "How long will the repairs take?"

Lando looked at where she was pointing. "Repairs? Oh, that. Don't worry about it. A little hydraulic problem, that's all. We'll lift on schedule."

Wendy looked doubtful but forced a smile. "If you say so."

"I certainly do," Lando replied confidently, as he took Wendy's med kit and led her towards the lock. "*The Tink's* a good old bird. You'll love her."

Lando continued his cheerful babble until they were inside the ship. Wendy stopped to look around. She was appalled by the filth and apparent lack of maintenance.

"No offense, Citizen Lando, but your ship has seen better days."

Warned by the use of his last name, Lando looked around. Suddenly he saw the worn fittings, the stained bulkheads, and the trash underfoot. There was no doubt about it. The ship *looked* like a deathtrap. He rushed to explain.

"Don't be fooled by appearances, Doc. *The Tink's* in tiptop shape. When you go through customs it pays to understate the condition of your ship."

Wendy nodded slowly. Lando had confirmed her worst fears. The attraction she'd felt the night before had been physical in nature. The man was little more than a common criminal, and a boorish one at that. Wendy's voice was as cold as the void itself.

"Well, you certainly succeeded. This is the most understated ship I've ever seen. And the name is Wendy, not *Doc.*"

More than a little chagrined, Lando showed Wendy to her tiny cabin, and spent the next half hour picking up the worst of the trash and wiping things down. The ship *was* filthy. Lord help him if the argrav failed during a run. The cabin would be full of floating trash. He made a note to clean up more often.

At precisely 0930 *The Tinker's Damn* lifted for space. The ship was little more than a vapor trail by the time the black limo screeched to a stop on the still-warm pad.

The woman with one eye stepped out into a pool of Number 3 lubricant. It stained her 500-credit boots. She swore and took a step forwards. "Damn." Just fifteen minutes earlier and she'd have had them. Unfortunately it had taken the rest of the night and part of the morning to find Troon's office, break in, locate his safe, blow it open, and scroll through the 167 data cubes stored inside.

In the meantime, one of her assistants had been hard at work identifying the spacer and his ship.

Finally, after hours of staring at boring junk, she'd hit pay dirt. It was just as her boss suspected. The Chosen *were* trying to import fertilizer. Fertilizer that would help them become self-sufficient, stay on Angel, and screw up the company's plans.

The woman forced herself to remain calm. They were gone. No big deal. Weller's World was only days away, and the Wendeen bitch was traveling on a piece of clapped-out space junk. The woman would charter a speedster and get there first.

She got in the limo and slammed the door. Her boots smeared oil on the expensive gray carpet. "The terminal and step on it," she ordered.

Tires screeched as the driver stepped on the gas. The woman was pushed deep into the soft leather seat. She ground her teeth in frustration. All this trouble over a shitload of chemicals. It didn't seem right.

Lando touched a key and watched data flood the screen. Destination, speed, ETA, a routine systems check, and so on. The NAVCOMP equivalent of "Hey, I've got things under control, go find something to do."

Good advice, but do what?

Lando took a sip of coffee. He'd done a lot cleaning during the last three days, performed maintenance checks on every system he could access, and started a dozen conversations with Wendy. Conversations that always seemed to end shortly after they began.

Oh, she was friendly in a distant sort of way, and willing to share in the chores, but seemed to prefer an unending series of medical texts to his company. So much for the Lando charm.

Lando decided to give it one last try. He left the cockpit, stopped off at his cabin, and grabbed a small box. He had it under his arm when he entered the lounge.

The main aisle split the lounge in half like line through the center of a circle. Wendy sat to port, so Lando chose that side as well.

Wendy looked up from her cube reader, nodded politely, and went back to her reading.

Lando sat down and unwrapped the package. His slug gun and a cleaning kit were inside. The smuggler thumbed the magazine release, worked the action to make sure the weapon was empty, and began to take it apart.

"Must you do that here?"

Lando looked up. "Do what?"

Wendy nodded towards the table. "Play around with that awful gun."

There was the rasp of metal on metal as Lando released the trigger mechanism and pulled it free of the pistol's stainless steel frame. Her comment annoyed him.

"I'm not playing. I'm cleaning a weapon. What's so awful about that?"

Wendy frowned. "That's rather obvious, isn't it? Guns are used to *kill* people."

Lando put a small drop of lubricant into the hole provided for that purpose.

"Well, that's one way to put it, although guns are also used to *protect* people."

"Only because guns are used to *kill* people," Wendy insisted stubbornly. "And I don't like them."

Lando held the barrel up to the light. The bore was clean and the rifling was intact. "Well, I don't *like* them either. But what's the alternative? It's a violent universe. You have to protect yourself."

"*Not* if it means taking a sentient life," Wendy replied. "Thou shalt not kill."

"An eye for an eye, and a tooth for a tooth," Lando answered, sliding the weapon's barrel into the receiver mechanism with a positive click. "Your pacifism is misguided."

Wendy stood. "And *you* are hopeless."

She left the lounge, stepped into her cabin, and closed the curtain with an angry jerk.

Lando looked at the magazine, checked to make sure it was full up, and slid it home. The smuggler shook his head ruefully. "Smooth, Pik. Real smooth."

The Tinker's Damn left hyperspace two days later and entered orbit a day after that. Weller's World was a blue marble surrounded by wispy white cotton. Blessed with broad temperate zones above and below its equator, it was an agricultural planet. Genetically modified Terran crops and animals had been crossed with native flora and fauna to produce a variety of hybrids. Some of the hybrids were quite valuable. Especially those that were used to make pharmaceuticals.

But Weller's World had other assets as well, including some apatite deposits from which phosphate fertilizers were made. All they had to do was land, pick up the shipment, and lift. Or so Lando hoped.

The trip down to the planet's surface was extremely smooth, which should have left Lando in a good mood, but didn't. The situation had gone from bad to worse after the discussion about guns. They barely spoke to each other now, and when they did, it was born of strict necessity.

They left the ship together, having secured the lock behind them. Wendy made it a point to ignore Lando's slug gun, and he made sure the mini-launcher was hidden inside his sleeve. There was no point in giving her something more to complain about.

Neither one of them noticed the weasel-faced boy at the spaceport, who slipped into a com booth, consulted a crumpled piece of paper, and keyed a number.

A comset chimed in a hotel room on the other side of town. The woman with one eye was busy doing sit-ups. She swore at the interruption, bounced to her feet with the energy of a woman half her age, and grabbed the handset next to her bed.

"Yeah?"

"They just arrived. You want me to follow?"

The woman wiped sweat from her forehead with a corner of the bedspread and looked at the resulting stain. "No, that won't be necessary."

The woman with one eye dropped the handset into its cradle. She knew where they were going, if not this minute, then very, very soon. The Wendeen bitch had arrived a full rotation earlier than expected. Pretty fast for a ship that seemed to be on its last legs. Interesting.

She lifted the handset and keyed a number. A male voice answered. "Dulo."

"They just arrived," the woman said. "Is everything ready?"

"Yes, ma'am. Ready and waiting."

"Good. I'll be there in fifteen or twenty minutes."

"Fifteen or twenty minutes. Yes, ma'am."

"And, Dulo . . ."

"Yes ma'am?"

"Don't screw this up." The phone made a hollow plastic sound as it hit the cradle.

Wendy got out of the autocab and looked around. Although the establishment looked like a muddy lot filled fender-to-fender with used vehicles, the electronic billboard claimed it was RUDY'S MOTOR MECCA, "where you can rent, buy, or practically steal the vehicle of your dreams. Come on in."

Wendy's boots made small sucking sounds as she followed Lando onto the lot. "Are you sure this is necessary? Couldn't we hire a freight company to move the fertilizer for us?"

Lando paused to kick the rubberized skirt of a used but still serviceable hover truck. "We could, but I'd rather not. It's like my father says: 'He who controls the most variables wins.' "

"What does that mean?"

"It *means*," Lando replied patiently, "that transportation is a variable, and since we have the power to control it, we should do so."

Wendy wondered if the transportation issue wasn't much ado about nothing, but decided to let it go. There was enough tension between the two of them already.

After protracted negotiations with no less a personage than Rudy himself, Lando handed over a deposit of 200 Imperials,

and received the ignition code for a decrepit ten-wheeled truck
in return. The vehicle came equipped with a light-duty crane,
a flatbed in back, and a world-class collection of dents. It
would have little difficulty coping with a ten-ton cargo
module.

Lando climbed up and into the driver's side of the cab.
Wendy entered from the opposite side. The seats sagged, the
paint was worn, and the interior smelled of stale cigar smoke.
Wendy tried to open a window. A motor hummed and nothing
happened.

Lando entered the ignition code, hit the START button, and
listened to the turbine spin up. A little tired but okay. He
smiled, touched another button, and felt the truck lift itself
up on a cushion of air. So far, so good.

Lando eased the truck out of its slot, waved at Rudy, and
slid out onto the street. The hover truck steered like a tank.
Lando's turn was too wide, but traffic was light, and no
harm was done. He was afraid to take even one hand off
the controls.

"See if the mapper works."

There was a screen set into the center of the dash. Wendy
touched the power button, and much to her surprise, a menu
appeared. She touched "path, most direct," and entered the
address Troon had provided.

The menu disappeared and a map took its place. The truck
was a bright red delta, their destination a glowing green circle, and the jagged blue line the most direct path between
the two.

Lando looked, nodded his understanding, and followed the
mapper's instructions.

Wendy watched as retail businesses disappeared and pro-
cessing plants and warehouses took their place. Long, low
affairs most of them, busy freeze-drying food, manufacturing
pharmaceuticals, or storing them prior to shipment.

And then the landscape changed again. The buildings became
taller and uglier. They sprouted tanks, cylinders, and pipes.
Wendy saw piles of ore, rivers of molten metal, and power
pallets piled high with shiny ingots.

Then the buildings shrank as a variety of retail establishments reemerged and stood shoulder-to-shoulder with their
larger two- and three-story cousins.

Lando pulled over to the curb. He cut the power and felt the truck sink onto its skirts. The turbine sighed as if exhausted by its labors.

"There's the building." Lando nodded towards a long, low warehouse on the far side of the intersection.

Wendy consulted the mapper. It agreed. "Okay, so what are we doing?"

Lando leaned back in his seat. "We're watching."

Wendy looked at the warehouse, then back to him. She was puzzled. "Watching for what?"

Lando shrugged. "For unusual activity, signs of an ambush. Who knows?"

Wendy considered the smuggler's comments. They might make sense if the cargo in question were something a little more exciting than a load of fertilizer. Mega-Metals might care, but they didn't know about it, so why the big deal?

No, the whole thing was a waste of time, and Wendy was tempted to tell Lando so. And she would've too, except for the fact that it would heighten the tension between the two of them and last leg of the journey even less pleasant. Wendy reconciled herself to a wait. What would it be? A half hour? She could handle that.

Time passed. One hour turned into two. Wendy wished that she'd brought something to read. Lando had insisted on her wearing body armor, and it felt uncomfortable under her clothes. Lando drummed his fingers on the side of his seat. It started to rain. The raindrops made little paths through the dirt on the windshield. Wendy imagined that she was in her father's house on Angel, staring out of her bedroom window.

The sound of Lando's voice jerked her back to the present.

"What did you say?"

Lando eyed her curiously. "The fertilizer. Once we get the stuff to Angel, then what? How will you get it dirtside?"

Wendy felt a sense of alarm. "What do you mean? That's *your* job!"

Lando lifted an eyebrow. "Oh really? I don't remember agreeing to that."

"Of course you did! You said . . ."

"I said I'd put the cargo 'in orbit,' " Lando finished for her. "It's *your* responsibility to get it dirtside."

"My responsibility? *You're* the smuggler!"

"True," Lando agreed calmly. "And a smart one. I would never agree to land a cargo without doing some research first. It's damned hard to put a ship down without someone noticing. What you need is a plan. A scam that'll get the fertilizer dirtside with no one the wiser."

Wendy crossed her arms and fumed. What was this? An attempt to hold her up for more money? Damn the man!

Lando sat up. "I don't know about you, but I'm hungry. I saw a greasy spoon a few blocks back. What would you like?"

Wendy ignored him.

Lando smiled and shrugged his shoulders. "Maybe they'll have something with vegetables in it. Keep an eye on the warehouse."

Lando opened the door, slid towards the ground, and disappeared.

The rain was coming down harder now, drumming on the metal roof and running in rivulets down the windshield. Blast him! Wendy opened her door and jumped to ground. Mud splashed onto her pants, and rain slapped her across the face.

She looked around, pulled up her collar, and started across the intersection. Lando was a jerk, so why humor him? She'd go inside, find the fertilizer, and force Lando to load it on the truck. After that she would . . . No . . . one thing at a time.

Her boots made a slapping sound as they hit the rain-shiny pavement. The building curved down on both sides like a cylinder buried in the ground. It had two doors. One was large enough to admit a good-sized truck, while the other was smaller, and would accommodate about 80 percent of known sentient races. The door opened to Wendy's touch. It felt good to step in out of the rain.

She found herself in an utterly unremarkable alcove. There was a door, durasteel this time, and a standard security console. The ceiling, walls, and floor were bare.

She fumbled around inside her jacket, found the piece of paper, and took it out. Troon's printing was neat and even. Using the console provided for that purpose, Wendy typed in her name, and a sixteen-digit authorization code.

There was a pause followed by a computer-generated voice. "You may enter. Your property is located in grid twenty-four.

Any attempt to remove property other than yours will result in a call to the police."

The durasteel door whirred open and Wendy stepped through. It was dim inside the warehouse and completely silent. A row of chem strips had been mounted high above and provided what little light there was. For one brief moment Wendy wished Lando was with her, but pushed the thought away. There was no one in the warehouse. There was nothing to fear.

She walked down the aisle that divided the warehouse in half. Mysterious piles of Lord-knew-what bulked to the right and left of her. Dark unlit passageways cut between the piles and disappeared towards distant walls. Something squeaked and skittered down an aisle. A rat or the local equivalent.

Wendy gritted her teeth and forced herself forward. Now she saw that slightly luminescent yellow-green lines had been used to divide the entire floor into boxes and that each section had a number. The one to her right glowed "3." Twenty-four would be a lot further back. Wendy's footsteps echoed off duracrete walls as she walked towards the back.

"Hold it right there!" The words and the hard white light came together. Wendy turned and saw two men. One was young, muscle-bound, and a little too pretty. The other was middle-aged and getting fat. Both were armed.

Something whirred and Wendy turned again. She couldn't see much more than a rectangle at first—a descending platform—but then it came level with her, and Wendy saw the woman. An older woman, with an electro-implant, and a nasty smile.

Wait a minute . . . No, it couldn't be . . . but yes, it definitely was! The woman who had asked her to say something for Wilf! She was a spy, an agent for Mega-Metals, and Wendy had led her to the concentrate. No, the woman was already here, so . . .

The platform made a dull clanging sound as it hit the duracrete floor. The woman with one eye stepped off. "Well, well, well. Look at what we have here. One of The Chosen." The woman drew a slug gun. "Where's your friend?"

Wendy swallowed. Her throat felt dry. Stall. Stall and pray for some sort of miracle. "He's at our hotel. How did you find this place anyway?"

The woman smiled and waved her weapon back and forth like a conductor's baton. "A rather tiresome cyborg told us. Not directly, you understand—no, not with a bullet through his head—but later, through the records in his office."

Troon! Troon was dead . . . murdered by this woman! Wendy was still thinking about that when the hover truck crashed through the cargo door and screeched to a halt.

Wendy heard a loud bang, felt something hard punch her in the chest, and fell over backwards. Cold duracrete hit the back of her head. She felt dizzy. It was hard to breathe. Why? Was she dying? No, the slug had smacked into the body armor, and knocked the wind out of her lungs. She rolled to the left.

She heard Lando's shout, the roar of his slug gun, and the grunt of expelled air. The older woman hit the floor only four feet away, light winking off her implant, the other eye empty of life. There was a dark spot at the center of her chest, and a rapidly expanding pool of blood. Wendy felt dizzy. Somebody should do something about that. A doctor . . . Wait a minute, *she* was a doctor . . . The world went black.

5

Wendy floated up through layers of soft grayness, not running from the darkness, but following the path of least resistance. She felt warmth touch her cheek, tasted the sweet scent of flowers, and heard the whisper of leaves playing in the breeze.

Her eyelids fluttered as she willed herself to see. Where was she? Could this be death? Was she in heaven?

Now she realized she was in a bed, a wonderful bed with crisp cotton sheets, and a quilt so light that she could barely feel its weight.

It rustled slightly as a breeze touched her face. Wendy smiled and swung her feet over the side of the bed. Her chest felt sore and she had a headache.

"And where are you going?"

The apparition was so sudden, so completely unexpected, that she shook her head in disbelief. Lando! What was he doing here? Had he been killed as well? No, if this was heaven, then he'd be somewhere else.

The smuggler smiled gently. "Sleeping Beauty awakes. Here, try some of this."

Wendy accepted the mug and took a tentative sip. It was full of hot creamy soup. It tasted good. She found she was hungry and swallowed the soup in greedy little gulps.

As Wendy ate, Lando sat on the edge of the bed and watched. Now Wendy remembered. The decision to enter the warehouse without him, the one-eyed woman, and the horrible fight. A fight that Lando had won.

She finished the soup and handed the empty mug to Lando. Suddenly tired, she fell back against the pillow. She smiled. "Hello, Pik."

Lando smiled back. "Hello, Wendy."

"I've got a feeling that I owe you a great deal." There was a bandage on the back of her head. She didn't remember her head hitting the floor but knew that it must have. She touched her chest. "Thanks for the armor."

Lando shrugged. "We were lucky."

Wendy shook her head. "No, *you* were lucky. I was stupid. *Stupid* to ignore your advice, *stupid* to go in there alone, and *stupid* to be taken by surprise. How many people did my stupidity kill?"

Lando shook his head slightly. "None. They died because they tried to kill us. The decision was theirs, not ours."

Wendy frowned. "You make it sound so reasonable. But they might be alive if I'd followed your orders. That's the trouble with evil. It *sounds* good."

Lando reached out to take her hand. His fingers were strong yet gentle. "How about a truce? You believe your way, and I'll believe mine. What's done is done, and there's no going back."

Wendy thought about that for a moment and nodded her head. Lando was right, this time, anyway.

"Well, if that's settled, I'd like to brush my teeth and see to some other needs as well."

Lando nodded understandingly. "The bathroom is nearby. I'll give you a hand."

Wendy took a peek under the sheet and felt blood rush to her cheeks. "Thanks, but I'd like to put some clothes on first."

Lando smiled. "Why? I've seen all there is to see. You're very pretty."

Wendy blushed and changed the subject. "Which brings us to an interesting question. Why a hotel rather than a hospital? And who's paying for all this?"

Lando disappeared for a moment and reappeared holding a long white terry cloth robe. It had the hotel's logo emblazoned on the breast pocket. He turned his back while Wendy put it on.

"We're staying in a hotel because it would be very difficult for me to protect you in the local hospital. As for the bill, well, consider yourself my guest."

Moving cautiously, Wendy once again swung her legs over the side of the bed. "You really think it's necessary? Protecting me, that is? You can turn around now."

Lando took Wendy's arm as her feet found the floor and she winced slightly. "Yeah, I think it's necessary. If stopping you was worth one team, then it's worth another. It will take some time for the news to make its way to Terra, and some more time for Mega-Metals to react, but they will."

Wendy supposed that he was right. She shuffled through a nicely furnished sitting area and into the bathroom.

"What about the local police?"

"We're free to leave whenever we want. The warehouse security cameras captured the whole thing. It was a clear-cut case of self-defense."

"No," Wendy said. "That's good news . . . but it's not what I meant. Wouldn't the police protect me?"

"Not really," Lando replied evenly. "They can't spare someone to guard you just on the chance that you'll be attacked."

Wendy stopped at the door. "Did you tell them about Mega-Metals and the fertilizer?"

"No. I told them the whole thing seemed like robbery pure and simple. And the stuff that woman said about killing Troon bore me out."

Lando laughed. "The hard part was convincing the police that your fertilizer was worth stealing. But the price listed on your invoice did a lot to convince them."

Wendy nodded. She'd forgotten about Troon. Another death, and even more proof that Lando was right. The company would stop at nothing.

Wendy closed the bathroom door and leaned on the sink. Troon was dead but she was alive. Not just alive, but *happy* to be alive. Was that right or wrong? The face in the mirror provided no clue.

Lando was an old hand at driving the hover truck by now. The fertilizer was stored in *The Tink's* hold, so free of any load, the truck made pretty good time.

They passed mile after mile of orderly fields. There were a variety of crops, but some low, leafy bushes seemed to be especially popular, and took up thousands of acres.

Wendy saw neat-looking farmhouses, hard-working robo-tillers, and the occasional agrobot. The newer ones stood about thirty feet tall, could perform a wide range of tasks, and crossed the fields with twenty-foot strides. They had a delicate mincing gait that ate a lot of ground without damaging the crops.

Wendy glanced at Lando. His attention was on the road. What was the smuggler up to, anyway? The ship was ready to lift, and outside of some residual soreness, so was she. And, given the fact that Mega-Metals would be extremely unhappy with them, there was every reason to leave.

She studied him more closely and wondered what he was thinking. The smuggler was a lot more complicated than he seemed. Mercenary yet altruistic. Violent yet gentle. And this trip to the country . . . What was it about?

As if in answer to her question, Lando pulled over to the side of the road and killed the turbine. The truck settled to the ground with an audible groan.

Wendy looked around. Lando had chosen a spot where other vehicles could pass. There were fields on one side and a dip on the other. It led upwards to a small hill and a copse of gently swaying trees.

Lando smiled. "The view from the top of that hill should be rather nice. Just right for a picnic."

"A picnic?"

"That's right," Lando said as he opened his door. "Some therapy for the invalid."

Wendy laughed. "I'll show you an invalid. Let's see who reaches the top of that hill first!"

Lando slid to the ground, grabbed the hotel's picnic hamper from the back of the truck, and scrambled down the side of the road.

Wendy had raced ahead and was already starting up the hill.

Lando put on a burst of speed, slipped, and fell. The fall cost him the race, but he did manage to hold on to the picnic basket.

Wendy scampered the rest of the way up the hill and stood victorious on the top. Her chest hurt a little. She waited for Lando to plod his way up the slope.

"Slowpoke."

"Cheat."

Both of them laughed. They looked around. The view was marvelous. Starting at the base of the hill, row after row of bluish green crops marched off to the horizon and disappeared. Some fluffy white clouds dotted the sky, gently pushed by a cooling breeze, all so much alike that they seemed like products of a vast machine.

Wendy breathed the beauty in and let it fill her soul. "Thank you."

Lando smiled. "For what?"

"For everything. For crashing through that door on the chance that I was in trouble, for nursing me back to health, and for bringing me here. Now I'll have good memories to balance out the bad."

Lando looked into her eyes and found himself drawn to the softness there. The hamper tell from his grasp to the ground. Their lips touched. The kiss was tentative at first, but the awkwardness soon passed.

Hands touched, bodies met, and hearts beat a little faster. It was Wendy who pulled Lando down towards the grass.

Lying there beside Wendy, his hand cupping a well-shaped breast, Lando brushed her lips with his. "Are you sure?"

Wendy smiled, one of her hands slipping down the front of the smuggler's body. "Yes, I'm sure."

Lando grinned. "It's not against your religion?"

Wendy laughed. "Of course not. Just shut up and take advantage of me. Watch my chest though . . . it's still a little sore."

Lando opened Wendy's shirt one closure at a time. "Guess what? Your chest looks fine."

Wendy raised an eyebrow. *The Tinker's Damn* was in hyperspace and had been for hours. They were seated in the ship's miniscule lounge. "Wait a minute. I thought you said it was my problem."

Lando grinned over his coffee cup. "I changed my mind."

Wendy did her best to look stern. "Oh? And why was that?"

"Because if I get the concentrate past the company's ships, and down to Angel's surface, I'll be able to spend more time with you."

Wendy laughed. "Nicely put! Realizing of course that your idea of spending time with me involves more than friendly conversation. So what's the plan? Remembering that violence is out."

"Well," Lando answered lightly, "while you were lying around the hotel room sleeping, I did some research. It seems that Mega-Metals runs a highly automated shipping operation. Rather than pay the higher costs associated with crewed ships the company runs a fleet of automated cargo carriers."

Wendy nodded her agreement. "That's true. They're cheaper to operate and carry larger payloads to boot. The company still charges us an arm and a leg, though. But so what? How does that help us?

Lando took a sip of coffee. "Answer the following question first. You indicated that your supplies arrive via Mega-Metals hulls. Does the company search your cargo prior to landing?"

Wendy shook her head. "No, that's done at the other end. The company's security police search our supply modules before they're loaded aboard. The company claims that they're looking for contraband, but the truth is that they're checking to see what we're up to. By analyzing what we import, they can tell which crops are doing well, which aren't, and where to put more pressure on us."

"So," Lando concluded, "it's fair to say that whatever cargo comes off the carrier is taken at face value?"

Wendy's face lit up with sudden understanding. "I get it! Somewhere between Earth orbit and Angel we load the concentrate aboard their own ship! The vessel arrives, and they bring the fertilizer dirtside along with everything else. Not only that, they deliver it right to our front door! It's brilliant!"

"Maybe," Lando said thoughtfully, "and maybe not. The timing would be absolutely critical. There's no way to locate, much less board, another ship in hyperspace. That means the cargo would have to be loaded just prior to, or just after the jump. Not only that, there's the matter of available space. Would there be enough room for the concentrate?"

"Yes, sometimes," Wendy answered eagerly. "The company man, a rather unpleasant individual named Lorenzo Pal, gripes about partially loaded supply ships all the time. They lower his profit margin. But there's no way to be sure that we'd get one.

"As for the other problem, well, that's a good deal more difficult. Tugs escort the carriers out from Terra and stand by until they enter hyperspace."

Lando nodded. "So it would be impossible to load the concentrate prior to the hyperspace jump. What about afterwards? Are tugs waiting at the other end?"

Wendy bit her lower lip. It was a nice lower lip, and something about the way it moved caused Lando to think about other activities. He forced himself back on track.

"No, I don't think so. We don't get much pirate activity around Angel, and the tugs are kept pretty busy, so Pal allows the carriers to drift for a while."

"How long would that be?"

Wendy shrugged. "It's hard to say exactly. Hours at least, days at most."

Lando gave it some thought. For the scam to work, they'd have to match speeds with the carrier, land on it, crack the company's security code, fine a place to stash the additional cargo module, shift the concentrate from *The Tink's* hold to the larger vessel, secure it, and escape. All without leaving any sign of their visit. Not an easy task. Still, it would be one helluva scam, and might even impress his father.

Lando thought about the problem for a moment longer, and then raised his cup. "To a first-class scam. Let's hope it works."

6

Lando glanced at Wendy, saw that she was absorbed in a medical text, and slid out from behind the table. He walked the few short steps to the cockpit, dropped into the command chair, and checked the ship's sensors. Nothing. Not too surprising, since a buzzer would sound if a ship came near.

Lando swore softly and wiped the sweat from his forehead. The main drives were shut down to avoid the possibility of detection. The result was an unusual amount of heat buildup, less than optimum air-recycling, and a shortage of water.

Three standard days had passed with no results. How long would it take for a cargo carrier to appear? A day? A week? A month?

Things had gone pretty well up till now. Sex is fun, and done properly, takes lots of time. But even that wears thin eventually. Both wanted to talk, to share more than their bodies, but were afraid to actually do so. They were very different people. What if they disagreed? Became angry? Had a fight? No, it seemed safer to stay with what they had. And what they had was a lot of time to kill.

Lando decided to wait a bit longer. One more day. If the cargo carrier didn't show up within one standard day, they'd call the whole thing off and try something else.

The smuggler got up, made his way back to his cabin, and stretched out on the bunk. Maybe some shut-eye would make the time pass more quickly.

The harsh sound of a buzzer brought Lando up and out of a shallow sleep. He rolled off the bunk, pulled the curtains aside, and slipped into the cockpit.

Wendy had heard the buzzer as well, and arrived a few

seconds later. She wore short-shorts and a sweat-stained halter top. "Is that what we hope it is?"

Lando activated the ship's tac tank. A star system appeared, complete with color-coded planets, a yellow-white sun, a green dot that represented *The Tinker's Damn*, and a red delta that symbolized the incoming vessel. The ship had dropped in-system about halfway between Angel and the sun.

Words appeared beneath the red delta. SHIP. TYPE UNDE-TERMINED.

"It's hard to tell," Lando replied. "It's too far away. We'll have to wait."

Time passed slowly, but the incoming object was following the right track, and decelerating all the way.

Then, when the object was only a few hundred thousand miles away, a radio beacon came on. It made an intermittent beeping sound, and according to *The Tink's* sensors, was easing into an orbit around Angel's sun. It had to be a cargo carrier. A crewed ship would keep on going.

The tac tank confirmed Lando's theory with the words: SHIP. CARGO CARRIER. TYPE TM49021. REGISTRY: TERRA/MEGA-METALS HN30-78965.

"That's our baby," Lando said happily. "Let's get to work."

Lando fired the drives, felt the temperature begin to drop, and imagined that he could taste the additional oxygen in the air. Now came the challenge. To match speeds, transfer the concentrate, and escape without detection.

Like most NAVCOMPs *The Tink's* would accept instructions via voice or keyboard. Lando preferred the keyboard except for rare emergencies. It gave him a feeling of direct control.

He typed some instructions into the NAVCOMP and watched the distance between the green dot and the red delta start to shrink. He scanned the tac tank. No tugs or other vessels on their way to retrieve the carrier. Good.

The next few hours passed with agonizing slowness. First came a long period of acceleration followed by an equally long period of deceleration. But finally, after what seemed like an eternity, the waiting was over and the cargo carrier appeared on Lando's viewscreens.

The carrier was little more than a gleam of light at first, but it quickly took on shape and size, and became a long rectangular box. Each corner of the hull was marked by a flashing beacon.

Knowing that the cargo carrier would never be called upon to negotiate a planetary atmosphere, the tech types had been free to ignore aerodynamic design. And, while the resulting shape brought joy to the hearts of Mega-Metal's accountants, it had none of the streamlined grace common to smaller vessels.

No, the box-shaped hull reflected the cargoes it would carry on the journey out, and raw ore on the return. Both would fit into the cargo carrier's hull with a minimum of wasted space.

The smuggler's fingers flew across the control panel, giving the NAVCOMP some necessary freedom, but reserving the right to override the computer's decisions.

While nothing less than a computer could guide a ship from system to system, there were times when facts weren't enough and intuition came into play. Although most NAVCOMPs were self-programming, and could acquire experience, they did make mistakes about *which* experiences to retain.

Most computers had a tendency to collect information around orthodox problems and accepted solutions. A tendency that made them somewhat less than useful when sentients decided to do something unusual, such as landing one ship on another.

Unusual for *The Tink* that is, not for the company's supply shuttles, which landed on cargo carriers all the time. Their computers knew what *The Tink's* didn't.

A double row of white landing lights came on and rippled the length of the ship. The letters M-E-G-A-M-E-T-A-L-S had been stenciled lengthwise along the hull, and a green X marked the landing zone.

Lando's heart tried to beat its way out of his chest. Was someone aboard? It was possible. There were emergency crew quarters on some cargo carriers. Had a tech type come along for the ride? Had they mistaken *The Tink* for one of the company's tugs and activated the landing lights? Should Lando abort the landing and run like hell?

No, wait a minute. They'd be on the comset by now. "Hi there, it's about time you showed up," or something like that.

Lando scanned the most commonly used radio frequencies,

just to make sure. Nothing. The most obvious explanation was best.

The cargo carrier's NAVCOMP sensors had detected another ship's presence and assumed that it would land. After all, *The Tink* was the approximate size and shape of a medium-sized tug. Lando released a long slow breath.

The Tink's NAVCOMP made its approach, disapproved of the landing zone, and started to abort. Lando switched the computer to standby and took control.

The cargo carrier was closer now, and Lando could see that the landing path was more like a channel than a flat surface. It had thick raised sides with nothing at either end.

The sides were far from empty, though. They contained cargo-handling equipment, a variety of ship's systems, and yes, the emergency crew quarters. An area that held increasing interest for him.

The ship jerked slightly and the larger ship rose with alarming speed. Wendy closed her eyes.

Lando cut power to the main drives, fired the ship's retros, and used steering jets to push *The Tink* towards the carrier.

Wendy opened her eyes and saw lights flashing by. The freighter skimmed only feet above the carrier's durasteel skin. The raised sides were only feet away from *The Tink's* stubby wings.

Then, just when it seemed certain that *The Tink* would zip through the landing zone and shoot off into space, the lights slowed to little more than a crawl. There was a gentle thump as Lando put the ship down at the very center of the green X and activated the electromagnets built into the ship's landing jacks.

Wendy let out a sigh of relief. "That was something to see . . . and I never want to see it again!"

Lando released his harness and laughed nervously. "Thanks. I think. So much for problem Number One. Now for problem Number Two."

"Which is?"

"Which is breaking and entering," Lando replied, getting up from his seat. "With the emphasis on 'entering.' Breakage could cause problems. We don't want the company to know that we've been here."

Wendy released her harness and also stood up. "Won't the carrier's NAVCOMP tell them that we landed?"

"It would if they asked," Lando replied. "But I'm banking on the fact that the company has no reason to ask. Not until they hear about what happened on Weller's World, anyway."

Wendy nodded. What Lando said made sense. But how would they get inside? Surely there was an access code or something.

Lando pulled a keyboard out of a wall recess and tapped on the keys. "How about it, Wendy? Have you ever gone for a walk outside?"

"As in *outside the ship*? In space armor?"

The words PROGRAM CHECK COMPLETE rolled up on a small screen. Lando eyed them and tapped a key. The words disappeared. "Yeah, as in 'outside the ship in space armor.'"

"Never."

Lando nodded and straightened up. "That's what I thought. But that's okay 'cause there's plenty for you to do right here. See this keyboard?"

"Yes?"

"Well, when I get outside I'll ask you to operate it. If the keyboard's a problem, use voice. Keep an eye peeled for visitors too. The sensors are set for max. If one goes off, then let me know right away. Got it?"

Wendy nodded. "Operate the keyboard and monitor the sensors. Got it."

Lando grinned. "Good. Then how about a kiss?"

Wendy slid into his arms and met his lips with hers. The kiss lasted a long time.

When it ended, Lando cleared his throat. His voice was hoarse. "You're a very distracting lady. Too distracting. Remind me to continue this conversation a little bit later."

Wendy smiled. "It's a deal."

It took Lando half an hour to gather what he needed, to don his space armor, and exit through the ship's tiny lock.

The white landing lights still rippled the length of the ship and the nav beacons still flashed. The endless void stretched off in every direction. It would be easy to unclip the safety line, push hard, and drift away.

Lando shook the idea off and moved away from *The Tink's* hull. Within a matter of three or four steps he left argrav behind and entered zero-G. He checked the safety line to make sure that it was secured. It was.

Two squirts from Lando's built-in jet pak carried him over to the cargo carrier's raised side. A series of yellow arrows interspersed with the words "Emergency Quarters-Oxygen Breathers Only" led him to the personnel lock.

The outer hatch was made of durasteel. Right next to it was a pressure plate and an internally lit numeric keypad. Lando palmed the pressure plate. Nothing. Surprise, surprise. The hatch was locked.

He anchored his self-closing supply sack to the cargo carrier's hull and fumbled through his gear.

"Hey, Wendy . . . you read me?"

"Loud and clear. I can see you, too. The port vid cam has a nice clean shot."

"Good. I'll need your help on the keyboard. Enter 'Test Sequence,' but don't execute."

"Roger."

Lando found the small self-powered transceiver, checked the setting, and turned it on. A magnet held it to the deck. Assuming that everything worked correctly, the transceiver would provide linkage with a small, highly specialized computer aboard *The Tink*. A computer equipped with some useful but rather illegal programs.

"Okay . . . execute."

"Executing."

Seconds passed, and Wendy returned. "I have 'Test Sequence complete.'"

"Good. Set up 'Run Program,' and wait to execute."

"Roger."

Lando attached two leads to the numeric keypad and connected the other ends to the transceiver. An indicator light glowed red. The smuggler checked to make sure the leads were properly seated. The red light disappeared.

"Okay," Lando said, "here goes nothing. Execute."

"Executing."

Time passed. Lando used it to sip water from his suit. Wendy's voice boomed inside his helmet.

"A series of numbers appeared on the screen."

"Excellent! What are they?"

"Ten . . . seventeen . . . twenty-three . . . and twelve."

Lando punched the numbers into the keypad and watched the indicator light flash green.

"Very tricky," Wendy said approvingly. "You used the computer to run all the possible combinations until it hit the right one. That's illegal, isn't it?"

"Is it?" Lando asked innocently. "I'll check the next time I visit a law library."

The hatch cycled open. Lando unclipped his safety line and attached it to one of the many tie-downs located just outside the lock.

He stepped inside. Lights came on and threw his shadow against the bulkhead. He waited while the outer door irised closed and the ship's computer pumped an atmosphere into the lock.

A "Pressurized" sign came on. Lando checked the heads-up display inside his helmet to make sure. It agreed.

Lando opened his visor and found that the cargo carrier's air tasted musty and stale.

"Pik?" Wendy sounded nervous.

"Yeah?"

"Is everything okay?"

Lando stepped out of the lock and into the ship's emergency quarters. There were some tidy bunk beds, a serviceable galley, and a wall full of electronics. Lando headed in that direction.

"Sure . . . everything's fine. I'm inside now. Any sign of company?"

"No, not so far."

"Good. Keep your eyes peeled."

There was a chair located in front of the electronics. Lando sat down. It made a whirring noise and adjusted to his frame.

The ship's central computer sensed his presence and activated the control panel. A screen came on, and rows of indicator lights glowed red, yellow, and green.

Lando grinned. It was just as he'd hoped. Since there was no way to anticipate who might use the emergency quarters, the company had dispensed with the usual security codes.

He spoke. "Show me how much of the cargo capacity has been utilized."

Silence. It seemed that Mega-Metals didn't waste money on voice-actuated computers for the emergency quarters on its cargo carriers. The keyboard would have to do.

Although his gloved fingers made it difficult to type, Lando entered: "Cargo . . . Percentage of capacity utilized this voyage."

Words flashed on the screen: CAPACITY UTILIZED 98.7%.

Lando swore under his breath. "Damn!" So much for slipping the concentrate into an empty slot. Every freighter lost some of its hold space to odd nooks and crannies, the gaps between cargo modules, and sloppy stowage. The 1.3 percent of supposedly available space wasn't really there.

"Did you say something?"

"Yeah," Lando replied. "I did. This baby's fully loaded."

"Oh," Wendy said, obviously disappointed. "Well, that's that, I guess."

Lando tapped his fingers on the console. His gloves made a clicking sound against the plastic. "Maybe, and maybe not. We could dump some of the company's cargo and replace it with the concentrate, or locate some of your supplies and do the same thing."

Wendy thought out loud. "If you dump the company's supplies, they're almost sure to notice the discrepancy and investigate. And if you dump our supplies, then we lose something we need."

"That's about the size of it," Lando agreed. "It's a tough decision."

A buzzer sounded in *The Tink's* cockpit and made itself heard over the radio.

"We've got company, Pik! It looks like there's a tug headed our way!"

Lando felt his pulse pound in his head. He knew he should pull out, run like hell, but they were so damned close. "So what's your decision?"

"My decision? You mean you're still willing to try?"

"It'll take them hours to get here. What's your decision?"

"But they'll detect us when we break away!"

"Maybe, and maybe not. What's your decision?"

Wendy killed the buzzer. The sudden silence helped her think. An investigation was out of the question. The timing would be terrible. What if the company found out about . . . No, she mustn't even think it.

That left the second alternative. Dumping some of their own supplies. Which would the elders prefer? The concentrate,

or whatever else was aboard this particular vessel? Short of
checking the manifest, and actually asking them, there was
no way to be sure. Wendy took a chance.

"Okay, dump some of our stuff. Anything but medical
supplies, replacement parts, or lab equipment."

"Roger."

Lando instructed the computer to display all non-company
cargoes. A manifest rolled up. He skimmed the list. Tools,
clothing, medical supplies, food paks, lab equipment, replacement parts, and a long list of data cubes.

"How about clothing, food, or data cubes?"

Wendy bit her lip in frustration. Every one of the things
Lando had named was desperately needed. Still, the concentrate was absolutely critical to Angel's future. "Dump the
clothing first, food second, and data cubes last."

"That's a roger," Lando replied and went to work. Here at
least he could get some help. The cargo carrier was highly
automated and capable of loading and unloading itself. The
first problem was to locate the cargo he wanted to dump.

Lando ran the cursor down the manifest and highlighted
the items in question. With that accomplished, the smuggler
asked for and received a 3-D schematic showing the location
of each item.

Now Lando saw that the cargo was stowed in vertical stacks
under the topmost surface of the ship. The same surface *The
Tink* had landed on. So, unless the cargo he wanted to dump
happened to be on top of a stack, other modules would have to
be removed and then put back. A time-consuming chore even
with automated equipment.

The clothes were towards the stern, packed under five of the
company's cargo modules, making them impossible to access
in the time available. They would stay.

The food was located amidships, not far from the landing
zone, second in a stack of twelve.

The data cubes were in a perfect location, extremely close to
the landing zone, and right up front with nothing blocking the
way.

The problem was that the data cubes had an insufficient
mass. The concentrate would require almost double the amount
of space that the cubes occupied.

There was no doubt about it. The food would have to go.

The computer keys were oversized to accommodate space-suited hands, but Lando still found it difficult to type with gloves on. He made mistakes, and ground his teeth as he used precious seconds to correct them. The company's tug got closer and closer with every moment that passed. Lando forced the thought out of his mind.

"Wendy."

"Yes?"

"Go back to the hold. Release the straps that hold the concentrate in place. Then return to the engineering space, seal the hatch, and depressurize the cargo bay. Once that's done, instruct *The Tink's* computer to open the outer doors. Got it?"

"Got it."

"Good. Give me a holler when the doors are open."

Part of the cargo carrier's automated equipment consisted of specially designed zero-G autoloaders.

Though built to shift cargo modules weighing thousands of pounds apiece under Earth normal gravity, the autoloaders were extremely light, and looked like eight-legged Terran spiders. Under zero gravity conditions agility and control were much more important than strength.

And, similar to Earth-type arachnids, these could also spin long safety lines, which allowed them to venture out half a mile or so from the ship whenever necessary.

But, even with help from two autoloaders, it still took an hour to open the proper stack, remove the company's cargo module, launch the food into space, replace it with the fertilizer, and doctor the cargo manifest to hide the switch.

The cargo carrier's computer would still rat on them if asked the right questions, but Lando continued to hope that no one would think to do so.

As he rose from the chair, the console turned itself off and the indicator lights went dark. The smuggler looked around, assured himself that everything looked just as it had when he arrived, then headed for the lock.

"How close is the tug?"

Wendy's voice was shaky. "Damned close. Their ETA is eight hours and twenty-six minutes. They'll pick us up the moment we separate from the carrier."

Lando waited for the lock to cycle him through. Wendy was right. The tug's crew would be sure to notice if he fired up *The Tink's* drives and took off in the normal manner. The combination of heat, radiation, and electromagnetic activity would light up half their control panel.

But what if he took another approach? What if he simply released *The Tink* and drifted away? Yes, the ship's life-support systems would generate some heat, but not enough to trigger the tug's sensors. Or so Lando hoped.

The lock irised open and closed automatically. The smuggler found the safety line, clipped it to his armor, and was halfway to *The Tink* when he remembered the transceiver. There was nothing he could do but go back and get it.

A full minute passed while Lando grabbed the transceiver and his other tools, stuffed them in the self-sealing bag, and headed for *The Tink's* lock. He nearly went crazy waiting for it to cycle him through.

Once inside, he went straight to the cockpit, clumsy in his space armor, but reluctant to take it off. Every second was precious.

As a tight-lipped Wendy looked on, Lando secured the ship for takeoff, and cut power to the electromagnets. The ships drifted apart. They were traveling at nearly the same speed and in almost the same direction.

Now came the tricky part. Lando used tiny bursts of power to push the ships apart and send them on two divergent courses. With each passing minute, they'd get farther and farther apart until they were separated by hundreds, then thousands, of miles.

Far enough so that Lando's NAVCOMP could take *The Tink* in and out of hyperspace so fast that only a computer analysis would reveal the truth of what had just occurred. To those on the tug, and those in orbit around Angel, it would appear that a ship had dropped in-system and was coming their way.

The next few hours passed slowly, but the tug showed no signs of heading their way and made no attempt to hail them. The plan had worked. The tug would escort the carrier into Angel orbit, shuttles would bring the cargo modules dirtside, and the company would deliver the fertilizer into the settlers' hands.

In spite of the heat, and in spite of ship's thick atmosphere, they found an enjoyable way to celebrate. What they did wasn't especially new, but it sure was fun.

7

The ring surrounded Angel like a shining halo. It was one of the most beautiful sights Lando had ever seen. Angel looked like a blue gem streaked with brown and partially obscured by wisps of white cotton.

Time passed and the planet grew to fill Lando's viewscreens. It became more spectacular with each passing moment.

But if Angel was beautiful, the halo that surrounded it was utterly magnificent. Five to six thousand miles wide, the ring glittered with reflected sunlight, and looked as if it were made of pure silver.

As the asteroid glanced off the planet some 100,000 years before, it pushed lots of debris in front of it. Some of this material escaped the planet's gravity-well and kept on going, but most of it remained in orbit.

During the period immediately after the collision, most of the debris had passed through a bath of vaporized material. Some of the stuff had condensed around the chunks of iron and nickel and hardened into a shiny coat. The effect was absolutely amazing. The halo seemed to glow as if invested with an inner light.

"So what do you think?" Wendy asked, her eyes on the main viewscreen.

"It's the most beautiful planet that I've ever seen," Lando answered. "Bar none."

Wendy nodded. "It doesn't take much imagination to see why the original survey team named the planet 'Angel,' or why it appealed to our elders. From space it looks like the Promised Land."

Lando looked her way. "And from the ground?"

Wendy smiled wryly. "That's another story. Life isn't easy on the surface, but it can be quite beautiful."

"Like you."

The smile Lando had expected failed to appear. The look Wendy gave him was serious, intent. "You're under no obligation to stay, Pik. I enjoyed our time together, but I don't expect anything more. You can drop me dirtside and lift."

"It isn't that easy, Wendy. . . . What about Weller's World? We left three of their people dead. Mega-Metals may be lying in wait for us down on the surface."

Wendy shook her head. "Not yet . . . You said so yourself. It will take some time before they figure out what happened and try to do something about it. You'll be gone by then."

"And you?"

"That's my problem."

"You could come with me."

Wendy's eyes held his. "We're very different people, Pik. More different than you may realize. You'll see that when we get dirtside."

Lando shrugged. "Maybe, but my father gave me some advice regarding situations like this."

Wendy smiled. "I'm not surprised. I'd like to meet your father someday. So, what did he say?"

"Never throw something away until you know what it is."

Wendy nodded soberly. "That sounds like pretty good advice, Pik. We should follow it."

Their conversation was interrupted by a burst of static. The voice was female and had an obvious edge to it. "Mega-Metals orbital control to incoming ship. Who the hell are you? And what do you want?"

They wanted him to smart off. Provide them with a reason to turn on the heat. Lando forced himself to remain calm. There was no sign of video, so the smuggler decided to respond in kind. He touched a key.

"This is the freighter *Tinker's Damn* in-bound with a passenger. Our ultimate destination is the planetary surface at . . ."

Lando accepted a piece of paper from Wendy and read it out loud. " . . . at a point known as Elder's Flat."

The radio was silent for a moment, as if the operator was consulting with someone else. Then she returned.

"And the passenger is?"

Lando looked at Wendy. She nodded grimly. Lando cleared his throat. "The passenger is Dr. Wendy Wendeen."

The reply came quickly. "That's a negative, *Tinker's Damn.* You will not, repeat *will not*, put down at Elder's Flat. By authority of Imperial Charter Number IC-890214, the corporation known as Mega-Metals, along with its duly authorized employees, has the right and obligation to search all incoming and outgoing vessels for contraband materials.

"You will land your vessel at the location known as PROS-PLANT 2, where it will be searched. The coordinates are being fed to your NAVCOMP on Channel Two."

Lando started to sweat. "That's a roger, Orbital Control. Out."

Lando turned to Wendy. "It's like I said. They're waiting for us."

Wendy shook her head. "No, I don't think so. They do this sort of thing all the time."

"They knew your name."

Wendy's face was pale. She crossed her arms on her chest. "Blopar Wendeen is my father. He's president of the council and a major thorn in the company's side. I come in for special treatment as a result."

"What sort of special treatment?"

Wendy refused to meet Lando's eyes. "Annoying stuff. Nothing I can't handle."

Lando wasn't so sure, and wanted to ask some more questions, but Wendy's expression made it clear that she wouldn't answer them.

The NAVCOMP took the little ship down well north of Angel's halo. There was no reason to risk collision with thousands of orbiting rocks.

Some interesting facts were included in the information that Mega-Metals had sent.

There were other things in orbit around Angel besides pieces of rock. There was one small moon, a space station, two company-owned cargo carriers waiting to take on ore, a tramp freighter, and a variety of tugs and shuttles.

Lando saw that the planet's gravity was 0.95 G, the days were 27 hours, 46 minutes, and 40 seconds long, and it was winter in the northern hemisphere.

A winter made more severe by the fact that the northern

land mass was currently shadowed by Angel's halo.

A halo that also dumped about 250 million tons of debris into the planet's atmosphere each year, making the equatorial zone look like a battlefield, and shortening the life expectancy of anyone who ventured into it.

As *The Tink* made its way down towards the surface, Lando saw that the planet had a relatively small north polar cap and some extremely large oceans. And, because large bodies of water are notoriously difficult to either heat or cool, the entire planet had a relatively mild climate.

The ring interfered with the natural progression of seasons, but the oceans tempered the effects and kept Angel habitable, if not exactly ideal.

Lando took over from the NAVCOMP as *The Tink* entered Angel's atmosphere. He enjoyed the feel of air under the ship's stubby wings.

"So, tell me about this PROS-PLANT 2 place."

Wendy grimaced. "Watch the screens. I think the view speaks for itself."

The approach vector had brought them in over the ocean. Wind-tossed waves, each topped with a whitecap, raced in to crash against vertical cliffs. Wherever the waves hit, enormous plumes of white spray exploded upwards, paused, and fell back into the maelstrom below.

Just before the ship passed over the cliff Lando glimpsed multiple layers of rock that had pushed their way up in response to the volcanic activity of 100,000 years before.

The ship flew low, not more than a hundred feet off the ground, rising and falling with the lay of the land. Twin crags appeared and flashed by to either side. Wendy's fingers were white where they gripped the armrests.

Lando's eyes were up ahead. Now he saw what Wendy meant. The picture *was* worth a thousand words. Millions of tons of earth had been stripped away, leaving a multitude of terraces, each one stair-stepping down towards the pit below.

A whole army of orange robo-scrapers, each one the size of a good-sized apartment complex, moved inexorably along the terraces and scooped ore into their metal bellies.

And there were other, smaller vehicles as well, some robotic, and some operated by men and women. They looked like mechanical maggots, swarming through the flesh of a recently dead corpse, eating their fill.

Then the scene was gone, lost in the semipermanent murk of dust and smoke, with only the vehicles' headlights to mark them from above.

Lando touched a key and a heads-up landing grid appeared before his eyes. *The Tink* was represented by a green delta against an amber grid. Various numbers flickered across the bottom of the screen.

Lando moved the joy stick a hair to the left, saw the delta center itself on the grid, and glanced over at a viewscreen. The murk parted for a moment and he caught a glimpse of the ground. There were some prefab domes, a cluster of storage tanks, and a conventional air strip, all of which were coming up fast. The murk closed in and he switched back to the heads-up display.

The smuggler moved the joy stick a little to the right and cut power. Then, just as *The Tink* shuddered on the edge of a stall, Lando touched a key and felt the repellors kick in. The ship popped upwards slightly, then sank towards the ground and the landing area below.

The freighter touched down with the usual groan of protest, slumped to the left, and started to leak Number 3 lube. If Mega-Metals personnel were inclined to underestimate *The Tink* and her capabilities, then so much the better.

A male voice came in over the comset. "Mega-Metals Security Control to *The Tinker's Damn*. All crew and passengers will report to the main terminal building. You will leave your main lock unsecured to facilitate a contraband search."

Lando looked at Wendy. She nodded grimly. He touched a key. "That's a roger, Security Control. We're on the way."

Wendy was extremely subdued as they waited for the lock to cycle open. Her head was down and her entire body signaled defeat.

Lando couldn't figure it out. Why was Wendy so depressed? It wasn't like her. Besides, Mega-Metals could search the ship all day without finding anything more than some dirty laundry. No, it had to be something else. He tried to make small talk, draw it out of her, but Wendy's replies were short and nonresponsive.

The lock cycled open and a gust of thick dust-laden air

blasted its way inside, peppered them with grit, and rushed back out.

It bothered Lando to leave *The Tink* unsecured, but those were the orders, so he forced himself to walk away. At least there was no reception party, no phalanx of corporate police, just waiting to avenge the deaths on Weller's World.

The main terminal was a large dome-shaped affair which predated the surrounding structures by ten or fifteen years. Originally intended as only temporary while other more durable buildings were erected, the dome had proved too useful to tear down.

And now, after countless patches and re-patches, its duraplast surface had a strange mottled appearance, as if the dome were dying of some strange skin disease.

There were two orange all-terrain vehicles parked out front, along with something that looked like a main battle tank, except that it had big crablike arms instead of energy cannon and slug throwers. It sat on a huge trailer, towering at least three stories off the ground, looking for all the world like an armored beetle.

Lando wanted to ask about the vehicle but Wendy's face was even darker than before, so he let the opportunity pass.

Once off the duracrete airstrip, Lando felt gravel crunch under his boots. Repeated gusts of wind raced down the valley and tried to push him off his feet. He pulled up his collar and stuck his hands in his pockets. The air wasn't especially cold, maybe thirty-five or forty degrees Fahrenheit, but the wind-chill factor made it seem much worse.

As they approached the terminal building, Lando saw that someone had taken the trouble to mount an electro-sign over the main entrance. The flashing letters spelled out SECURITY CO TROL with boring regularity.

A stocky woman stepped out of the double doors, pulled a hood up around her face, and walked towards an all-terrain vehicle. She didn't look at them or acknowledge their existence.

Lando watched Wendy pause in front of the doors, draw herself up straight, and march forward. On the surface she looked strong, purposeful, and in control.

But Lando saw the fear in her eyes, the slight trembling of her lower lip, and knew something was terribly wrong. But what? The smuggler frowned and followed her inside.

The reception area looked as if it hadn't been cleaned or painted in years. Green paint had peeled away to reveal more green paint. There was a large, rather modern-looking reception console, but the rest of the room was a total disaster.

The floor was covered with a thick layer of semiliquid mud, the modular furniture was filthy, and a dead plant stood in one corner.

It bore a hand-lettered sign which said "To Diane, Best Wishes, The Crew."

Two doors opened into the reception area and each had a faded sign. One said OFFICE, and the other said RESTRICTED.

As Lando and Wendy came to a stop in front of the console, the "Restricted" door swung open and a middle-aged man entered the room.

The man was almost entirely bald. What little hair he had hung like a greasy curtain around the sides of his head and brushed the top of his shoulders as he moved.

The man wore a dirty orange jumpsuit with "Pops" embroidered over the left breast pocket. Having just come from the toilet, he was still in the process of zipping the suit over a hairy pot belly.

Pops stopped, looked at Wendy, and smiled. "Well, hi there, sweet lips. Nice of you to drop in. Mr. Pal is waiting. You know the way." He jerked a thumb towards the door marked "Office."

Wendy gave a short jerky nod and walked towards the door. It opened inward to let her pass.

Lando started to follow, but the big man blocked the way. He held up a huge paw.

"As you were, son. This may take a while . . . so take a load off."

The look in the man's piggy little eyes, the set of his body, signaled his readiness to fight if that's what Lando wanted to do.

Lando met the man's challenge with a smile and a nonchalant shrug. Pops outweighed him by a good sixty pounds. That, plus the possibility that there might be some muscle under all that blubber, suggested a less direct approach.

"Sounds good, Pops. The truth is that I can't wait to get rid of her. There's nothing worse than a spending a week aboard ship with a religious nut."

Pops chuckled understandingly and moved around behind the console. "She wouldn't put out, huh? Well, it's all in knowing how. You take Mr. Pal, for example. Now there's a man who knows how to get what he wants. Wish I was boss. Some people have all the luck."

Lando felt his belly tighten up, and fought to control his voice. He moved forward to lean on the console. "It sounds like Mr. Pal has a good thing going."

Pops nodded as he dropped into an oversized chair. It creaked under his considerable weight. "Yup, that's for sure."

The older man took a quick look around as if checking for witnesses, then lowered his voice to a conspiratorial whisper. "You wanta see what you were missing?"

Lando nodded eagerly and resisted the temptation to shoot Pops right between the eyes. "I sure would."

"Come around here," Pops said, motioning Lando behind the console.

The smuggler obeyed, coming around the far end of the counter, to stand by the other man's left shoulder. Now Lando understood why the security console looked better than everything else in the room. It was packed with com gear, sensor readouts, and vid screens. Some showed huge robo-scrapers moving through the murk, others showed Mega-Metals personnel going about their various jobs, and still others were blank.

"Watch this," Pops whispered, and flipped a series of switches. Suddenly Lando found himself looking at three different angles of the same room. In comparison to the reception area it was nicely furnished and spotlessly clean. But Lando had no interest in the room or its furnishings. His eyes were on Wendy and a man standing directly in front of her.

Pal was a small man, an inch or two shorter than Wendy, and rail-thin. He had dark, almost black hair, which he wore combed straight back, and even, almost handsome features. He wore the same sort of jumpsuit that Pops did, except that his was clean and pressed. In spite of his size, the company man's voice was deep and commanding.

"Look at me!"

Wendy stood completely still, her eyes focused on some point over Pal's head. The scene reminded Lando of a recruit standing in front of her drill instructor.

Pal slapped her across the face. "I said, look at me!"

Wendy's head tilted so that her eyes were in line with Pal's, but they were out of focus, as if her mind were somewhere else.

The company man nodded approvingly. "That's better. Now, given the fact that you are a member of a known subversive group, it will be necessary to search your body for illegal substances. Take off your clothes."

Wendy's face was completely expressionless as her hands came up and her fingers started to unsnap her blouse.

Pops never knew what hit him. Lando's handgun made a solid thunk where it hit the back of the older man's head. The smuggler felt reasonably sure that Pops would live, but really didn't care.

A quick check showed a selection of handguns and stunners neatly racked to one side of the console. Lando selected a stunner, aimed it at Pop's head, and pressed the firing stud.

The security man gave an involuntary jerk as his entire nervous system went into temporary spasm. The effect would last a good thirty minutes.

Lando glanced at the monitors. Pal was watching with obvious enjoyment as Wendy removed her blouse. A comset started to buzz, and Lando ignored it.

The smuggler stepped over to the entryway marked "Office," touched the plastic access panel, and waited for the door to open. Nothing. Locked from the inside.

Lando took a step backwards, kicked the door open, and walked through. Pal took his hands off Wendy's breasts, spun towards his desk, and dived for the gun belt hung on the back of his chair.

Lando yelled something incoherent as he squeezed the trigger. The slug gun made a loud booming sound as the bullet creased the corpo's side and spun him around. Blood sprayed across the beige carpet as Pal went down. He swore and went for his blaster.

The slug gun boomed again. A large hole appeared in the center of Pal's hand. He screamed and held it to his chest.

"Lando! No!"

The smuggler heard Wendy's voice but paid no attention. All the blood drained from Pal's face as he looked up into the bore of Lando's slug gun and waited to die.

Wendy hit Lando's arm just as the gun went off, causing the bullet to slide along the side of Pal's head instead of passing through his brain. The security man slumped backwards.

Lando tried to bring the gun back up, but Wendy was holding his arm. "No! Not for me! You've done enough harm already!"

Lando let the gun fall. "Harm? Done enough harm? What the hell are you talking about? That man was going to rape you!"

Wendy's eyes blazed with open fury. "That man has already raped me! He rapes me every time I come back! It's the price I pay for going off-planet."

Lando looked at her incredulously. "Are you crazy? Is that the problem? Or do you *like* being raped?"

Wendy slapped him across the face. "Damn you! And damn your mindless violence!

"Killing Pal would accomplish nothing. There are millions more just like him. That's why we must have the entire planet, that's why I allowed him to abuse me, and that's why *you* are an idiot! Thanks to you, the company has an excuse to search our settlements, and depending on what they find, people may die."

Wendy ignored Lando's astonished expression, and felt for Pal's pulse. "He'll live. Come. We must warn the elders."

Wendy picked up her clothes, turned on her heel, and headed for the door. She dressed as she went.

Lando took one last look around, and followed. By the time he reached the reception console, Wendy was already outside and headed for the ship.

Lando ignored the cacophony of buzzers, chimes, and bells, and pulled Pops away from the counter. The man slumped back in his chair.

Lando frowned as he scanned the electronics for the inevitable recorders, found the appropriate data cube, and pulled it out. A tidy little record of everything that had happened. Not much, but better than nothing. Lando slipped the cube into his pocket.

He stepped out through the front doors, took a quick look

around, and jogged towards the ship. Wendy stood in the lock and waved him on. Was she crazy or was it him? Either way they were in a heap of trouble. Lando swore and ran a little faster.

8

"This is Mega-Metals orbital control. Return to PROS-PLANT 2 at once. Failure to comply with this order will result in serious consequences."

Lando keyed his mike. "And what 'serious consequences' might those be? What will you do? Nudge me to death with a tug? Give it a rest, Orbital Control. I'll get back to you in ten or fifteen minutes."

There was a squawk of outrage, but Lando keyed the comset off. Angel loomed large below. A luminous ball surrounded by a skirt of silver. The view was spectacular, but Lando had little time to enjoy it.

The smuggler's fingers fairly flew over the keyboard as he gave the NAVCOMP control of the ship, pulled the data cube out of his pocket, and dropped it into a player.

"What are you doing?" Wendy demanded angrily. "Land this ship immediately!"

"In a few minutes," Lando answered grimly. "After we buy ourselves some insurance."

A green COPY COMPLETE light came on. Lando pushed a button and caught the new cube as it popped out. He slipped it into a pocket. Now for the next step.

"Does the Church have an attorney or business agent on Terra?"

Wendy frowned. "Yes, but I don't see what . . ."

"I need his or her name and some sort of address," Lando interrupted. "We don't have a lot of time."

"Alexis Strasser, the Imperial Tower, in Main Port."

Lando nodded and his fingers danced across the keyboard. A RECORDING light came on.

"Now will you tell me what you're doing?" Wendy asked.

"Sure. Did you see the data cube I put in the player? Well, I took it from the company's security console. It shows Pal trying to rape you."

Blood surged into Wendy's face. "It *what*?"

"It shows Pal attempting to rape you," Lando repeated patiently. "And your lawyer can use it to light a fire under the company. The Imperial Court may be jaded . . . but I think this will get their attention."

Wendy looked both shocked and confused. "You mean he taped what he did to me?"

"Yes," Lando replied gently. "That's exactly what I mean. I'm sorry."

Wendy remembered the two previous occasions when Pal had abused her. How many of the company's employees had watched and vicariously enjoyed it?

Hatred boiled up from deep inside, overflowed her self-control, and filled her with rage. Every atom of her being wanted Pal dead. She knew it was wrong, knew she should feel otherwise, but couldn't help it.

The COPY COMPLETE light came on.

Wendy's voice shook with emotion. She used the back of her hand to wipe a tear away. "So, how will you get the information to Terra?"

"*The Tink* carries two message torps," Lando replied. "One should be enough, but I'll use both just to make sure."

Wendy nodded her understanding. Due to the fact that no one had figured out how to ram a radio signal through hyperspace, ships were still the fastest way to move information from one system to another.

So, in order to meet the need for a less expensive way to move information from one place to another, the tech types invented message torpedos. The torps had hyperspace drives, a tremendous amount of memory, and could move faster than all but the most advanced speedsters.

"I'm sorry," Wendy said. "Message torps are very expensive."

Lando tapped some keys. The words "Torpedo Armed" appeared. The smuggler pushed another button and *The Tink* jerked slightly as both message torps surged away, fired their main drives, and headed out towards the nearest nav beacon.

In a week or so the torps would emerge from hyperspace near Jupiter, head in towards Earth, and announce their presence. One of the many recovery firms would pick them up and charge Alexis Strasser a stiff fee for delivery. The NAVCOMP indicated that both missiles were running straight and true.

Lando said, "Forget it," but his emotions belied the words. The message torps had been modified to carry small and somewhat illegal cargos. Each torp was worth twenty thousand Imperials. Counting the cost of the hotel on Weller's World, and Wendy's medical expenses, Lando's profit margin had fallen from a tidy half million to around four hundred and fifty thousand.

The time had come to quit goofing around and pick up his pay. All sixty-nine pounds of it.

A sensor beeped. The tac tank came to life. Lando saw that a small ship was closing in on his position. A Mega-Metals tug or shuttle. Easy fodder for *The Tink's* energy cannon and missiles. But Lando wanted to avoid conflict if at all possible.

It was like his father always said. "I've been in a lot of fights, son, and never made money off one of them yet."

Lando keyed the comset. *"Tinker's Damn* to Orbital Control. We're heading for Elder's Flat. Have your security people meet us there."

There was a burst of outraged protest, but Lando flicked the set off.

Wendy bit her lip and clutched her armrests as Lando headed for the surface. The ship bucked up and down and jerked back and forth as the smuggler forced it down through the atmosphere.

Lando watched to see if the pursuing ship would try to catch them. It didn't. Good. Someone had decided to send surface forces instead. That would take some time, and the more the better.

They came in over the ocean just as they had done before. Wendy watched the wave tops whip by to either side, and felt slightly ill.

Tall cliffs made a jagged line against the sky, and Lando was about to pull up when he saw the river. It was wide but still strong after the rough-and-tumble journey down from the mountains.

Lando moved the stick to the left just as the sun appeared.

The river turned into a highway of light and the smuggler followed it upstream.

Rocky cliffs flashed by to either side, sometimes giving way to green valleys, but always closing ranks again.

Then the walls crept in. The river became smaller, faster, and broken by rapids. As Lando pulled the ship up and out, he was surprised by what he saw.

The plateau, or "flat" as Wendy would call it, was like a pan onto which wind and rain had deposited what little topsoil the mountains had to offer.

There was low-lying scrub at first, cut here and there by man-made roads, eventually giving way to carefully tended fields.

Some fields were planted, and some weren't. All of them had been contoured to minimize soil loss. No wonder the settlers were willing to pay such a high price for fertilizer. Farming had always been tough, but the conditions on Angel made it close to impossible.

There were houses as well, each one neat as a pin, surrounded by a cluster of sheds. Most were made of stone, something Angel had plenty of, but were missing the chimneys that one would normally expect to see.

Given the lack of forests, or nearby coal deposits, the settlers had nothing to burn. As a result, each house had to be equipped with its own fusion plant imported at great expense from one of the inner planets.

The town was small and carefully laid out. It consisted of two- and three-story buildings, an arrow-straight street, and a large church with an old-fashioned steeple. The whole thing looked like a scene from ancient Earth.

"There," Wendy said, pointing towards the bow viewscreen. "That's the airfield."

Viewed from above, the airfield looked like little more than a giant "X" that someone had scraped out of the ground. Lando saw a prefab hangar and a couple of beat-up planes, but nothing big or fancy enough to be corporate.

Good. It would be nice to have a little time before Mega-Metal's goons arrived and started to throw their weight around.

Lando killed speed, switched to repellors, and felt the landing jacks thump down a few moments later.

The Tink slumped to the left, but Lando decided to dispense with the phony leak. Might as well save the Number 3 lube for someone who cared.

He did leave the ship's systems on standby, however. He hoped the Mega-Metals rep would listen to reason, but you never knew. He could run if push came to shove. Assuming they let him get aboard the ship, that is.

The Tink was almost entirely surrounded by ground vehicles by the time Lando and Wendy climbed down from the lock. There were beat-up trucks, tractors, and homemade creations that defied description.

Behind them Lando saw flat, uncultivated ground, the dark clustering of the town, and the white-capped mountains beyond. He noticed that clouds had moved in to hide the sun and erase most of the shadows.

Lando watched as men, women, children, and dogs crowded in and around Wendy, all talking, laughing and barking at once, each eager to hug, kiss, or in some cases, lick her hand.

Lando felt envious. He had many things, not the least of which was *The Tink* and the freedom that the freighter represented. But Wendy had her people, a place to call home, and a cause that she believed in. It looked like a lot.

The crowd parted suddenly and people looked his way. Wendy moved forward with a large, awkward-looking man at her side.

The man's bones were visible under the surface of his wind-reddened skin. A shock of white hair stood straight up from the back of his head, and that, along with the beard that whipped sideways in the wind, gave him the look of an old-time prophet. He was dressed in heavy work clothes and wore a circle-and-triangle pendant around his neck.

But it was the man's eyes that caught and held Lando's attention. They were brown like Wendy's, warm in a way, but almost fanatically determined.

Lando knew that this was Wendy's father, the source of her strong personality, and a force to be reckoned with. It was something they had in common. Strong fathers and mothers who died young.

The man extended his hand and Lando took it. Wendy performed the introductions.

"Pik Lando, I'd like you to meet my father, Blopar Wendeen. Father, this is Pik Lando."

Lando found tremendous strength in the other man's hand. A hand heavily scarred by endless hours spent repairing machinery, and callused by hard physical labor.

"It's a pleasure to meet you, sir."

Wendeen nodded pleasantly, but his eyes were like lasers, cutting through the surface to see within.

"The pleasure is mutual, Citizen Lando," Blopar Wendeen replied gravely. "I look forward to giving you a proper welcome and hearing of your adventures. Unfortunately, Wendy informs me that there are other, more pressing matters to deal with first."

"Look!" a little boy yelled. "The corpos are coming!"

Lando turned in the direction of the boy's pointing finger and saw that he was correct. A VTOL aircraft had made its way through the mountain pass to the north and was coming in for a landing. It made a wide turn, and Lando saw the Mega-Metal markings and the words "Corporate Police" stenciled along the fuselage.

He turned back to Wendeen. "Yes, sir. I had a little disagreement with a man named Lorenzo Pal. He was wounded."

Blopar Wendeen frowned. "No offense, Citizen Lando, but we abhor violence, and I don't see why we should be held responsible for *your* actions."

Lando felt the blood rush to his face. He fought to control his voice. The sound of the VTOL's engines grew louder.

Wendy held up a hand, as if anticipating what Lando would say. "Pik . . . please . . ."

But Lando's attention was focused on her father. He raised his voice in order to be heard over the sound of the aircraft engines. "Well, *Citizen* Wendeen, maybe *you* think Lorenzo Pal has the right to rape your daughter each time she returns to this planet, but *I* don't!"

Wendeen looked at Wendy, saw the confirmation in her eyes, and dropped his head. A full minute passed before he spoke. "Some say that we're fanatics . . . and at times like this . . . I wonder if they're right. If only I had known."

Wendeen looked lovingly at his daughter. Tears ran down his cheeks and into his beard. "I helped create the situation in which this could happen. Later, when this is settled, I will beg my daughter's forgiveness."

The VTOL settled into a cloud of dust. Its engines wound down.

Lando nodded. "We're out of time. Will you allow me to speak for you?"

Wendeen looked at the smuggler. "Nonviolently?"

Lando gestured towards the VTOL and the heavily armed corpos. "I'm tempted to shoot all twelve of them, but I'll try to control myself."

Wendeen frowned, realized that it was a joke, and smiled. "Yes, Citizen Lando. You may speak for us."

Lando nodded. "Good. But just because I promised to be non-violent doesn't mean they did. Tell your people to clear out."

Fire flashed deep in Wendeen's eyes. "No, Citizen Lando, such is not our way. We will stand at your side. If the security police open fire they must kill us as well."

Lando couldn't see the logic of this, and thought it was similar to the way that Wendy had sacrificed herself to Pal, but didn't say so. Why bother? It wouldn't do any good.

Lando turned and walked towards the corpos. Wendy, her father, and all the rest followed. It was important to be aggressive, to gain the upper hand.

It made a strange scene, the heavily armed corpos, marching shoulder to shoulder towards the unruly crowd of men, women, and children, the clustering of vehicles, and the wind-swept plain beyond.

Then the corpos began to spread out, making themselves harder to hit, and doing their best to look tough. But it seemed kind of silly, given the circumstances.

Outside of Lando's slug gun, and the mini-launcher up his sleeve, the settlers were armed with nothing more lethal than a shovel or two.

Then as both groups slowed, and came to a halt, a woman stepped forward. She wore brand new body armor and looked scared.

Lando's first reaction was surprise. He'd expected something in the Pal mode. A lean, mean, enforcement machine.

Still, it made a kind of sense. A man like Pal would never tolerate someone like himself as a Number Two. Too damned threatening. No, he'd choose a toady, a yes person, and here she was.

The woman cleared her throat. She wore her hair in a no-nonsense crew cut. She crossed her arms to hide the fact that her hands were shaking.

"My name's Corvo. Which one of you owns that ship?"

Lando stepped forward. "I do. Are you in charge of corporate security?"

The woman flinched as if surprised by Lando's aggressive tone. "Yes, for the moment anyway. Now, see here. I . . ."

"No, *you* see here," Lando said angrily. "I wish to file formal charges against one of your employees. Lorenzo Pal tried to force his attentions on my client through an inappropriate use of his quasi-governmental powers. I insist that he be arrested and shipped to Earth for trial."

One of the woman's goons, a skinny man with a weasel-like face, whispered in her ear. Corvo nodded and looked triumphant. Lando groaned to himself. One of Pal's more experienced assistants was trying to regain the upper hand.

Corvo managed something resembling a sneer. "Nice try, spacer. But I know the truth."

The corpo turned to the crowd. She pointed at Lando. "This scum attacked our receptionist, beat him unconscious, and shot Mr. Pal. Fearing for Dr. Wendeen's life, Mr. Pal sent us here to place this man under arrest and put him away where he belongs. Like you, we detest violence."

There was anger in Blopar Wendeen's eyes. He started to say something but stopped when Lando held up a hand.

The corpos reached for their guns as the smuggler dipped his other hand into a pocket and withdrew the cube.

Lando shook his head in amusement. "You're pretty well-armed for a bunch of pacifists. Here, take a look at this." He tossed the cube to Corvo.

She fumbled the catch and dropped the cube, then bent to pick it up. "What's this supposed to be?"

Lando smiled. "Proof. Proof taken from your own surveillance system. Sound and pix of Lorenzo Pal forcing himself on Dr. Wendeen, going for his blaster, and paying the price."

A crafty look came over Corvo's face. She allowed the cube to fall, then stepped on it. The plastic shell made a crunching sound. "Oops! Silly me! Oh well, that's the way it goes sometimes. Now . . . put your hands on top of your head and turn around."

Lando made no move to obey. "You can step on as many copies as you like . . . the original is still on its way to Earth. I launched two message torps just outside the atmosphere."

Corvo frowned and looked at weasel-face. He shrugged, said something inaudible into a boom mike, and waited for a reply.

With their attention spans exhausted, children and dogs both began to play. Shouting and barking with excitement, they darted here and there, running between the goons, making them nervous.

It's hard to maintain an atmosphere of confrontation with children playing around you, and Lando could feel the tension ease. At least two of the tough-looking corpos broke into grins and petted dogs or winked at the children.

Then the reply came. Weasel-face said something angry, shot a mean look in Lando's direction, and whispered in Corvo's ear.

The administrator eyed the crowd and wished that she was somewhere else. She cleared her throat and looked uncertain.

"Orbital control confirms a launch. What message did you send?"

Lando considered the various possibilities. One part of him, the more emotional part, urged him to go for broke. He could tell the big lie, claim friends in high places, and suggest that legal action was inevitable. By doing so, he'd scare the hell out of Corvo and maybe Pal.

There was a down side however. Scared people do stupid things. Innocent people might get hurt. That suggested another approach. It wasn't as satisfying, but it would prevent the situation from escalating out of control. Lando felt the pressure of many eyes and forced a smile.

"Both torps carried the same message. The recipient was requested to hold the evidence for thirty days. Should they receive no further instructions within that period of time, they were instructed to file formal charges against Mega-Metals Incorporated. I don't know what you think, but I believe that once introduced into evidence, Mr. Pal's footage would create quite a stir. Enough to bring one of Prince Alexander's investigators out for a little look-see."

Lando gestured towards the crowd. "They wouldn't mind. Would you?"

Lando could almost see the wheels turn as Corvo struggled to take it in. He waited breathlessly to see if she'd bite, and took a deep breath when she did. Though a good deal less physical than Pal, Corvo was no fool, and she knew an escape clause when she saw one.

"So it's your opinion that our, ah, differences could be settled locally?" Corvo ventured.

Lando shrugged and looked around. "Well, given the fact that Mr. Pal has already suffered some degree of punishment, I think an agreement could be reached. Providing that you leave these people alone."

Corvo looked relieved. "Good. And who shall we contact for further discussions?"

Lando looked at Wendy. She looked at her father. Blopar Wendeen smiled thinly and inclined his head.

Lando turned back towards Corvo. "Citizen Wendeen will speak on behalf of his daughter and the settlers."

Corvo nodded and started to turn away. Weasel-face touched her arm and whispered something in her ear. The administrator frowned and turned back.

"And you?"

Lando lifted an eyebrow. "I'll stay for a few days in order to make sure that things go smoothly."

Corvo mustered her courage. "Three days and no more."

Lando had every intention of leaving in less. News of the fracas on Weller's World could arrive at any time, and once it did, all hell would break loose. He nodded his agreement.

The goons disengaged themselves from the children, backed away, and headed for the VTOL. Starters whined, engines caught, and the aircraft lifted off.

Lando felt very exposed, and very much aware of the VTOL's guns as it swept over the crowd, blasting them with grit. He could almost hear the roar of the aircraft's cannons and feel the impact of the slugs. But nothing happened and the plane was soon gone.

Wendy touched his arm. "I didn't know about the thirty-day thing. That was extremely clever."

Lando smiled. "Yeah. Too bad I didn't think of it at the time. Sol only knows what your attorney will do when those torps arrive."

Wendy looked surprised and started to laugh.

Lando laughed too, and discovered that it felt very, very good.

9

Lando felt around for a handhold, found one, and gathered his strength. He was almost there. The spire of granite called Elder's Rock stood towards the west side of the flat and pointed towards the sky like an accusing finger. For reasons of stubbornness and male pride Lando had agreed to climb it.

Wendy had scampered up the spire like one of the bioengineered rock goats on Lando's native Ithro. She was on the summit by now, enjoying the view, and no doubt laughing at her less gainly companion.

Lando pulled with his arms and pushed with his legs. The top part of his body scraped up and over the edge of the cliff. Good. He heard Wendy's voice but refused to listen. He was almost there and would make it on his own. It was evening and the light had started to fade.

Lando scrabbled for a new handhold, found one, and swore as it came loose. The rock made a clattering sound, followed by silence, followed by a distant thump as it hit the talus a hundred feet below. Lando didn't look. He was afraid to.

His hand found a small crevice. He pulled. One leg came up over the edge and was quickly followed by the other. He rolled to the right and found that a pair of petite climbing boots blocked the way.

"You can get up now."

Lando did a push-up and got to his feet. A cold wind tried to find a hole in his jacket and failed. The smuggler brushed himself off.

"Thanks. Remind me to ask some questions the next time you suggest a 'nice little walk.' "

Wendy was contrite. She took his hand and looked up into his face. "I'm sorry, Pik. It's just that it's so beautiful up here. I wanted you to see it."

Pik looked around. There wasn't much room, just a few square yards of relatively flat space, and a low windbreak made from loose rock.

Wendy saw the direction of his gaze and smiled. "I made that when I was a little girl. I used to sleep up here. I was scared, but the view was worth it."

Lando thought about a little girl brave enough to climb a cliff and stay all night on the summit by herself. Enduring the cold and loneliness to fulfill some inner need.

Wendy took the smuggler's arm and turned him towards the south. "Look, Pik."

There was the town in the foreground, and the mountains beyond, but they were nothing compared to Angel's halo. It was as reflective as a field of freshly fallen snow. The much-elongated reflection of the sun, dazzlingly bright, bounced off the halo and speared Lando's eyes. He squinted and looked away.

The same ring that looked like silver from space was white when viewed from the planet's surface during the late afternoon. It arched over the mountains like a rainbow pointing towards a distant pot of gold.

"Beautiful, isn't it?" Wendy asked. "But you should see it at night. That's why I used to come up here."

Lando *had* seen the halo the night before. A part of the ring had been obscured by the planet's shadow. The edge of the lighted area had been reddened by the passage of sunlight through Angel's atmosphere at first; then, as the night wore on, the shadowed portion of the halo had risen higher in the sky. And, about three hours after sunset, the far edge of the shadow became visible as the reddened dawnside rose in the east.

By midnight there was a fully illuminated white ring visible to both east and west, fading into red, and then black to the south. Seen from the top of the spire and unobscured by the surrounding mountains it would be unbelievably beautiful.

"The view's gorgeous," Lando agreed.

Wendy looked up into his eyes. "Was it worth the climb?"

"Well worth the climb," Lando said solemnly, looking at her instead of the halo.

The kiss lasted a long time. It was warm flesh and cold wind all mixed together.

Both were silent for a while after the kiss ended. Wendy spoke first.

"You're lifting tomorrow?"

She knew the answer, but Lando replied anyway. "Yes. Enjoyable though my stay's been, it's time to make some money."

"Some *more* money," Wendy said tartly. "You already have sixty-nine pounds of gold in *The Tink's* hold."

Lando nodded. Wendy was right. He'd loaded the nugget the night before. Mega-Metals used a whole array of surveillance satellites to spy on the settlers. Satellites so sophisticated that they could read a book over your shoulder. But there was a small gap in the coverage between two and three in the morning and Lando had taken advantage of it to load the nugget. *The Tink* was ready to lift.

But was he? He had something with Wendy, but what? And was it worth giving up his profession for?

The smuggler knew Wendy well enough by now to realize that she wouldn't settle for anything less than everything.

The questions brought no easy answers, and besides, there was Corvo to consider. Corvo and Pal both. He should leave before they heard about Weller's World. The message torps might protect the colonists for a while, but Lando fell into a somewhat different category.

Wendy interrupted his thoughts. "Will you join us for dinner? Father would like to talk with you."

Lando looked into her eyes. He saw the same mixture of things that he felt. He smiled.

"Sure, providing that I survive the climb down."

Lando did survive the climb down, but was grateful when his boots touched solid ground.

Wendy had borrowed her father's beat-up utility vehicle for the trip to Elder's Rock. The UV was little more than a platform on four wheels. There were two seats, one in front of the other, and handlebars instead of a steering wheel.

Lando climbed into the seat directly behind Wendy, and held on for dear life as she took off across the plain.

Wendy seemed to delight in tight turns, spine-jarring jumps, and gravel-spewing speed. Lando didn't know it, but she was exacting a measure of revenge for the landing aboard the cargo carrier, as well as their most recent reentry.

It was dark by the time they pulled into the gravel-covered parking area behind Blopar Wendeen's house. It was a low, rambling structure, half underground to conserve energy, and almost invisible against the night. Only the bright rectangles of yellow light served to show where it was.

Gravel crunched under their boots as they approached the back door. Wendy pulled on the old-fashioned string latch and the door swung open on well-oiled hinges.

Lando followed her into an anteroom. It was small, and except for the work clothes that hung along both walls, completely bare. The only light came from a single chem strip on the ceiling. Lando waited for Wendy to open the next door, but she didn't. She looked embarrassed.

"I'm sorry, Pik, but to the best of my knowledge, no one has ever worn a weapon inside our house."

Lando nodded, unbuckled his gun belt, and hung it on a peg. He still had the mini-launcher up his sleeve, but figured what Wendy didn't know wouldn't hurt her.

She smiled her thanks and opened the inner door.

Lando felt a wall of warm air touch his face, and smelled a wonderful combination of food and aromatic tobacco. There was a short flight of stairs that led down into a combination kitchen-living room. It was a large, cheerful affair full of improvised furniture, family mementos, and warm colors.

There was light from above, and Lando looked up to see where it came from. A large skylight had been cut into the south side of the slightly pitched roof. It made a perfect frame for Angel's halo, and was also a source of illumination since the ring would reflect sunlight throughout the night.

Blopar Wendeen apologized as he hurried forward to shake Lando's hand. He wore a smile and a long white apron. "Sorry about the tobacco smoke, son. It's a nasty habit . . . but I enjoy it thoroughly. Thanks for coming."

Lando took note of his sudden elevation from "Citizen Lando" to "son," and wondered if it signaled acceptance or something a little less obvious.

But if the other man's motives were less than pure, there

was no sign of it in his handshake or friendly smile. "I hope you like stew . . . minus the meat of course."

Lando said that he did, and sat next to the kitchen counter, as Wendeen cooked, and told some well-rehearsed stories.

But if Wendeen was an amiable host, he was a father as well, which Lando learned as the two of them sampled some stew. Wendeen took a bite and looked up from the steaming spoon.

"So, did Wendy take you to the top of Elder's Rock?"

Lando nodded. "Sort of. She ran to the top and waited for me to arrive."

Wendeen laughed and scattered some seasonings over the stew. "That's Wendy, all right. She wanted to climb that spire from the time she could walk. Never would've allowed it myself, but her mother had a different turn of mind, and you can see who won."

Lando had wondered about Wendy's mother, but never worked up the nerve to ask. Wendeen seemed to read his mind.

"My wife took a bad fall when Wendy was twelve. We did the best we could, and they might've saved her on one of the inner planets, but she passed away. We didn't have a real doctor back in those days."

Lando nodded soberly. It all made sense. Wendy's interest in medicine, her father's influence, and her strong personality. "I'm sorry."

Wendeen shrugged as he ladled generous helpings of stew into mismatched earthenware bowls. "God gives, and God takes away. That's how it is."

Wendeen glanced towards Wendy, assured himself that she was out of earshot, and smiled.

"Just a word to the wise, son. Wendy likes you. The trip to Elder's Rock proved that. And if you like her too, then well and good. But cause her pain . . . and you'll answer to me."

Lando nodded dutifully, but wasn't impressed. What sort of punishment could a pacifist mete out? And besides, where the hell was Blopar Wendeen when Lorenzo Pal was molesting his daughter?

The meal went well. Wendeen steered the conversation away from The Church of Free Choice and towards other matters. He had some fascinating stories to tell, and Lando enjoyed hearing them.

Wendy was uncharacteristically silent during most of dinner, glancing from one man to the other, apparently content to listen rather than speak. This seemed strange and caused Lando to wonder where things were headed.

So, while he enjoyed himself, the smuggler was careful to consume only one glass of the wine which was served with dinner.

"Always check the menu to see if you're on it," his father liked to say. And sure enough, more visitors started to arrive the moment they cleared the table.

They came in singly and in two's and three's. Older men and women mostly, but with a scattering of the middle-aged, and one or two younger people. Most wore the triangle-and-circle pendants favored by Wendy and her father. Wendy introduced them as "Elder" this and that, so Lando knew that his suspicions had been correct. Blopar Wendeen *was* up to something. But what? There was no way to tell.

It took a while for the elders to arrive. But finally, when the living area was full of people, and the air was thick with tobacco smoke, Wendeen stood and held his hand up for silence. The low murmur that filled the room died away.

"Welcome. And thank you for leaving the comfort of your homes to join me in mine."

There was a chorus of "glad to be here's" followed by curious stares as the visitors switched their attention to Lando.

The smuggler looked at Wendy, but she refused to meet his eyes. There was something afoot and she knew what it was.

Wendeen relit his pipe and spoke between puffs of blue smoke. "By now you've noticed that there's a stranger among us. Some of you have met him and some haven't.

"His name is Pik Lando. Thanks to him, and my daughter Wendy, we'll soon have the fertilizer we need. Fertilizer that is only part of a rather ambitious plan."

Lando saw heads nod in agreement and wondered what was going on. Plan? What plan?

Wendeen nodded as if acknowledging Lando's question. "I'll return to that in a moment. First we must vote.

"As all of you know, our plan depends on obtaining some rather critical items, and given the current state of tension between ourselves and the corpos, that becomes more difficult with each passing hour. Lorenzo Pal will be up and around pretty soon. The corpos will clamp down the moment that occurs."

Wendeen looked around as if making sure that the elders understood the seriousness of what he'd said. Satisfied that they did he continued.

"In order to obtain the items we need, and bring them to Angel, we'll need some transportation. Not just *any* transportation, but the kind that Citizen Lando supplies, the kind that goes around the corpos.

"We had originally planned to wait a little longer, to finish the laboratory first, but time is of the essence. Each passing day brings with it the threat that the corpos will discover our plan, that one of our own will betray us, that everything we've worked for will be destroyed."

Lando paid close attention, not just to the part that referred to him, but to the rest as well. The fact that some members of the Church might betray the rest was especially interesting. It made the entire organization seem more human.

Blopar Wendeen cleared his throat. His voice cracked. "I allowed Wendy to undertake this last mission based on the belief that the corpos trusted her and would pay less attention to her activities than they would to mine. I thought they were human beings, who, having benefited from my daughter's services as a doctor, would allow her to come and go unmolested. I was wrong."

There was a long moment of silence. Heads nodded in agreement. This was a small community. Everyone knew what had happened. Lando looked at Wendy. She met his eyes and smiled rigidly.

Blopar Wendeen looked around the room. "I am not a violent man."

Lando heard a scattering of "amens." The feeling was different now. It was as if a hard and determined spirit had entered the room. A spirit that had been born on a hundred rim worlds, nurtured deep within a thousand hearts, and brought here to flower.

Wendeen's eyes flashed and his body seemed to swell with power. "The Church Of Free Choice will run no further. This is *our* planet, *our* heritage, *our* home. We will not stoop to violence, but we *will* keep that which is ours, even if that means war!"

Lando was truly confused now. A nonviolent war? How could that be? But a loud chorus of "hear! hear's!" and "so be it's," drowned the thought out.

"So," Wendeen continued, "the choice is this. Shall we take Citizen Lando into our confidence? Shall we secure his services? Or wait until later, in the hope that conditions will improve?"

A tough-looking middle-aged man with wind-roughened skin and a deeply lined face jumped to his feet. "I say we should act now! Blood has already been spilled over this matter. Let's move now before things get even worse!"

"Maybe, and maybe not," an elderly woman said, her voice hard and unyielding. "Patience is a virtue. Besides, how do we know we can trust this man?"

Now Wendy got to her feet. "I am not an elder, but request permission to speak."

Five or six voices said, "Granted," and Wendy nodded her thanks.

"I, better than any of you, can answer the question posed by Elder Nakasoni. Pik Lando saved my life. First on Weller's World and then on Angel. On both occasions he acted without expectation of a reward. My mission would've ended in failure without his help. I didn't know Jonathan Troon was a member of our Church, but I liked him, and he liked Pik Lando. Troon called Pik a man of honor, and I agree."

Wendy took her seat to mild applause, and the debate raged on for another fifteen or twenty minutes.

Lando was annoyed at first, but by the time a vote was taken, he was angry.

The meeting, and the vote which followed, assumed his cooperation. With the exception of Wendy, everyone else had discussed him as though he were little more than a robot who would automatically do whatever they ordered.

Lando came close to walking out. Only Wendy's anxious expression kept him from doing so.

The vote was overwhelmingly in favor of action, and Blopar Wendeen nodded his head in satisfaction. His eyes swept the room and came to rest on Lando.

"Thank you. The next order of business involves an apology

to Citizen Lando. Pik, I apologize for the way we treated you just now. We must seem extremely arrogant. Can you possibly forgive us?"

Faced with such a sincere and straightforward apology, Lando felt his anger dissipate like the air from a punctured balloon. He still felt resentful, but could hardly admit it.

"Apology accepted."

The elders murmured their approval, and Wendy smiled encouragingly.

Blopar Wendeen beamed his approval. "Good. I can see why my daughter likes you."

Most of the elders laughed, and Wendy blushed. Lando felt himself smile, realized that the older man had played him like a well-tuned violin, and felt helpless to stop it.

Wendeen made a gesture with his pipe. "So, let's get down to business."

The words were addressed to the entire group, but his eyes were on Lando.

"I'm going to entrust you with a secret. The same secret that cost Jonathan Troon his life. We are about to declare war on the corpos. No, not the kind of war that most of us are used to, but an open conflict nonetheless. A conflict that we didn't start."

Wendeen made an expansive gesture. "We wanted to buy this entire world, settle here, and live out our lives in peace and harmony.

"Then Mega-Metals came along with their hired help, robotic equipment, and limitless greed. The law requires that they remain on their half of the world, but many are the times that we've found their robo-prospectors searching our land for mineral deposits. It would be naive to think that such occurrences are 'system malfunctions' as they claim. And it would be equally naive to think that they are satisfied with only half the planet.

"But that's not all. Bit by bit, hour by hour, and day by day the corpos are killing this world. Their drills reach deep into the ground, pump out the water, and replace it with liquid waste. Their airborne emissions pour into the atmosphere, are caught by the winds, and carried to our lungs.

"Their machines strip away the surface of the planet, destroy what little topsoil there is, and breed new wastelands."

Wendeen paused dramatically, his eyes flashing, and pointed out towards the world beyond. "What the corpos have launched is nothing less than ecological war! They know of our agrarian ways, of our distaste for violence, and are determined to use that knowledge against us!

"By exploiting their half of the world, and poisoning the rest, they hope to drive us away as others have done in the past. They think we'll pack our bags and run! But we're through running! It's they who shall run, and damned fast too!"

There was a chorus of "hear! hear's!" Lando cleared his throat.

"You mentioned a secret."

Wendeen nodded. "In order to understand the secret you must first understand our history. The secret is this: There are a number of highly trained scientists sitting in this room. Men and women with advanced degrees from all over the empire. Working together, they've designed a new ecosystem for Angel. An entire scheme of plant and animal life custom-designed to meet the conditions found on this planet."

Lando nodded his understanding. Many colonies tinkered with their new homes, and in some extreme cases, entire planets had been terraformed. But such efforts were extremely expensive, and therefore rare.

Wendeen held up a hand. "I know what you're thinking, and that's not what I mean. *What I'm talking about is an ecosystem that's compatible with our philosophy.* Think of it! An ecosystem that devours most forms of metal! An ecosystem that consumes robo-crawlers, tractors and weapons, and returns them to the soil. In short, an ecosystem that will drive Mega-Metals off our planet!"

Lando started to say something but Wendeen interrupted.

"Yes, we'll be forced to give up some of the technology we presently use, and we'll have to find a way to seal off some of our laboratory facilities, but the results will be worth it."

Lando gave it some thought. It was a radical idea. To shape a world for an agrarian society rather than a techno-logical one. If the idea worked, the value of Mega-Metals' investment would plummet, and the settlers would be able to buy the other half of the planet for a song and live happily ever after.

Suddenly Lando realized that everyone was waiting for him

to speak. "It's a brilliant concept but where do I come in? Where is this ecosystem now? And how does one transport an entire ecosystem? If memory serves me correctly, a man named Noah was the last one to try it."

It was Wendy who replied. "The ecosystem was designed here, but manufactured on Techno. And you won't have to move the mature ecosystem. Just the microorganisms that pave the way for the rest. The higher life forms will come later. *The Tink* could handle the whole thing in one trip."

Lando had heard of Techno but had never actually been there. Techno had started life hundreds of years before as a small research lab orbiting Terra.

But a dispute with the planetary government had caused the scientists and technicians who ran the habitat to declare their independence and remove the lab from Earth's gravity well.

Techno had its own orbit now, conveniently located between Earth and Mars, but much, much larger than its original size. Over the years it had grown, one module at a time, until it was a third the size of Terra's moon.

As such, it was a small, independent, and self-sufficient universe, inhabited by some of the best scientists in known space, all working for the highest bidder. If anyone could manufacture a custom designed ecosystem, they could.

Blopar Wendeen interrupted his thoughts. "So you'll help us? We're a little short of cash at the moment . . . but we'll make regular payments . . . and pay reasonable interest."

Lando looked at Wendy. She shrugged her shoulders and smiled.

The smuggler looked around the room. The elders looked back. The whole thing was crazy. A nonviolent war waged against a violent opponent. Lando knew he should say "no," should climb in his ship, lift, and never look back. They couldn't pay him, for Sol's sake. Not right away, and who knew if they ever would?

Lando's eyes met Wendy's. They were filled with a combination of hope and despair. He tried to open his mouth, tried to say "no," and found he couldn't. Not with Wendy sitting right there.

"I'll sleep on it."

There was a collective sigh. Faces dropped. The elders were disappointed.

Blopar Wendeen was no exception, but he nodded his understanding, and brought the meeting to a close.

There was a silent prayer, a quick kiss from Wendy, and a promise to see her in the morning.

A scientist named Nelson Lakowski offered Lando a ride in his truck and he accepted.

Lakowski's wife was with him, so there was no room in the vehicle's tiny cab, but Lando welcomed the chance to be alone in the back.

Angel's halo was gorgeous. It arched from horizon to horizon like a bridge of light. But even its glory was put to shame by the steady stream of meteors that flashed across the sky, maybe one a second, falling on the equatorial zone like a fiery rain. Lando leaned back against the bulk of a folded tarp and let the beauty of it carry him away.

It seemed like only seconds had passed when Lakowski came to a jerky stop off *The Tink's* starboard wing. The spaceship was a black blot against the stars. A single greenish-blue light hung over the door of the distant hangar.

Lando jumped down from the truck, thanked Lakowski for the ride, and strolled towards the ship. Somehow, without even trying, his mind was made up. He liked Wendy, but this eco-war thing was half-baked at best, and could go seriously wrong. His answer would have to be "no."

He passed under a stubby wing, checked to make sure that a tie-down wire was sufficiently taut, and headed for the ship's lock. He was tired and couldn't wait to climb into his bunk. He needed some sleep, a shower, and a big breakfast. Maybe then he'd feel up to seeing Wendy.

The blow took him completely by surprise. It hit him in the side of the head and hurt like hell. Lando stumbled, reached for his gun, but it was too late. Powerful arms wrapped themselves around his midsection and immobilized his hands.

He saw a foot and stomped on it. His reward was a blow to the face.

He heard someone say, "take his gun," and felt it jerked from his holster.

The arms around his midsection disappeared and were replaced by a half nelson.

"Hold him up." The voice was familiar but Lando couldn't quite place it. Then he didn't have to, as Lorenzo Pal stepped out of the shadows and stood before him. The corpo wasn't so pretty anymore. He favored his left side, carried his right arm in a sling, and had a bandage wrapped around his head. The corpo's eyes were black with fury.

"Do you know me?"

Lando forced a smile. "Of course. I know shit when I see it."

Lorenzo Pal delivered the first backhanded blow. But there were more, so many more that Lando lost count, and was only half conscious when the combat boot connected with his head. The darkness felt good.

10

Lando awoke to complete and utter darkness. He tried to open his eyes but found that he couldn't. It felt as if the darkness would swallow him. He threw an arm out and winced when it hit solid durasteel. That pain summoned more pain, and his entire body began to ache.

"Pik? Was that you?"

Lando saw filtered light and struggled to see. There was gooey stuff all around his eyes. His eyelids were cemented shut. The smuggler managed to wipe some of it away. He felt his right eye pop open. Wendy was blurred but recognizable. His left eye opened. She sounded concerned.

"Pik, stop that. You need rest. Give yourself a chance to heal."

He grunted something inarticulate and swung his legs off the bunk. *The Tink*. The beating. It came flooding back.

The pain swept over him in waves. Lando tried to find some part of his body that felt good, but couldn't. He gathered his strength, gritted his teeth, and stood. He swayed dangerously and Wendy grabbed his arm.

"Damn it, Pik! This is crazy! Get back in bed!"

Lando waited for the dizziness to ebb. His voice was little more than a croak. "Not right now, honey . . . I've got a headache."

It took forever to traverse the few feet between the cabin and the head. Each step brought new pain. It felt as if Pal and his thugs had beaten every square inch of his body.

He lurched through the door and was shocked by what he saw in the mirror. His eyes were little more than reddened slits, nearly invisible within blue-black pockets of swollen flesh.

There were bruises everywhere, a carefully sutured cut on his right temple, and more scratches than he cared to count.

Wendy managed a smile. "I couldn't find any broken bones or internal injuries. You did receive a nasty crack on the head, though. Maybe they thought you were dead."

Lando nodded and wished that he hadn't. "I certainly *look* like I'm dead."

But he knew it wasn't true. If Pal had wanted him dead, then he'd be dead. No, the corpo wanted him off-planet and out of the way. The beating had served to even the score.

Carefully, and with lots of help from Wendy, Lando dabbed at his face, brushed his teeth, and shuffled into the lounge.

None of this met with Wendy's approval, but she was powerless to stop it. Some coffee, a little bit of fruit juice, and four pain tabs later, Lando felt like he might survive.

"Did they damage the ship?"

Wendy shook her head. "Not that I could see."

Lando nodded. It confirmed his suspicions. They wanted him to leave. If the message torps triggered some sort of investigation, a murder would make things worse.

The whole thing had seemed slightly silly the night before, a wild-eyed scheme by a bunch of religious fanatics, but now it was different. Now it was personal.

Lando cleared his throat. "What time is it?"

Wendy glanced at her wrist term. "Almost noon."

"Okay. Get your stuff. We'll lift in four hours."

Wendy shook her head. "No, Pik. Your body needs time to recover. I won't allow it."

"We have no choice," Lando insisted gently. "News of what happened on Weller's World will arrive any day now. Besides, once we clear the atmosphere I'll hand the ship over to the NAVCOMP and sleep all the way to Techno."

Wendy didn't like it, but knew that Lando was correct. The sooner he left, the better. And her too, for that matter. She had no desire to face Lorenzo Pal. Not yet anyway. She stood up. "All right . . . if you promise to take easy until I come back."

Lando smiled and winced when it hurt. "Yes ma'am, doctor ma'am. But there's one more thing. We're going to need some help. The cargo carrier trick won't work twice. We need someone on the ground. Someone who knows the equatorial zone. Someone who's willing to take a few risks."

Wendy frowned. The equatorial zone was the ten-to-fifteen mile-wide strip of land located directly under Angel's halo. It covered some three hundred thousand square miles of surface area and was an extremely dangerous place to go. Roughly 250 million tons of debris fell into the equatorial zone each year, with individual chunks ranging in size from bullets to ground cars. The corpos used huge armor-plated crawlers to scavenge for metals in their half of the zone and lost one or two a year.

Wendy considered telling Lando that, but one look at his beat-up face convinced her to let it go. The less talking the better. She nodded.

"I know just the man. He goes into the equatorial zone all the time, and believe me, that's risky. I think he's in town but I'm not sure."

"Good," Lando answered. "Bring him here. Oh, and bring some maps of the equatorial zone. We're going to need them."

It took Wendy more than an hour to rush home, shove some clean clothes into her backpack, and find her father.

Blopar Wendeen was out in the equipment shed as usual, his large bony hands working to replace the drive assembly on Elder O'Brien's number two robo-tiller while his mind dwelt on events long past. The sun slashed down through a large skylight to bathe him in gold.

Wendy paused for a moment, determined to lock the picture away in her memory, insurance against the possibility that she'd never see it again. She'd grown up here, playing among the machinery, asking her father endless questions. The look of it, the smell of it, were an important part of her childhood memories.

The workshop was a large but almost fanatically tidy place, full of chain hoists, power tools, spare parts, and equipment awaiting repair. Although Wendy's father thought of himself as a farmer, and did sow some fields each year, he made most of his money by repairing other people's machinery. Machinery that would cease to exist if the plan worked.

A power wrench whined and chattered in Blopar Wendeen's hand. Then he saw his daughter, the backpack that dangled from its strap, and knew she was leaving. Wendeen turned the wrench off and put it down. He wiped his hands with a dirty rag.

"So, he's well enough to lift?"

Wendy shrugged. "No, not really, but he's determined to do it anyway."

Wendeen nodded. "I have a feeling that Citizen Pal did us an enormous favor last night. Pik had 'no' written all over his face as he left the house. The beating changed his mind."

Wendy thought about it and decided that her father was probably right. She felt disappointed. It always seemed as though Pik did the right things for the wrong reasons.

"Yes," Wendy replied soberly. "I suspect you're right. Well, we're lucky to have him. If anyone can get the cargo through, Pik can. By the way, he wants me to bring him someone who knows the surface, especially the equatorial zone."

Wendeen frowned. "The equatorial zone? Why there? It's extremely dangerous."

Wendy nodded. "Yes, I know. But that's what he wants."

Blopar Wendeen looked thoughtful. "Okay, but don't let him risk the shipment on any stupid schemes. You thought of Lars?"

"Yes, that's where I'm headed next. I hope he's in town."

Her father nodded. "He is. I saw him yesterday. He asked after you."

Wendy made a face. Lars Schmidt had asked her to marry him. Twice. She had refused on both occasions. She could hardly say "yes," knowing it would put Lars on a collision course with Lorenzo Pal.

And there was something else too. Was this what she really wanted? Life on a rim world? Lando had offered to take her with him, not just to Techno but wherever he went. Part of her wanted to say "yes."

"You could do a lot worse," her father cautioned sternly. "Lars has a good head on his shoulders."

Wendeen regretted the words the moment they left his mouth. He started to apologize but it was too late.

"And *you* should mind your own business," Wendy replied tartly. "Who I marry is my business. Take care, Father. And watch out for Lorenzo Pal. He'll be back."

Wendeen bent over to kiss his daughter's cheek, cursed himself for a fool, and watched her leave the shed. A large part of his heart went with her. She was right about Pal. The next few months would be extremely difficult. But difficulty was nothing new. Not for The Church of Free Choice. The wrench chattered in his hand.

Lars Schmidt was right where Wendy had expected him to be, deep beneath the city's library, busily tapping data into the colony's mainframe computer. A computer that the corpos knew nothing about.

The brightly lit room held six terminals, and all of them were in use. Two of the scientists nodded to Wendy as she walked down the center aisle, but the rest didn't even look up. Computer time was precious and they were determined to use every second. One of them wore a bulbous helmet that allowed him to use verbal commands without disturbing the others.

Most were hard at work on computer-aided models that simulated the interaction between the planet and the custom-designed ecosystem now waiting on Techno. It would be too late to correct mistakes once the organisms had been dispersed.

Schmidt was the single exception. He was the colony's chief geologist and had just returned from a field trip. His research had a bearing not only on the eco-design project but more general applications as well.

It was Schmidt's job to assess their half of the planet's mineral resources, investigate the many active volcanos, and pass that information along to the rest of the scientific community. There was absolutely no chance that he'd accomplish the task in his lifetime.

The geologist was a large man. He filled the chair to overflowing and tapped the computer keys with big blunt fingers. He wore a set of beat-up leathers, a utility belt, and some scruffy boots.

The man was handsome, there was no doubt about that, and Wendy could feel his raw physical power from ten feet away. He had a neatly trimmed beard and bright green eyes. They lit up with pleasure as Wendy appeared.

"Wendy! It's good to see you. I heard about the trouble. Are you all right?"

There was genuine concern in Schmidt's voice. He knew what Pal had done, and was worried about Wendy. There was no trace of the distaste or curiosity that some men would have displayed. Wendy felt grateful. She smiled. "Hello, Lars. It's good to see you too. I'm fine, thanks."

Wendy gestured towards the computer. "I'm sorry to interrupt, but I need your help. I also need the latest maps, surveys, and photos of the equatorial zone."

Lars looked curious, but nodded, and produced a big smile. His teeth were extremely white in contrast to his beard. "For you, anything. I'll dump what you want to a data cube, log off, and be right with you."

Schmidt was as good as his as his word. Fifteen minutes later they were aboard Blopar Wendeen's UV and racing towards the airstrip. The geologist did his best to listen and hang on at the same time. Wendy drove with her usual abandon and yelled to make herself heard over the engine.

The more Schmidt heard, the less he liked it. He didn't like the fact that Wendy was spending time with another man, he didn't like plans that involved the equatorial zone, and he didn't like being so helpless.

But Schmidt knew Wendy, and knew that one wrong word could drive a wedge between them, so he kept his reservations to himself.

Wendy sprayed gravel against *The Tink's* starboard landing jack and brought the vehicle to a sliding halt. Schmidt followed her into the ship's lock, waited for it to cycle them through, and felt increasingly jealous. The way Wendy operated the lock, the way she moved down the vessel's main corridor, all signified a degree of intimacy that he envied. Who was this Lando guy anyway? And what made him so special?

Then Wendy stepped out of the way and the geologist was taken aback by what he saw. In spite of the smuggler's fresh coverall it was obvious that he'd been severely beaten. Something Schmidt knew a lot about, since unlike the other colonists, he was well acquainted with violence.

Not even Wendy knew that the soft-spoken scientist had served a six-year hitch in the Imperial marines, fought on three different worlds, and been decorated twice. Nor did she know that the second decoration was the Imperial Battle Star, the empire's highest medal of valor, or what Schmidt had done to get it. A deed so horrible that it still haunted his dreams.

Wendy smiled hesitantly. "Lars Schmidt . . . Pik Lando. Pik . . . this is Lars. He heads up our geological team."

Lando winced as he got to his feet. "Welcome aboard, Lars. Thanks for coming."

Schmidt wanted to dislike the other man, wanted to find fault with him, wanted to reject him. But it was impossible to do. Long before Schmidt had heard of the Church, or embraced a life of nonviolence, the marine corps had trained him to respect honesty, strength, and courage. And like it or not, Lando looked like a man with all of those traits. No wonder Wendy liked him. Schmidt forced a smile.

"Glad to do it. I'm sorry about the beating. It looks like a rather professional job."

Lando raised an eyebrow, one of the few facial expressions that didn't hurt. A nonviolent geologist who knew a professional beating when he saw one. Interesting.

"Yeah, they knew what they were doing all right. Which brings us to the present. I've agreed to take my ship to Techno, pick up your custom-designed ecosystem, and bring it back."

Schmidt nodded his understanding. "The first part being relatively easy, the second being a good deal more difficult."

Lando smiled. "Exactly. And that's where you come in."

The ensuing conversation lasted for more than an hour. During that time, information about the planet's surface was dumped into the ship's computer, and various plans were considered and rejected before a compromise was reached.

It would require lots of luck, no small amount of courage, and considerable skill.

Schmidt had mixed feelings as he drove away in Blopar Wendeen's utility vehicle and paused to watch the liftoff. He wished Wendy were on the ground with him. The entire plan was iffy, but Schmidt's part, the part on the ground, was the worst of all. What would he do if it came to a fight? Give up, or . . . ?

There was a roar of sound as Lando activated the main drive and pushed his ship up through the atmosphere. Within a matter of minutes the *The Tink* was little more than a speck at the far end of a long white contrail. The contrail intersected Angel's halo and made an enormous white cross. The speck disappeared.

Schmidt sat for a moment, stared at the cross, and wished that things were different. It seemed that the very thing he had run away from had tracked him down.

He started the UV's engine and headed back towards town. He would return the vehicle to Blopar Wendeen later. The thought of making conversation with Wendy's father was too much to face right now. Why hadn't he told her how he felt? That he was worried about her? That he cared about her?

Because she'd think he was being possessive, that's why, or jealous, or God knows what. Schmidt remembered the marriage proposals. Awkward blurted things that seemed to fall from his lips like stones. He winced, and drove a little faster.

Schmidt's house was half underground like all the rest, a small affair, but more than adequate for a bachelor who spent most of his time in the field.

Schmidt parked the UV out front, entered through the front door, and headed for the bedroom. The house was sparsely furnished. There was only one of everything and no provision for guests. Every available surface was littered with core samples, pieces of rock, and stacks of hard copy. Boots, packs, and other oddments of outdoor gear filled the corners.

Schmidt entered the bedroom, went straight to the closet, and brushed a pile of dirty laundry off the top of a gray duraplast trunk. He paused for a moment, grabbed a handle, and dragged the chest out into the room. Schmidt pressed his thumb against the print lock, heard a distinct click, and felt the lid move under his hand.

There was a long moment during which Lars Schmidt did nothing at all. It had been five years since he'd sealed the trunk. What would happen if it were opened? Would it be like Pandora's box? A source of pent-up evil?

Moving slowly, Schmidt lifted the lid. There were four separate bundles inside. He lifted them out one by one and placed them on the unmade bed. Carefully, almost reverently, he unwrapped each bundle.

Then, when all the objects had been laid side by side, he sat down to look at them. The bed hissed under his weight. There was a blast rifle, an assault gun, a hand blaster, and a slug thrower. All artifacts of an earlier life. A life in which he had understood and treasured such things.

Were they the very embodiment of evil? Why had he kept them? And what would he do now?

Schmidt heard no answer beyond the sound of his own breathing.

_11_

Lester Haas was bored and had been for some time. He was a small man, strong for his size, and as plain as an unmarked envelope. That's why it was so easy for him to sit in the middle of the arrival lounge without attracting attention. Something he'd done every day for the past three weeks.

It was fun at first, a nice change from life as a bounty hunter, living off a Mega-Metals expense account while waiting for people to happen by. But it was extremely boring. You spot someone, file a report, and sit around some more. Haas would have enough money to buy his passage out in another week or two. Maybe he'd try his hand at roid mining or join someone's army. Anything would be better than this.

Haas crossed his legs, refolded the news fax to the sports section, and scanned the immediate area. The synthi-leather-covered seats started right in front of Techno's entry point and radiated outward like ripples in a pond. About a third were occupied.

Very few of the people around Haas were waiting for incoming passengers. Most were too poor to live in anything more spacious than an hourly sleep slot, and used the lounge as a communal sitting room. They read, watched portable holo players, or munched on the wide variety of food available from the roving robo-vendors.

And others, even those with a bit more money, came to enjoy the high ceiling, the lush islands of green plants that dotted the lounge, and the slowly moving star field that could be seen through the transparent duraplast high overhead.

Bit by bit the lounge had come to serve as a social center,

much like the town squares common to recently settled rim worlds, or the gigantic shopping malls of Terra.

So there were all sorts of people in the lounge, long-time residents and newcomers alike, walking, talking, or just taking a nap.

Haas compared their faces and body types to the hundreds that had been chemically and electronically memprinted onto his cerebral cortex, found a zero correlation, and turned his attention to the sports page.

Like any large corporation, Mega-Metals had a lot of friends and a lot of enemies. Both bore watching. In the dog-eat-dog world of competition, today's friend could be tomorrow's enemy. Information could spell the difference between profit and loss.

That's why Mega-Metals paid Haas, and thousands of others, to gather information. And Techno was the perfect place to do it. The scientific habitat functioned as a sort of economic and political crossroads, a place where all sorts of sentients met, and intrigue was a way of life.

That made the place worth watching, not just by Mega-Metals, but by all the larger corporations, and the government as well.

Haas smiled to himself. He wondered what would happen if he stood on his chair and asked all the spies to raise their right hands. The ex-bounty hunter imagined a hundred hands stabbing the air all at once. Would anyone be left? Was anyone an innocent? Or were all of them watching each other?

Haas felt a chill run down his spine. Was that possible? Did Mega-Metals have someone watching him? And if so, what had they reported about his occasional drunks?

Haas looked around, suddenly paranoid, wondering if he was under surveillance. But the lounge was huge and there was no way to tell.

Then Haas saw a face, followed by another face, and heard mental alarm bells start to ring. A match! Finally! Something to break the monotony.

He was up and moving. The couple were just ahead talking to each other and consulting one of the schematics given out to arriving passengers. The map would show their destination, the services available en route, and the shortest way to get there.

Haas wished they'd throw the schematic away so he could retrieve and use it. That had happened once. He'd been after a man. No, a woman. In any case an informant had sold him a map neatly annotated by the fugitive herself and left in some bar.

But this pair showed no signs of doing anything quite that stupid. No, he'd have to follow them, and that meant leaving the vicinity of the checkpoint. What if someone else came along? Haas smiled wryly. Another spy could handle that.

The man and the woman stopped next to a slowly creeping robo-vendor, bought something to drink, and looked around. But Haas was so plain, so ordinary, that their eyes swept right past him.

The corpo noticed the tiny cut on Lando's forehead, the puffy look around his eyes, and the greenish-blue cast to his skin. A beating? And if so, did it have anything to do with the company?

Haas called for Lando's memprint and it appeared inside his head. This particular memprint was quite different from the usual beat-up holo pix and semiaccurate description.

The first thing Haas saw was a shot of a very attractive woman taking her clothes off. The same woman who stood in front of him. She dropped her top and looked into the camera with empty eyes. The corpo heard the name "Wendy Wendeen" inside his head and knew it was she.

Then a man moved into the shot. Not her present companion, but someone else, seen from behind. Haas wondered why. No camera to shoot the other angle? A VIP of some sort? He'd never know.

The man moved in, placed his hands on the woman's breasts, and said something that had been omitted from Haas's memprint.

Then all hell broke loose as the man called Pik Lando appeared at the edge of the frame, mouthed silent words, and fired a slug gun.

That was the end of the artificially implanted memory, except for orders to follow either one or both of the subjects, and report to Mega-Metals HQ open-budget priority-one.

Haas blinked. Open-budget priority-one! What the hell had this pair done? Used the executive washroom without permission? Greased the entire board of directors?

Wendeen and Lando finished their drinks, threw their cups into the nearest trash chute, and consulted their schematic.

Haas licked his lips in anticipation. He smelled a big fat bonus somewhere down the line. The couple moved and he followed. They went to their right, paused, and turned left.

Lando took Wendy's arm. "Don't look now, but we're being followed."

Wendy resisted the impulse to turn her head.

"How can you tell?"

Lando's eyes were up ahead. "Because when we change direction, he does too. Not only that, but he's closing in."

"A corpo?"

"Maybe," Lando answered uncertainly. "But why here? We could be anywhere. No, chances are that he's a snatch, looking to steal whatever he can, or a con man hoping to slip us the pitch. Let's get rid of him. Stay by my side."

There was a whole bank of see-through lift tubes up ahead. The doors hissed open and closed as hundreds of people came and went. It was a mixed crowd, tech types mostly, but well-sprinkled with military uniforms and business suits.

Lando approached the tubes, realized that they'd arrived seconds too early, and paused as if unsure of which tube to take.

He looked at the schematic, smiled stupidly, and moved towards the nearest tube. Wendy stayed right by his side. Lando timed their movement so they were the last ones aboard an already crowded lift. The door slid closed behind them.

A tech type swore and gave Lando a dirty look. The smuggler smiled vacantly and the platform moved upwards.

The floor was transparent like everything else. Lando looked down between his feet and saw their tail hurry towards the nearest up-tube. Stubborn little bastard.

Wendy nudged Lando's arm. "Aren't we supposed to be going down instead of up?"

The smuggler nodded as the platform coasted to a stop. "Yup, we'll get off here."

The door hissed open and the crowd pushed them out. Lando looked around, saw some passengers spill out of a down-tube, and headed that way. They were aboard a few seconds later.

There was another tube only inches away, and as their platform started to fall, the other flashed upwards. Lando caught a brief glimpse of their tail then he was gone. Good. The smuggler allowed himself to relax.

The platform stopped twice before a computer-generated voice said "Level Two," and they got off.

Microcircuitry embedded in the schematic's plastic weave responded to tiny transmitters concealed in the habitat's bulkheads. The Techno branch of Lando's bank glowed green, and an unending series of full-color ads slid across the bottom of the page.

"Turn right at the next intersection," the current advertisement suggested. "The firm of Hurley & Hurley can meet all of your investment needs."

Lando and Wendy turned left instead, and followed a plush red carpet into a nicely appointed lobby.

There were the usual robo-tellers, cash machines, and computerized transaction booths. The walls were covered with electronic wallpaper, with the words "Planetary Bank of New Britain" programmed into the constantly shifting patterns. Various kinds of information appeared as well, including stock quotes, bond prices, and other business briefs.

Lando looked around, spotted a solitary human being towards the back of the room, and headed in that direction. The bank manager was pretty in a carefully calculated sort of way. She was up and around the glass-topped desk in the wink of an eye. She held out a hand with blood-red nails.

"Hello! My name's Carol. Welcome to the Bank of New Britain. How can I help you?"

Lando smiled. "I have an account with your bank and some gold to sell."

Carol frowned. "I'd like to help . . . but we don't deal in jewelry and such. A pawn shop perhaps . . ."

Lando shook his head. "No, you don't understand. I'm talking about a single nugget that weighs sixty-nine pounds."

Carol gulped. "Sixty-nine pounds? Yes, of course. Please take a seat."

Most of the larger banks maintained high-security storage facilities in Techno's main landing bay. Knowing that, Lando had stopped off long enough to unload the nugget and receive a notarized receipt.

That should have shortened the sales process. But by the time the bank's assayer had examined the gold for purity, and both parties had agreed on a price, more than two hours had passed.

With the deal finally completed, Lando stood, shook hands with Carol, and left the bank considerably richer than when he'd arrived. Gold prices had taken a dip due to a major find out along the rim, but he'd done well just the same.

From there it was a short trip up to Level 3. Their new destination was a place identified as "Production Lab 43." Lando found the listing on the index, touched it with his finger, and saw a green glow appear on the map.

Lando and Wendy got off the lift tube, took a hard right turn, and proceeded down a gleaming hall. This area had a completely different feel from the financial section.

They saw laboratory equipment, smelled a variety of strange odors, and brushed elbows with people dressed in disposable lab smocks. This was just one of the many levels dedicated to scientific research. Techno's one and only product.

They took another turn. The hustle and bustle gave way to a long hallway. It was empty except for a lone maintenance bot. Brushes whirred as it polished the floor.

Lando watched the doors. "45, 44" and there it was, "PL 43." It was the last door in corridor, and was mounted in what should be Techno's outer hull.

Wendy touched the glowing green access panel and they heard a whirring sound as a tiny security camera turned slightly and zoomed in.

"Yeah?" The voice was male and far from friendly.

Wendy addressed herself to the camera. "This is Dr. Wendy Wendeen. I was told to provide you with the following identi- fication code: PESP-TS-9816."

There was thirty seconds of silence followed by a loud click. The door hissed as it slid open. The voice sounded friendly now. "Customers are always welcome. Come on in. Be sure to follow the instructions. This area has been quarantined."

Wendy entered first and Lando followed. The hatch slid closed behind them, a lock clicked, and they found themselves in a small room with shiny white walls. The room was suffused with light that came from no discernible source. Another door blocked their way. A large sign covered most of its surface:

YOU ARE ENTERING A BIOLOGICAL QUARANTINE AREA.
VISITORS MUST STRIP AND SHOWER.

A computer-synthesized voice issued instructions: "Please
remove all your clothing and place it in an empty wall locker.
No tools or weapons will be allowed inside the quarantine area.
Violators will be ejected from the habitat."

Lando smiled. "Well, you heard the computer . . . take off
your clothes."

Wendy made a face and looked around. There were no
cameras in sight. Lando removed his top. She did likewise.

Once both of them were nude and had placed their clothes
in otherwise empty wall lockers, the shower came on.

The water was warm and smelled strongly of chemicals. It
came from everywhere at once, powerful jets of slightly green
liquid, squirting from tiny nozzles hidden within the ceiling
and walls.

The water that fell to the floor disappeared quickly, sucked
up through slots located along the bottoms of the walls, to be
recycled and used again.

The shower stopped and a blast of warm air blew them dry.
The voice returned.

"Please open the wall lockers labeled Q-SUITS, select a garment in your size, and put it on."

Lando touched an appropriate panel, waited for it to slide
out of the way, and saw three stacks of clothing. Each suit
was stored in a clear plastic bag. The smuggler pulled one
out, saw the label SMALL, and tossed it to Wendy.

Then it was a simple matter to find a package marked
LARGE, open the plastic bag, and step into the suit. The
one-piece white garment included booties and a hood, and
made a raspy sound when Lando moved. The suit had been
chemically treated and smelled of disinfectant.

Lando smiled. "Do I look as silly as you do?"

Wendy laughed. "Worse. You look like a large white rodent."

The door slid open and they stepped through. The next
room was extremely small and provided access to a standard lock.

A man waited to greet them. He was prematurely bald,
athletically handsome, and dressed in a disposable jumpsuit.
He had brown skin, bright intelligent eyes, and a big grin.

"Sorry about the suits . . . but we're still doing some last-minute tests. My name is Hooks, Dr. Robert Hooks, but friends call me Bob."

The scientist held out his hand. "Welcome aboard, Dr. Wendeen. Your uncle speaks very highly of you."

Wendy smiled. Uncle Syd had negotiated the contract with Techno. "Thanks, it's a pleasure to meet you. Friends call me Wendy."

"Wendy it is," Hooks replied, and turned to Lando. "And you are?"

Lando took the other man's hand. Hooks had one helluva strong grip for a microbiologist. "Pik Lando. I'm Wendy's chauffeur."

Hooks smiled. "Glad to meet you, Pik. Be careful how you handle Wendy's cargo. It would love to eat your ship!"

The scientist gestured towards the nearest bulkhead. "That's why we take all these precautions. Your custom-designed bugs could turn Techno into a pile of orbiting bug poop if they ever got loose."

Wendy knew that wasn't entirely true, but laughed just the same. The truth was that many elements of the ecosystem would die without support from laboratory equipment or the planet that they'd been designed to live on.

Still, microorganisms that liked to eat metal could cause a lot of problems, and the scientists were wise to protect themselves.

"So the ecosystem is ready for shipment?"

Hooks nodded. "More or less. I wish we could do some fine-tuning, but I understand that time is of the essence, so we'll ship the system as is."

Wendy nodded soberly. "We need to disperse it soon. Otherwise Mega-Metals will . . ."

Hooks held up a hand in protest. "We value *all* of our clients, including Mega-Metals. We never take sides."

"Which means that your knowledge goes to the highest bidder," Lando observed cynically.

Hooks grinned. "Has it ever been otherwise? And would it be better if all of our scientists were owned body and soul by governments and large corporations?"

"I don't know," Lando answered honestly.

"And neither do I," Hooks replied. "Come on . . . let's take a look at the lab."

• • •

Lester Haas was bathed in sweat by the time the com
call ended. The actual conversation had been rather brief.
But each word took eleven minutes to travel from Techno
to one of Terra's many comsats, make its way to the planet's
surface, and come out of a comset on the seventy-third floor
of Mega-Metals HQ.

And, given the fact that the return message took an equally
long time to reach Techno, the whole affair had occupied
something approaching four hours. Faster than a message torp,
but still frustratingly slow.

Haas wiped his forehead with his sleeve. It came away wet.
Every second that he continued to sit here cost Mega-Metals
another ten Imperials. But the corpo needed time. Time to
compose himself, time to prepare.

His orders were simple. Find out what Wendeen and Lando
were doing, then kill them. The first part was fine. Haas had
already agreed to that. But what about the second? What about
cold-blooded murder? Could he do it?

Bounty hunting was okay. When you greased someone they
deserved it and you could sleep at night.

But was this any different? Hadn't he seen the Lando guy
shoot someone? And what would happen if he refused? Mega-
Metals pulled some heavy G's.

Haas wiped his forehead once more, opened the door, and
stepped out of the booth. His enclosure was one of four. There
were ten or fifteen people waiting to use each com booth. A
man brushed past and slammed the door. The corpo didn't
notice.

Haas looked down at the information written on the palm of
his hand. *The Tinker's Damn.* That shouldn't be hard to find.
He headed towards the lift tubes.

Production Lab 43 consisted of a single large cylinder. It
was connected to the larger habitat by a fifty-foot umbilical.
The tube-like umbilical had a lock at each end, was made out
of pleated duraplast, and could be mechanically severed.

A reasonable precaution when dealing with custom-designed
microorganisms. In the case of a really bad accident, or a
plague, the scientists would cut the umbilical and drift free
of Techno.

That was the plan at least, but Lando wondered if the tech types would actually do it. Actually sacrifice themselves for the greater good. He wasn't sure that he would.

All of the environmental conditions matched those on Angel. The argrav was set for 0.95, the atmosphere contained the same mixture of gases, and the temperature followed a pattern typical of the temperate zones.

That was mostly by way of a backup however, in case one of the carefully sealed experimental compartments was accidentally exposed to the lab's atmosphere.

The lab had been in use for more than three standard years. It looked lived in, but was well equipped, and very clean. Most of the staff were human, but Lando saw two Finthians, and something he wasn't quite sure of. A lizardlike sentient that relied on a complex breathing device.

The smuggler was fascinated as Hooks led them from one section of the lab to another, introducing his colleagues along the way, and pointing out the results of various experiments.

"Now," the scientist said as he led them into a well-lit compartment, "my pride and joy. Dr. Bob's magnificent metal munchers."

Transparent cubes lined the bulkheads. Each one contained a computer-controlled chunk of Angel-normal environment. Lando approached the nearest container and looked inside. All he saw was dirt, rocks, and some scrubby plants. He looked at Hooks.

"I don't get it. What am I supposed to see?"

The scientist smiled smugly. "Look again."

Lando looked. Something caught his eye. He bent over. There it was, the last remnants of some copper tubing, now reduced to little more than reddish dust.

Lando moved to the next box. What had been a sheet of aluminum now looked like a piece of Swiss cheese. And so on, until he'd seen half a dozen commonly used metals reduced to waste.

It was amazing. Lando pictured what would happen when the microorganisms were turned loose. Gradually, bit by tiny bit, the bacteria would destroy almost every machine on the planet. Only those made from a rather expensive kind of durasteel would survive.

Yes, they'd have hand tools and plows, but little more. No

ground vehicles outside of those drawn by imported animals, no aircraft inside the atmosphere, and no computers besides the ones sealed inside atmosphere-controlled labs.

And then, after the bacteria were finished eating the machines, they would go to work on the planet itself, consuming the very minerals Mega-Metals had worked so hard to mine.

Wendy stood next to him, examining the damage done to a piece of lead. "Will it be worth it?" he asked her.

She turned to face him. Her eyes were determined. "Yes, if it brings us freedom and peace."

Lando thought about it for a moment and shook his head. "If you say so. But it's kind of like my father used to say: 'When a man shoots someone, it's silly to hang his gun.' "

Wendy's eyes flashed with sudden anger. "Life, *real* life, is a bit more complicated than one of your father's clever sayings. We're tired of running. Tired of being victims. A life without technology, or a great deal less of it at any rate, looks pretty attractive to us. Once the new ecosystem is in place Mega-Metals will be forced to leave. We'll be safe."

Lando shook his head sadly. "Safe, but stagnant. It won't work, Wendy. You can't go back. Someone will introduce new bacteria that can kill yours, or develop machines that can tolerate your microorganisms, or Sol knows what. The truth is that there's no place to hide."

There was silence for a moment as they stared into each other's eyes, both certain that they were right, and both unwilling to back down.

Hooks chose that particular moment to step in from a connecting compartment. "Seen enough? If so, it's time to do some work. The system's ready to go but there's a lot of paperwork left to do."

Lando and Wendy nodded in unison. Both were glad of the interruption.

The next two hours were dedicated to a series of complex financial arrangements. Lando was more spectator than participant, but found the transaction interesting nonetheless. It seemed that Wendy's uncle had negotiated the agreement some two years before. The proposal had been simple but rather daring.

The Church planned to use their half of Angel as collater-

al and then borrow enough money to pay for the necessary
ecosystem.

At first Techno had refused, arguing that the settlers planned
to destroy the very minerals that made Angel valuable in the
first place. They wondered how something without value could
be used to secure a loan.

Wendy's uncle had responded by pointing out that Angel's
halo contained more than enough mineral wealth to repay the
loan, and would remain unaffected by the new ecosystem. By
mortgaging half the planet the colonists were mortgaging half
the halo as well.

After some quick research by their attorneys, Techno's man-
agement team had agreed and a deal had been done. Despite
completion of the heavy-duty negotiations, there were still tons
of documents to sign.

It was a good two hours before Lando and Wendy were able
to leave Techno's business offices and make their way back to
the ship.

Like most of the visiting vessels, *The Tinker's Damn* was
moored on Level 5. After the pair had checked themselves
through customs, they jumped aboard one of the many trams,
and rode it halfway around the habitat's circumference to
Robo-lock 64.

The Tink could be seen about a hundred feet out, held in
place by the snakelike umbilical and some reciprocal tractor
beams.

Lando palmed the access panel, waited for Wendy to enter,
and followed her inside the lock.

It took them about ten minutes to cycle through both locks
and make their way into the ship.

Once aboard, Lando wasted little time requesting permission
to break contact and pick up their cargo. The sooner he got the
ecosystem to Angel, the better it would be.

The moment Techno Control released the habitat's tractor beams Lando did likewise. *The Tinker's Damn* drifted
free.

Things got a bit tricky after that. Lando steered *The Tink*
around to the other side of the habitat, waited while a tubby
little freighter blasted into space, and eased his way into the
cavernous landing bay.

White light flooded the area, threw hard shadows down

across durasteel decks, and shimmered over heavily armored hulls.

A large green delta appeared on the deck in front of him. Beads of sweet formed on the smuggler's forehead as he followed the green delta back towards the rear of the bay, maneuvered his way between dozens of ships, and did his best to ignore the robo-tugs, scooters, and maintenance sleds that zipped over and around his ship.

Finally he was there, sliding through a matrix of alignment beams, dropping into Loading Bay C-22.

The ecosystem had been packed into six specially designed cargo modules. They were metal and lined with plastic. Each one had its own power source, its own computer, and a special life-support system. They were triple sealed and covered with warnings.

Lando had little to do but wait while the modules were loaded into *The Tink's* depressurized hold and strapped down.

Some spindly looking robots did most of the work, with occasional help from a pressure suited human.

Then, when the cargo was securely in place, and the hold had been secured, the green delta reappeared. Techno Control provided an "all clear" and Lando lifted.

It took ten minutes to follow the green delta out through the constantly changing mosaic of ships. It felt like twenty.

Then they were through, with nothing but stars up ahead. Lando stayed at the controls long enough to put Techno behind them, entered a course for the nearest NAV beacon, and handed control to the ship's NAVCOMP.

He looked around. Wendy had disappeared. Lando shrugged, got up from the controls, and headed for the lounge. What waited there took him completely by surprise. Wendy was there all right, but so was the man who'd been following them. His blaster was aimed at Wendy's head.

12

Haas smiled. "Come in. Have a seat." The blaster described an arc next to Wendy's head.

Lando did as he was told. He moved slowly, trying to close the distance without seeming to do so. The vinyl seat made a squeaking sound as he sat down. He put his hands on top of the table. The mini-launcher in his sleeve was aimed toward the man, but would kill Wendy too.

Sweat glistened on the man's forehead. He wiped it with a sleeve. "I hope you won't do anything stupid, Pik. I'd hate to mess up the upholstery."

Lando looked at Wendy. Her mouth was a hard straight line. "He was hiding in my cabin," she said.

Haas smiled. "You've got some fancy security aboard this tub . . . but not fancy enough."

Lando forced himself to remain calm. This man was dangerous as hell. It showed in his eyes and the sweat that had already reappeared on his forehead. One wrong word, one wrong move, and he'd put a hole through Wendy's head. There was little doubt that Lando would die a fraction of a second later.

Haas nodded as if reading Lando's thoughts and endorsing them. "Good. Now, using your left hand, reach over and remove that nasty-looking slug gun from its holster."

Lando did as he was told. He held the handgun between thumb and forefinger.

"Excellent. Let's check to make sure the safety's on. It is? Good. Now, put the weapon down and slide it towards me."

Lando obeyed. The slug gun made a scraping sound as it slid across the table. Haas intercepted the weapon and picked it up. Light glinted off the barrel. He nodded approvingly.

"Nice choice. Reactive grips, high-capacity magazine, moderate recoil." Haas stuck the gun into the inside pocket of his jacket.

"My name's Haas. I work for Mega-Metals. They're sending a ship to pick you up. Nice comset by the way. A little *too* nice for a ship that's falling apart."

Lando forced a smile. "Glad you approve. How much are they paying you? I'll double it."

Haas chuckled. "I like your style. Right to the point. I think I'll pass, though. Dead people don't need money. Which brings us back to you. What kind of cargo did you load?"

Lando ignored the corpo's question. "You plan to kill us, don't you?"

The shake of Haas's head said "no" but his eyes said "yes."

Wendy saw it too. She felt an almost overwhelming sense of anger and frustration. Where was God? Why didn't She intervene? Would the strongest always rule?

Something hit the ship. A cacophony of alarms went off. Haas swayed, the blaster drifted to one side, and Wendy grabbed it. The corpo tried to jerk the weapon away but Wendy hung on. This was wrong, violence is always wrong, she told herself, but she'd acted automatically. Something hot sizzled past her ear. The energy beam hit the bulkhead and she felt little bits of red-hot metal sting the back of her neck.

Then Lando was there, pulling Haas away, fighting for the blaster. The corpo's hand hit the durasteel bulkhead. The weapon spun away. It hit a cushion and bounced. Wendy grabbed and missed. The blaster clattered to the deck. She dived after it.

Haas was strong, and mean as hell. Lando found himself on the defensive, as fists, elbows, and knees slammed into his still sore body. Not only that, but his larger frame was a real disadvantage. There wasn't much room down on the deck, and Lando made the bigger target.

The corpo was on top. He wrapped wiry fingers around the smuggler's neck. Lando made a gurgling sound as Haas choked him. The smuggler tried for the other man's groin and failed to connect. His vision started to blur.

Wendy was crouched only inches away. She wanted to stand but the tabletop blocked her way. The blaster felt warm and slick in her hand. She aimed it at the back of the corpo's head.

What should she do? To pull the trigger would be to violate everything she believed in . . . yet the alternative was completely unacceptable. Lando was losing, and so were her people. Mega-Metals would capture the ecosystem, destroy it, and drive her people off-planet.

Wendy swallowed, closed her eyes, and squeezed the trigger. A thin beam of blue energy burned its way through the corpo's brain and scorched the bulkhead beyond. Haas collapsed on top of Lando. The odor of singed hair filled the air.

It took Lando a moment to suck in some oxygen and clear his head. He pushed Haas up and away. The body fell over sideways. The corpo's eyes were rolled upwards as if trying to see the exit wound at the center of his forehead.

Lando looked at Wendy, saw the blaster, and knew what she'd done. Her eyes were shut tight, as if that would delay the unpleasant reality of what lay before her.

Lando wanted to thank her, to tell her that it was okay, but the steady bleat of alarms pulled him towards the control room. Something had hit the ship and hit her hard. What was it?

He made his way forward and dropped into the command chair. The buzzers and Klaxons died away as his hands moved over the board. The NAVCOMP sensed Lando's presence and activated its voice synthesizer.

"A Jupiter-Class in-system freighter hailed this ship twelve minutes and forty-three seconds ago. Would you like a playback?"

"No," Lando replied. "Continue with your report."

"Affirmative," the NAVCOMP answered. "Shortly after the attempt to communicate, a pair of Force Nine tractor beams were locked onto the hull."

That explained the impact. Someone had nudged them with a tractor beam. It was easy to do. All it took was one little mistake, one little uncontrolled twitch of the joy stick, and whammo. A Force Nine tractor beam could knock a ship like *The Tink* into the next solar system. Lando almost wished that it had.

The NAVCOMP continued: "I made two attempts to break

free of the tractor beams. Both failed. The freighter continues to pull us in. Estimated time of arrival: three minutes and fourteen seconds from now."

Lando looked at the main viewscreen. The other ship was visible now, black on black, blotting out a section of stars. He could see the white rectangle of the ship's huge landing bay. It grew larger with each passing second.

This was the time to call for help. The emperor lived on Terra. There should be navy ships all over the place. "Send the following message. 'All standard freqs. Ithro-registered ship *Tinker's Damn* under attack by unknown forces. Request assistance.' Add our present position."

The NAVCOMP replied three seconds later. "I am unable to comply with your last order. The freighter is jamming all standard freqs."

Wendy looked at Lando as she dropped into the co-pilot's position. She still felt the horror of what she'd done, but was determined to make the death count for something. "I've been listening. What now?"

Lando leaned backwards and tried to look casual. "We wait."

Wendy looked at the viewscreen and then back to Lando. She forced a smile. "Don't tell me; let me guess. Your father has a saying for this situation."

"Why, yes, he does," Lando replied thoughtfully. "My father would say, 'Son, people who eat spicy food deserve indigestion.'"

Wendy frowned. "I don't get it."

Lando up at the viewscreen. The freighter was huge. Large enough to swallow a hundred *Tinks* with space left over. The smuggler smiled grimly. "You will. You will."

Captain Orlow was a middle-aged woman with a utilitarian haircut and a stocky frame. She stood in the middle of the control room, with her arms folded and feet spread wide apart. Orlow had a ship to run, cargo to move, and no time for this sort of nonsense. The expression on her plain, bulldog face was anything but happy.

She turned to the tall, thin man on her right. He was vice-president of morale, or something equally stupid, and was hitching a ride back from the roids. Sol only knew why, but he outranked her, and had insisted on responding to the company's "all ships" message.

"Listen, Tawson, I don't have time for this kind of crap. How the hell can we stay on schedule if we diddle around with this kind of stuff?"

Tawson didn't even look her way. His hard blue eyes were locked on the main viewscreen. *The Tinker's Damn* was larger now.

"Captain Orlow, I would remind you that the corporation cares more about 'this kind of stuff,' as you call it, than whether your load of ore reaches the refinery on time."

Tawson gestured towards the com screen. "You saw the holo. These people are criminals. They deactivated a Mega-Metals security team on Weller's World, and tried to neutralize the manager on a planet called Angel. It should've ended there, but some idiot allowed them to escape. What would you have us do? Ignore their crimes? Let them go?"

Orlow wanted to say "yes," but shook her head instead.

"Besides," Tawson said smugly, "if all goes well, you and your crew will receive a bonus."

Money didn't mean much to Orlow. She loved the process of running her ship. Had it been up to her, Orlow would've said, "To hell with the bonus, let's stay on schedule."

But Tawson was an exec, the kind that gets ahead more on politics than profit, and wouldn't understand. And neither would Orlow's crew. They *liked* money, and the ones near enough to hear were grinning with anticipation, eager to grab an easy bonus.

The captain sighed. She had very little choice but to see it through. She issued a stream of orders.

Lando's hands were damp. He wiped them on his thighs. The freighter was close now, so close that its huge landing bay filled the main screen and flooded the control room with light.

He saw acres of scarred deck, worn traffic decals, and a double row of beat-up shuttles. They were short, stubby ships, equipped with in-system drives, and used for bringing ore out of the asteroids. Each vessel had a large white number painted along its flank.

Wendy licked dry lips and looked at Lando. What would

he do? The edges of the hatch slid by and she felt something heavy land in the pit of her stomach. They had arrived in the monster's belly.

Lando fired the ship's repellors as *The Tink* came under the influence of the larger vessel's powerful argrav generators.

There was movement over to the right, and Wendy saw some space-armored figures spill out of a lock and take up positions along the right side of the bay.

Lando lifted an eyebrow in surprise. Either the vessel's captain had stripped the crew or called out the shuttle pilots. The second possibility seemed most likely.

A voice came over the comset. "This is Dulo Tawson, Executive Vice President Employee Utilization, Sector One. Put Lester Haas on-screen."

Lando looked at Wendy, and she shrugged. Lando replied voice only. "Haas here. Sorry about the video, sir. Most of the gear aboard this ship is little more than junk."

There was silence for a moment as Tawson thought that over. Given the circumstances, there wasn't much he could do but go along with it. "I understand. You're in control?"

Lando smiled. "Yes, sir. No problems here."

"Good. We're releasing the tractor beams. Follow the yellow robo-guide and land as indicated."

"Yes, sir."

Lando felt *The Tink* jerk slightly as the tractor beams were released. This was the moment that he'd been waiting for. He ignored the hovering robo-guide, activated the ship's weapons systems, and started to turn.

Tawson sounded angry. "Haas? What the hell are you doing? Turn that . . ." Lando killed the comset.

Blue light flared as the freighter's crew opened fire with blast rifles. The energy beams didn't even register on *The Tink's* force field.

The smuggler spun the ship on its axis. The hatch was straight ahead. Safety beacons strobed bright red as the massive black- and yellow-striped doors started to close. The bastards were trying to trap him inside the bay!

Lando thumbed a protective cover out of the way and touched a button. *The Tink* shuddered as a pair of missiles raced for the doors.

"Hang on!"

The words and the explosions came together. Wendy was pressed back into her seat as Lando applied full emergency power and blasted towards the hatch. She closed her eyes and waited for the impact. It never came.

She opened her eyes. Man-made lightning probed the darkness around them as it tried to find and destroy their ship.

Lando smiled and started to speak. Something hit *The Tink* and sent her spinning out of control. Most likely a missile, since energy beams don't pack any mass.

Alarms began to hoot, bleat, and wail. The NAVCOMP spoke in its usual measured sentences:

"This ship has sustained major damage. I repeat, this ship has sustained major damage. The hyperdrive is inoperable, the in-system drive is seventy-percent effective, the life-support system is ninety-one percent and falling . . ."

Lando decided to ignore the rest and concentrate on controlling the ship. Some of the ship's main steering jets had been destroyed and others damaged. Gradually, bit by bit, the smuggler found ways to balance the ones that still worked against those that were damaged but still operable.

Control was reestablished seventy-four seconds later. Lando activated the tac tank and took a look. The freighter was still there, a blinking red blob, and made no attempt to follow. Lando knew that might change, and change fast, once they realized that *The Tink* was something more than a drifting hulk.

Lando scanned both the systems readouts and the tac tank, looking for options. There weren't any. He couldn't jump to another system as long as the hyperdrive remained belly-up, and he couldn't outrun them with a damaged in-system drive. And, just to keep things interesting, the life-support systems were heading south as well. They'd be wearing space armor in another fifteen or twenty minutes. He had to hide, but where?

Wendy bit her lip as Lando looked at the tac tank. It was a tossup between Terra and Mars in terms of distance, but while the red planet was still a little bit wild and woolly, Earth was the province of government and the large corporations. Not a place where smugglers spent much time. Lando touched some keys. Mars it would be.

The freighter was not a warship, so the com officer doubled

on weapons. "They have the ship under control, Captain. They're heading for Mars."

"So what?" Captain Orlow said sourly. "We have a landing bay that can't be pressurized, plus damage to the Number Four power feed. Why did they route the damn thing past the hatch anyway?"

"Never mind that," Tawson said tersely. "Get this bucket going. I want those people, and I want them now."

Orlow turned towards the executive and placed her hands on her meaty hips. "Oh, you do, do you? Well, guess what? We're done playing cops and robbers. This ship's damaged and I'm taking her in."

Tawson's face grew dark with anger. "You forget yourself, Captain! I'm an executive and you'll do what I say!"

Orlow's mouth turned downwards. "What you say doesn't pull any G's out here, mister. I'm the master of this ship. Besides, it will take about a quarter-million to repair the damage to this ship, and we'll see how the home office likes that."

Tawson swallowed. Orlow had a point. What had seemed like a sure-fire opportunity to impress his boss had turned into a full-scale disaster.

It wasn't clear what had transpired aboard the other ship, but it seemed likely that Haas was dead, or being held prisoner.

Although Tawson didn't really care what happened to the ex-bounty hunter, he *did* care about his reputation in the company, and couldn't afford to back off. No, he'd have to see the whole thing through. Headquarters would ignore the quarter-million if he succeeded, but Sol help him if he failed.

Tawson cleared his throat. "I'm sorry about the damage, Captain Orlow, but if they get away it will reflect poorly on both of us, and we should do our best to stop them. Surely you can see that?"

Orlow was somewhat mollified by the executive's more reasonable tone, and knew that he was right. Right or wrong, the incident would reflect on her as well, and given the shortage of commands, she couldn't afford to ignore politics altogether. Still, Orlow had to think about the safety of the ship, and any further risk was completely unacceptable. A compromise was in order and the Captain had an idea that might work.

Orlow forced a smile. "You have a point, Executive Tawson. And, although I can't go along with any plan that would place this ship in further peril, I can still offer some assistance."

Orlow explained her plan to Tawson, and his face lit up with grim excitement. He nodded enthusiastically. "Captain, I like the way you think. We make a good team. We'll find those vermin and stamp them out. The credit will be shared equally."

13

The Tink came in low and slow, her nav beacons blinking on
and off, sliding into an awkward turn as the smuggler babied
the damaged thrusters. Mars had very little atmosphere, so it
took lots of power to hold the ship up. Lando had been living
in his space armor for the better part of a day. His hands felt
clumsy.

Mars Prime was huge. The city rose before them like a
dark blanket of plastic and steel, once home to seventeen
million souls, now little more than shattered domes and empty
streets.

Oh, there was life all right, dark forms that scuffled, whirred,
and clanked through the city on even darker errands. They
were all that was left of a brighter past in which heavily
laden colony ships had landed every day of the year to
be stripped of useful metal and absorbed into the city.
Mars Prime had grown at the rate of one square mile per
month back then, absorbing some of Terra's excess popu-
lation, and functioning as a sort of socioeconomic relief
valve.

But history is fickle, and what might have been one of the
empire's great cities had become a monument to technological
change instead. Just when Mars Prime had reached its height,
and seemed assured of lasting status, a woman named Dortoro
Nakula had perfected the Nakula Drive.

Though slower than the speed of light, the Nakula Drive
was a huge improvement over the propulsion systems available at that time, and when combined with recently developed
suspended animation techniques, it made travel to other solar
systems a real possibility.

It was only a matter of months before huge colony ships were under construction and thousands of would-be settlers had signed on to fill them. There were paradise planets to be settled, or so the promoters promised, and the land rush was on.

Why so many of the residents of Mars Prime were willing to fling themselves into space aboard untried ships will never be fully understood. Maybe it was the fact that Mars Prime was packed full of people with nothing to lose; maybe conditions were so bad that a roll of the dice looked better than what they had; or maybe it was a form of mass hysteria.

Whatever the reason, Lando knew that within a period of ten short years Mars Prime had become little more than a ghost town. Now it was almost empty, populated by the leavings of the great exodus, and the ghosts of those who had died in the blackness of space. Their ships were little more than drifting graveyards, their desiccated bodies sealed inside coffinlike animation chambers, their dreams fallen like dust around them.

Some of those ships were still being found, distress signals beeping, hundreds, or even thousands, of lights away from their original destinations. The thought made Lando shiver.

Mars had other cities, of course, bright, well-kept places, built since the early days of space travel, since the time of the great leaving, but they were elsewhere and out of sight.

Darkness gathered as Lando skimmed the periphery of the city. Phobos was low on the horizon. A speck of white against the backdrop of space. Lights could be seen below, pinpoints of life in the dark warren of broken domes and wreckage-strewn streets, maggots living within the corpse of a long-dead city.

Wendy wrinkled her nose. The instrument panel threw greenish-gold light up across the lower part of her helmet.

"It looks pretty ominous down there. Are you sure this is the best place to land?"

Lando gave a shrug. "No, but the other possibilities would be even worse. This isn't the rim, you know . . . they have rules around here. Lots of them.

"If we land at one of the nicer domes, they'll want to know how we got shot up, who did it, and why. We'd give our version, Mega-Metals would provide theirs, and you can imagine the rest. We'd be ass-deep in lawyers, your cargo would end up under a battalion of microscopes, and the entire plan would go belly-up. Mars Prime might be ugly, but it's relatively safe."

Wendy frowned. "Okay . . . but how does that square with your call to the navy?"

"That was different," the smuggler said evenly. "Mega-Metals was busy hauling us in. The navy looked pretty good right about then."

A diamond-shaped pattern of lights snapped into existence below. No radio procedures, no formalities, just a "come on down."

Lando killed speed and fired the ship's repellors. Some worked and some didn't. Gloved fingers poked here and there as he tried to balance them out.

"And now we're doing just fine," Wendy said, watching dark duracrete rush up to meet them.

"Yeah," Lando said as he glanced her way. "Now we're doing just fine."

One of the damaged thrusters went belly-up right at the critical moment, and *The Tink* hit with a spine-jarring thump.

As usual, the ship gave a groan of protest, slumped to port, and leaked fluid. Only this time the leaks were real and would have to be fixed.

A figure in shiny black armor appeared in front of the ship, held up a pair of luminescent light batons, and waved them to the right.

Lando swore, fired *The Tink's* repellors, and followed the green cones into a dimly lit bay. Then, on a signal from the figure in black, he lowered the ship onto blast-scarred duracrete.

"Look!" Wendy pointed to the stern monitor. Lando watched as a heavily armored door slid into place. They were in deep trouble if this was a trap. *The Tink* might be able to fight her way out, but the outcome was far from certain.

A cultured voice came over the comset. It sounded neither male nor female. "Welcome to Mars Prime. Your ship is currently located within Bay Four of the Mars Prime Class "C" Maintenance and Repair Facility, a wholly owned subsidiary of Lucky Lou Enterprises. The minimum fee for safeguarding your vessel, and estimating the cost of repairs to your ship, will be two thousand Imperials. Please indicate whether you still wish to utilize our services or would like to depart."

Lando winced. Two thousand Imperials was an outrageous sum, but he'd have to pay it. He'd been to Mars Prime before and knew that a lot of unpleasant things could and would happen to vessels that were left unguarded. Lucky Lou Enterprises had lots of overhead, some of which came in the form of a sizeable security force. He triggered the comset.

"We accept your terms and wish to stay."

"Excellent," the voice replied. "A security team will inspect your ship. Please open your lock."

Wendy looked at Lando as she released her harness. "Security team? What for?"

"Lucky Lou's been alive for a long time," Lando explained. "Some say for more than a hundred years . . . and luck had very little to do with it. He's careful, that's all. What if the ship were packed with mercs all set to take over his operation?"

Wendy was amazed. "That could happen?"

Lando nodded grimly. "You bet. Anything can happen and usually does. It pays to be careful."

The next few hours were very busy. First, a squad of tough-looking security types came aboard and searched the ship from bow to stern. They were extremely thorough, spoke in mono-syllabic grunts, and wore an impressive array of weapons.

The moment the security team left, Lando and Wendy stripped off their rather ripe pressure suits and took showers. They had to put the armor on again before they left the ship, however. The repair bay was pressurized, but there was the ever-present possibility of a blowout, so suits were a must. They left their visors open for the sake of convenience.

The air inside the hanger was cold and smelled of ozone. The lights were brighter now, and Lando could see a variety of maintenance bots, racks of shiny power tools, coils of black power cable, and banks of computerized diagnostic equipment. Lucky Lou Enterprises could do the job all right . . . but at what price?

Wendy had difficulty walking in the lighter gravity. Everything was easy, too easy, and she had an unsettling tendency to bounce up and down. Not only that, her armor had been made for someone a full size larger, and lagged behind her movements.

Lando seemed completely unaffected. And, although the smuggler's face was completely blank whenever Wendy looked his way, she couldn't escape the feeling that he was laughing behind her back.

Wendy heard a whirring sound and turned around. The cyborg had been there all the time, hidden in the darkness up towards the ceiling, waiting until now to make his entrance. And a dramatic entrance it was.

Wendy had been exposed to a lot of cyborgs, and even studied their biomechanical support systems while in medical school, but had never seen one exactly like this. Unlike Troon, who had opted for a somewhat humanoid appearance, this individual had allowed form to follow function.

The cyborg had two parts. The first part consisted of a boxy-looking support unit that floated on a cushion of air, its extendable arm reaching cranelike towards the ceiling, where the rest of the creature hung like fruit at the end of a branch.

The second part of the cyborg was shaped like a globe, with four articulated tool arms, each one capable of interfacing with a wide variety of power tools.

Most of the cyborg's vid-cam eyes were located where they'd do the most good, out towards the ends of its tool arms, but two were mounted on stalks that protruded from the upper surface of the creature's metal torso. One of these swiveled towards Lando while the other scanned the ship.

"My, my. What have we here? Damaged thrusters, a hole in the drive compartment, and sundry other problems. Don't tell me, let me guess. Someone dislikes you!"

Lando laughed. "Right the first time."

The cyborg dipped lower, whirred its way under a stubby wing, and looked at the port hydraulics.

"What gives? You've got some damage here . . . but not enough to cause this degree of list."

Lando revised his level of respect upwards. The borg was sharp.

"The list is window-dressing. It pays to let people underestimate your capabilities."

The cyborg bobbed his agreement and continued to examine *The Tink's* hull. The ensuing inspection took another hour or so. During that time a battery of diagnostic computers ran tests on all of the ship's command and control systems; a squad of vid cam-equipped mini-bots scurried through the hull and documented the interior damage, while the cyborg whirred hither and yon humming to itself.

Finally, after consulting a computer console, the cyborg whirred its way over to where Lando and Wendy waited. Both of its general-purpose vid cams swiveled in their direction. "You won't like this."

Lando shrugged philosophically. It didn't show through his suit. "So what else is new? What's the tab?"

The cyborg tilted a couple of degrees to the right. "To repair the hyperdrive, replace the damaged thrusters, plug the holes, and fix various subsystems will cost you two hundred and thirty-seven big ones. Half in advance."

Wendy looked concerned, and Lando swallowed hard. There went a big chunk of his remaining profit. "All right, I want her in tiptop shape. How long will it take?"

The cyborg waved one of its tool arms. "Two days, maybe less if things go especially well."

Lando nodded. "Two days it is. I'll thumbprint a fund transfer, grab a toothbrush, and we'll clear out."

Wendy raised an eyebrow. "Clear out? What for?"

Lando gestured towards the nearest bulkhead. "Lucky Lou runs a hotel but it's two miles away. The cost is included in the overall bill. They won't allow us to stay here."

Wendy followed Lando towards the ship. "Another security measure?"

"Exactly. Get enough people inside the place and they could take over. It's like I said before, Lou's longevity is due more to common sense than to luck."

Thirty minutes later a pair of heavily armed security types escorted them to a utilitarian lock, handed Lando a map, and grunted their goodbyes.

Wendy looked around. There was graffiti all over the inside of the lock. None of it was especially enlightening.

Lando sealed his suit and gestured for Wendy to do likewise. He chinned the radio. "Can you read me?"

"Loud and clear," Wendy replied. "I wish this suit was smaller, though."

Lando nodded sympathetically. "Sorry, *The Tink* isn't large enough to carry a full selection of passenger suits."

The smuggler held out one of two blast rifles he'd taken from *The Tink's* arms locker. "Here, take one of these."

Wendy made no move to accept it. She could still feel the weight of the blaster in her hand, smell the odor of burned hair, and taste the bile that had forced its way up from her stomach. She searched for and found Lando's eyes behind his visor. "No, Pik. I won't do it again. I can't."

Lando nodded understandingly. "Okay . . . but carry it anyway. Unarmed people attract trouble."

There was no denying the truth of what Lando said, so Wendy accepted the rifle, and slung it over her shoulder. She'd carry the damned thing, but that was all.

The hatch cycled open and they stepped out into a trash-strewn street. It was cold, and Wendy turned her heater up. The dark metal walls of high-rise buildings boxed them in, multicolored lights strobed the night, and a dozen people dressed in space armor turned in their direction. Wendy couldn't see their faces through the reflective visors but got the impression that they were extremely bored.

One of them wore an electro-sign over his suit. It urged them to "Eat at Sam's." Another stood beside a full-sized holo. It showed a man and woman having sex. The words "come with me" flashed on and off.

Wendy heard Lando's voice in her helmet. "Well, here it is . . . Mars Prime at night. Kind of pathetic, isn't it?"

Wendy had to agree. It *was* pathetic. The signs that announced this or that bar, the brightly lit gaudiness, and the erie silence that went with wearing a suit. The entire area wasn't more than a block long.

"You wanta ride?" The voice was male and slightly hoarse. Wendy flinched and then felt stupid. Anyone could use the standard suit-to-suit frequency.

An unlikely-looking vehicle came to a halt in front of them. It was actually little more than a platform on wheels, open to the atmosphere, and equipped with rudimentary seats. The single concession to safety was a full roll cage with a pair of sensor-targeted energy projectors mounted on top. The cab had four headlights, all of which had been taped to reduce the amount of light they put out.

The word "taxi" had been scrawled along the side of the vehicle with spray paint. The driver was invisible behind his

visor, and the armor he wore was old and worn. The suit had
been spray-painted pink at one time, but only islands of color
had survived.

Lando chinned his radio. "We're headed for Lucky Lou's
hotel. How much?"

"Forty Imperials."

"Twenty."

"Thirty."

"Done," Lando agreed, and motioned for Wendy to get in.

The onlookers seemed to lose interest in Lando and Wendy
at the moment they climbed aboard the taxi. Wendy figured
they were talking to each other on some other channel. She
thought about scanning for it, but decided to let it go.

The cab jerked into motion and so did the computer-controlled
energy projectors mounted over Lando's head. They swiveled
this way and that, their infrared and motion-sensitive scanners
searching for targets, ready to fire the moment the on-board
computer gave them permission.

The energy projectors should've made Lando feel secure,
but they didn't. The fact that they were necessary, and a
part of the cab's standard equipment, said something about
the conditions in and around Mars Prime.

The taxi was forced to take an indirect route in spite of the
relatively short distance it was going. Piles of rubble loomed
up out of the darkness, burned-out vehicles blocked some of
the side streets, storefronts gaped open, and at one point a
thrown-together wall blocked the way. It had been there a
long time, and their driver had little difficulty pulling around
the far end of it, but the wall made Wendy shiver. Who had
built it and why?

The cab made a tight turn around the end of the barricade
and the headlights swept over a pile of space-suited bodies.
There were four, maybe five of them, and their armor was
twisted as if it had been subjected to intense heat. Someone
had stacked the bodies there like so much cordwood. An act
of grief? A warning?

There was no way to tell.

The headlights danced across graffiti-covered walls, lit up
a series of empty doorways, and speared something black.

The twin energy weapons burped blue light, a section of
wall turned cherry red, and the black thing disappeared.

Wendy was surprised by the loudness of her own voice. "What was that?"

"No big deal," the anonymous driver replied. "That's just a metal scav, or an oxy vamp making his evening rounds."

"Oh good," Lando said dryly. "I feel better now."

The rest of their journey passed without incident up until the moment they approached Lucky Lou's hotel. The high-rise was, for reasons of security, located on a small hill. Lucky Lou's people had made it even more impregnable by clearing a free-fire zone all the way around it and installing a variety of automatic weapons emplacements. A series of interlocking floodlights bathed the area in a blue-white glare.

A long, curving driveway led up to the hotel, and when they passed the large LUCKY LOU'S sign, Lando thought he could make out the vague outline of the words "Hilton Hotel" in the background.

Wendy saw two space-suited figures up ahead, and wondered why they stood with legs spread, and arms straight out. Then the cab came closer and she saw that both sets of armor had been welded to a pair of X-shaped durasteel beams.

"They showed up about a week ago," the cab driver volunteered cheerfully. "Used to work at the hotel. Tried to sabotage the security systems and let some friends in. Ole Lou caught 'em, welded their suits to those beams, and left 'em there to enjoy the view."

As the taxi rolled by, Wendy caught a glimpse of bulging eyes, blue skin, and features locked in agony. Suffocation is not a pleasant way to go. She gave a little gasp of horror and looked away. Was there no end to the violence? The cruelty? The death? Wendy wanted to cry but refused to do so.

The cab dropped them in front of a large, heavily secured lock. Lando paid the driver with cash taken from an external suit pocket, identified himself to one of four heavily armed guards, and waited while they ran a security check.

The check must have cleared, because they were waved inside. The lock was large, spotlessly clean, and well decorated with high definition 3-D ads that promoted various aspects of Lucky Lou's considerable empire.

A green light came on and an extremely solicitous man in a black uniform appeared. He ushered them into a luxurious lobby, helped them off with their pressure suits, hung both

suits on a cart designed for that purpose, and took their bags.
The man didn't ask for their weapons, nor did Lando offer to
hand them over.

A sea of blood-red carpet stretched off in all directions,
interrupted here and there by islands of leather-covered furniture, and lapped against a massive slab of Martian basalt.
The basalt had been fashioned into a long, curved reception
counter. It was black like the rest of the lobby's fittings
and reflected some of the light that came from the crystal
chandelier high overhead.

A pretty blond woman appeared behind the counter. She
had biosculpted features that bore a strong resemblance to one
of the empire's holo stars, surgically augmented breasts, and
teeth so white that they gleamed.

"Good evening, Citizen Lando, Citizen Wendeen, and welcome to Lucky Lou's. Will that be one room or two?"

Lando looked at Wendy. The words that came out of her
mouth were a surprise to both of them.

"Two rooms, please."

Wendy saw the hurt in Lando's eyes, and felt some of
it deep inside herself, but couldn't say anything with the
receptionist standing right there.

What *could* she have said, anyway? That the smell of singed
hair had helped her to decide? That Lando's world was too
violent for her to live in? And that he was too violent to live
in hers? Not the one that existed now . . . but the one that she
hoped to help build?

The receptionist's voice pulled Wendy back. "If you'll place
your thumb here . . . our security system will record your
print . . . and that will serve as your key. You have rooms
fourteen-oh-four and fourteen-oh-five. Maurice will take your
things up."

Wendy placed her thumb on the electro-pad, waited for
Lando to do likewise, and followed him to the lift tubes.
Both were silent during the ride up.

The doors hissed open open and Lando stepped out into
the hall, looked both ways, and turned to the left. Wendy
followed. The hallway was long, plushly carpeted, and outside
of a small maintenance bot, completely empty. Where were
the other guests? And how could a nearly empty hotel make
money? The prices must be astronomical.

Wendy felt suddenly guilty. Guilty about the money that Lando had spent, guilty about the way she'd rejected him, and guilty about feeling guilty.

They passed the maintenance bot and Lando stopped outside an open door. Maurice had somehow managed to get there before them and was unloading the smuggler's pressure suit.

Lando turned. "Well, here we are."

Wendy looked up into his eyes. They were cautious now, wary of what she might say. Damn, damn, damn. The physical attraction was there. If only . . .

"Pik, I'm sorry."

Lando forced a smile. "It's okay . . . I understand."

Wendy searched his eyes, trying to make sure that he really did. Standing on tiptoes she kissed him on the cheek. "Good night."

"Good night."

Fifteen minutes later Wendy crawled between clean crisp sheets, realized that she was very, very tired, and fell instantly asleep.

14

Lando awoke with the knowledge that something was very, very wrong. He sat up in bed. The room sensed the motion and brought the lights to dim. He looked around. Nothing. He was all alone.

But the feeling remained. Something was wrong.

"When you feel an itch, then scratch it." That's what Lando's father always said, and it seemed like good advice.

The smuggler swung his legs over the side of the bed, felt his feet sink into the plush carpet, and headed for the large floor-to-ceiling window.

The curtains whirred aside and daylight flooded the room. An interior heat source kept the double-paned window free of frost.

Lando looked, and looked again. Thanks to the hotel's height, and the fact that it was located on top of a hill, the smuggler had a good view to the west.

First came Lucky Lou's free-fire zone, followed by two miles of tumbledown domes, and the spaceport beyond. And there, parked in a row, were three ships. There was something familiar about those ships, but Lando wasn't sure what it was.

The smuggler went over to his armor, opened an external pocket, and removed a pair of binoculars. The glasses had large, oversized controls to accommodate clumsy space-suited fingers.

He returned to the window and brought the binoculars to his eyes. The ruins jumped forward. He saw the remains of a curtain whipped sideways in the breeze, a set of grid coordinates that had been etched into the side of a building, and some scorch marks where something had exploded. The city seemed a little less ominous during the day, but still had a brooding air, as if thinking about the fate that had somehow befallen it.

The ruins blurred as Lando tipped the binoculars upwards. He found the spaceport, stopped, and pressed auto-focus. The ships appeared as if by magic, short stubby things, with large white numbers stenciled along their flanks. Shuttles with large white numbers . . .

Then it hit him. Mega-Metals! The shuttles looked exactly like the ones he'd seen parked inside the freighter's bay! They'd followed him!

He made his way to the comset. His fingers stabbed the buttons. Wendy sounded sleepy. "Hello?"

"Get up. There are three Mega-Metals shuttles waiting for us at the spaceport. We need to move, and move fast."

Now Wendy was wide-awake. "Shuttles? Like the ones on the freighter?"

"Exactly. Be ready in ten minutes. I'll meet you in the hall."

Lando hung up and the comset chirped softly. He hit a button. "Yeah?"

"Citizen Lando?" The voice was male but rather soft.

"Yes?"

"My name is Lou. Some people call me Lucky Lou. I'd like a moment of your time."

"And I'd like to oblige," Lando replied evenly, "but I'm in something of a hurry at the moment. Maybe later."

"No," the voice whispered, "I'm not *asking* you to come, I'm *telling* you to come. Meet my people in the hall." Lando heard a click as Lucky Lou broke the connection.

Damn. Why now? And what did the old geezer want anyway? Well, there was no helping it. Given the fact that Lucky Lou had a small army at his command, Lando was left with very little choice.

Wendy was already in the hallway by the time Lando stepped out his door. She wore her space armor. The blast rifle hung over one shoulder and the pack over the other. She looked rather small standing between four of the largest people Lando had ever seen. There were three men and a woman, all clad in pressure suits, all armed to the teeth.

It was the woman who spoke first. She had a helmet tucked under one arm, a poorly healed blaster burn down the right side of her face, and a pair of stainless steel canines.

"Well?"

Coming from her, the single word spoke volumes. It said, "Well, if you're stupid enough to make some kind of trouble, then go ahead and make it because we're ready to pound you senseless."

Lando forced a smile. "Sorry to keep you waiting."

The woman nodded curtly and headed down the hall. Lando and Wendy followed, with the men bringing up the rear.

The doors to the down-tube were open and the lift was waiting. The woman waited until everyone had stepped inside, tapped some numbers into the keypad, and crossed her arms. The lift dropped like a rock.

Lando watched the amber-colored numbers dwindle from 14 to 1 and keep on going. The display read "6-B" by the time the lift coasted to a stop. Lucky Lou lived six levels underground. Deep enough to survive a direct hit from anything short of a nuclear weapon. The doors slid open.

"Out."

There was little point in doing anything else, so they obeyed. The woman led the way once again. This carpet was even deeper than the one in the lobby, and the walls were covered with the most beautiful electro-murals that Lando had ever seen, animated planetscapes that looked absolutely real.

Then they passed through double doors and entered a darkened room. One entire wall had been given over to a computerized diagram. Part of it was blocked by a tall, rectangular structure but the rest was clear to see.

There were hundreds of boxes, each with a name inside, countless intersecting lines, marginal notes, numerical readouts, and multicolored status lights. It was a business plan, an organizational chart, and a status display all in one.

There was a whirring sound as the rectangular structure started to rotate. A spotlight came on as the box completed its turn. What Lando saw took him completely by surprise.

The long rectangular box looked very much like an open coffin, except this corpse was alive, and kept that way by the latest in life-support technology.

Lucky Lou was tall, at least seven feet, and very, very skinny. His hair was white, but his skin was black, and wrinkled like that of a raisin. He wore a full set of formal evening clothes, and if it hadn't been for the multicolored wires and tubes that ran in and out of his body, he would have been quite presentable.

Intelligent brown eyes swiveled towards Wendy and Lando. His voice was gentle. "Good morning. Excuse me if I don't get up."

Wendy wasn't sure how to respond, but Lando laughed, and Lucky Lou smiled approvingly.

His gaze was directed at Lando. "You don't remember me, do you?"

"No, I've heard of you . . . and visited Mars Prime once or twice before . . . but I don't think that we've met."

"That's where you're wrong," the older man replied levelly. "Your father introduced us more than twenty years ago. I was still up and around back then. You were four or five years old and a real pain in the ass. And still are for that matter. Mega-Metals wants the two of you real bad. They offered me two hundred and fifty-thou to hand you over."

"And?" Lando's voice was cool, cooler than he felt.

"And I told 'em to shove it," the man in the box replied. "Lucky Lou never takes sides. It's bad for business. They waste you, your father comes after me, I waste him. . . . Like I said, it's bad for business."

"So?"

"So I want you out of here . . . preferably in one piece. I checked, and your ship is nearly ready."

Wendy remembered the cab ride from the spaceport to the hotel. "And how will we reach the spaceport?"

Lucky Lou's eyes turned her way. A leg twitched. "That's an excellent question. Mega-Metals has six people on the ground, vacuum jockeys mostly, but they look fairly competent. They know that you're here, and know that I'll protect you inside the repair facility, so they'll ambush you along the way."

Lando thought it over. There were a lot of streets out there, and six people couldn't cover very many of them. It seemed as though Lucky Lou had overstated the odds.

Lucky Lou shook his head sadly, as if he could see what Lando was thinking. "You're wrong. Dead wrong. They've got help, a gang of oxy vamps called the Air Heads, and they're just waiting to pop your suits."

Wendy felt a vortex of violence swirl around her, always there, waiting to pull her down. What should she do? Fight? Or stop, having seen that killing leads to more killing, with no end in sight? But the questions seemed pointless since events were racing out of control.

Lando felt the old man was leading them somewhere, providing information in dribs and drabs, so they'd arrive at the conclusion that he wanted.

"Okay . . . Mega-Metals hired some guns. So what would you suggest?"

Lucky Lou smiled. His teeth were perfect. "I thought you'd never ask. The problem is transportation. You'll never make it on foot. We tried to call a cab but the word is out. No one wants your business. What you need is some sort of vehicle."

Lando held up a hand. "Don't tell me . . . let me guess. You just happen to have one for sale."

Lucky Lou frowned. "Maybe I'm wasting my time here. Your father's fairly smart . . . I wonder what happened to you."

Lando saw that the other man was genuinely offended. For all his commercialism, Lucky Lou saw himself as a good Samaritan. For the moment at least. "Sorry . . . I retract the comment."

Lucky Lou nodded slowly. "That's more like it. As I was saying, you need some sort of vehicle, and I have something that might do the trick. And it's on the house."

All Lando could do was nod and say, "Thanks."

The old man's eyelids fluttered for a moment and then returned to normal. "You're welcome, son. Good luck. And say hello to your father for me."

Lando said that he would, and watched as the coffinlike box turned back towards the huge wall display. Lights were blinking, warning Lucky Lou of money that could be made or lost, demanding his attention.

Acting on orders that Lando had neither seen nor heard, the security team led them out of Lucky Lou's office and into a heavily defended checkpoint. It included a lock, where they were told to seal their suits, and a huge set of armored doors. When the doors closed there was no light except that provided by their helmets. White blobs danced across the walls and ceiling.

The security team spread out, weapons up, helmets swiveling back and forth.

Lando checked his blast rifle and swallowed to lubricate a dry throat. The tunnel was dark and ominous. Anything could be waiting to ambush them.

The woman and two of the men took the point, followed by Lando and Wendy, followed by the fourth member of the security team.

They walked for a good twenty minutes or so, long enough to be well beyond the perimeter of the hotel's free-fire zone, and under the ruins.

The tunnels varied. Those closest to the hotel were relatively new and graffiti-free. The rest dated back to the glory days. Some had been used for maintenance, others had provided access to long-dead shopping centers, and at least one was part of a now-ruined subway system.

They followed that one for quite a while, walking along the still shiny power rail, and squeezing by a frozen trans car. Lando's helmet beam danced across the interior as he edged along the side of the vehicle, boots seeking purchase on the tiny ledge, but there was nothing to see. Only dust-covered seats and ads for products that were no longer available.

Then they were clear, and climbing a long inoperative escalator, its metal stairs almost invisible under the accumulated dust and debris.

Once, as they passed a side passage near the head of the escalator, Lando saw boot prints in the dust. Boot prints that were crisp and well-defined around the edges. The team leader saw them too, and motioned for everyone to remain silent, gliding down the hall with her autoblaster ready to fire.

But time passed and nothing happened. Gradually, bit by bit, Wendy allowed herself to relax. Then, about five minutes later, they arrived at their destination.

The security team came to a halt, signaled for Lando and Wendy to do likewise, and took a quick look around. Satisfied with what they'd found, or hadn't found, two of the team stood guard while the others worked on a large pile of trash.

Some of the debris was heavy, and would've been difficult to move on Terra, but was fairly easy on Mars.

Lando caught nothing more than glimpses at first, sections of curved metal, and glints of colored duraplast. Then a cover was pulled away, and as the cloud of dust settled slowly towards the floor, a scooter was revealed.

It was a two-seater, complete with dual antigrav units, and more power than was necessary on a planet like Mars. With very little gravity to overcome, and hardly any atmosphere to slow it down, the scooter would go like a bat out of hell.

Lando saw that a rotary missile launcher had been built into the vehicle's front fairing. He bumped helmets with the team leader and pointed towards the launcher.

"Does that thing work?"

The team leader laughed. "Who the hell knows? You'd better hope so."

One of the men did something to the scooter's controls and it lifted itself off the ground. The small instrument panel glowed green and the vehicle swayed slightly as the man got aboard.

A new source of static rattled in Wendy's ears. She imagined riding the scooter and felt something hard and cold in the pit of her stomach. They'd be like targets in a video game as they threaded their way through the broken streets.

One of the men touched Wendy's arm and motioned her forward. The woman moved up the corridor, with the scooter right behind, and left the rest of them to bring up the rear.

The strange assemblage had traveled only a short distance when the woman signaled for them to stop.

Lando saw a large bank of old-fashioned elevators and wondered what the woman was up to. He watched as she produced a small tool, unscrewed a metal plate, and did something to the wires inside. An UP sign appeared, nearly invisible through layers of dust, and a pair of doors slid open.

Amazing! Lucky Lou had restored power to at least one of the elevators. Just one of hundreds or maybe even thousands of contingency plans the old man had put in place during his extra long lifetime.

The scooter took up a lot of room, but all six of them managed to crowd aboard nonetheless, and waited while the ancient elevator carried them slowly upwards.

The letter *G* lit up and one of the doors slid open.

One of the men put his shoulder against the second door and forced it open.

Now they were in some sort of lobby, a one-time bank lobby from the look of the old-fashioned teller machines and the huge chrome-plated vault that stood open along one wall.

Lando noticed the bullet-riddled wall, the section of counter that had been melted by blaster fire, and the dust-covered mounds. Vacuum-preserved bodies, still clad in their punctured armor, awaited a burial that would never come.

A bank robbery? No, the dust wasn't thick enough for that. The bank had been deserted for hundreds of years. This was something more recent, a dispute over money, or a blood feud of some kind.

Dust sprayed sideways as the scooter's antigrav units counteracted what little gravity Mars had to offer, and a set of swivel-mounted thrusters propelled the vehicle forward. The driver stopped just short of the door and got off. The woman pressed her helmet against Lando's.

"This is where we part company. I attached a mapper to the console, and no matter which way you go, it will always show the shortest route to the spaceport."

The woman smiled cynically. "Of course that assumes that the mutes haven't barricaded any more streets during the last twenty-four hours."

Lando forced a smile. "Does the local Chamber of Commerce know about you?"

The woman shrugged and was large enough to make the armor shrug with her. "It's my job. Good luck."

Lando nodded and swung a leg over the scooter's seat. He felt the vehicle bob slightly as Wendy did the same. Something bumped into the back of his helmet and he heard Wendy's voice. "What now?"

Lando rearranged the sling on his blast rifle so that the barrel of the weapon was pointed to the right. "We go like hell and hope for the best. Sling your blast rifle so that the barrel points left. We'll cover both flanks that way."

"I don't know if I can shoot someone again."

Lando knew better than to insist. "Okay . . . but you could fire for effect. Just to keep their heads down."

Wendy said, "Okay," but knew it was a cop-out. Random death is death just the same.

Lando took one last look around. The security team had vanished back into the tunnels whence they'd come. He tilted his helmet back to make contact with Wendy's. "Hang on . . . here we go!"

Lando twisted the throttle. The scooter's thrusters fired and pushed him out into the light of day.

Tawson tripped over a dirt-covered pipe and swore under his breath.

The sound was picked up by his mike, transmitted over his suit radio, and received by all those around him.

The shuttle pilots grinned and looked at each other through darkened visors. They worked for Orlow. The Mega-Metals exec might pull some heavy G's back on Terra but he didn't know diddly out here. An open mike was real stupid. Fortunately the gaffe wouldn't make any difference. The targets weren't close enough to hear.

Tawson shifted the unfamiliar weight of the blast rifle from one shoulder to the other. Sol help him if anything went wrong. He'd never fired a weapon in his entire life.

It was a mistake to be here. Tawson knew that. But circumstances had left him with very little choice. He was committed now, so deeply committed that success was a must, even if that meant his personal involvement.

Damn Orlow anyway. This was her fault for allowing the fugitives to escape. To hell with asking them questions. Shoot on sight. That was the way to handle it.

Tawson shifted his weight from one foot to the other and used his binoculars to look around. The view from the top of his makeshift command post was excellent. Not the highest point around, but high enough to spot anything that approached the spaceport and nail it if need be.

Not that it would be necessary to dirty his hands. No, the somewhat repulsive group who referred to themselves as the Air Heads would see to that.

Tawson, and the five pilots who'd agreed to come with him, were nothing more than backups. A last line of defense in case Lando and the Wendeen bitch managed to slip past the oxy vamps.

Yes, money could work absolute miracles, raising entire armies when necessary and solving all manner of problems.

That's why Tawson was so fond of it.

Tawson felt a trickle of sweat run down his temple and wished that he could wipe it away. He turned his heater down instead. The sun was high in the sky and beating down through the thin Martian atmosphere.

The executive took a sip of water and looked out over the ruins. Wisps of dust, thin as smoke, rose like spirits from their graves.

When Tawson spoke he was unaware that the pilots could hear every word he said. "Hurry up, damn it. Hurry up and come."

Lando turned the handlebars to the right, realized that he'd turned them too far, and overcorrected in the other direction. The scooter bobbed, tilted dangerously, and straightened out. There was a pile of rubble in the middle of the street and he guided the scooter around it.

The smuggler glanced down at the mapper and saw that there was a turn coming up. He triggered the reverse thrusters in a series of short bursts, felt the scooter start to slow, and accelerated into the turn.

Lando felt better now, connected to the machine, and somewhat more confident of his ability to control it.

He saw a short stretch of open street up ahead. He twisted the throttle and felt the little vehicle leap forward.

Deeber fingered his talisman and prayed. "Eeny, meeny, miny, mo, let the holy Oh-Two flow."

Deeber hoped that the prayer would bring today's quarry in his direction. The first one to see and attack the norms would save half their oxygen. That, plus his share of the tribe's fee, would make this a profitable day. He squinted into the unaccustomed light.

"Night, night, that's the way, hunt at night not the day. Thus it is, thus it was, thus it shall always be, amen."

Deeber turned and his reflection turned with him. It was distorted by flaws in the ancient chrome but was better than nothing. He preened for a moment.

Though deformed from birth, Deeber's body was closer to norm than most, and he was proud of it. Unrestrained by gravity, and lacking in sufficient calcium, bones grew in strange ways. Deeber had a reasonably normal skull, narrow shoulders, a long twisted spine, and short stumpy legs.

His armor had been custom-made to fit his deformed body. His mother had assembled it from bits and pieces that she'd salvaged herself or purchased from the metal scavs. Deeber had decorated the pressure suit with more than a thousand pieces of plastic. They made the sunlight hop, skip, and jump as he moved.

He jerked around as a series of tones sounded inside his helmet. The oxy vamps used their children as scouts. This was Skizy, or maybe Pullo, slipping him the jump. His prayer had been answered.

Deeber's short stumpy legs carried him out the door of the one-time cafe and into the street. Two norms came straight at him. Wait a minute! They weren't supposed to have a scooter. What the . . . ?

Okay, ignore the scooter and concentrate. Raise the kill tube, aim carefully, take a deep breath, and fire. "Missile, missile, white and red, find the norm and kill him dead."

Lando swerved as the weirdly shaped alien thing aimed some sort of tube at him.

The tiny, heat-seeking missile identified two different heat sources, and true to its programming, chose the stronger of the two. It soared towards the sun.

The mute cursed. This sort of thing didn't happen at night. Deeber tried to turn, tried to run, but his short little legs weren't fast enough.

Leaving his right hand on the handlebars, Lando used his left to pull the blast rifle's trigger. A shaft of blue light shot out at right angles to the scooter and burned a black groove along the front of the buildings on that side. It cut through Deeber's homemade armor like a knife through warm butter. The oxy vamp exploded inside his suit.

A horrible series of screams filled Wendy's helmet. They were part sorrow and part anger as the rest of the oxy vamps rushed to avenge Deeber's death.

Unthinking, Wendy let go of the passenger bar and put both her hands to her helmeted ears, at the very moment Lando swerved sharply. Toppling sideways, she grabbed desperately for the bar, and just barely managed to seize it and right herself.

The screaming filled Lando's helmet. He wanted to turn his radio off but resisted the impulse to do so. No radio meant no Wendy.

Five pressure-suited somethings scurried, limped, and crawled out into the street. Each of them was armed and leveled some sort of weapon in his direction. The smuggler flipped a protective cover up, pressed the red button, and watched the missiles surge away. They had no guidance systems whatsoever and exploded on impact.

The oxy vamps became pillars of flame. Lando drove between them and out the other side.

A heat-seeking missile came from somewhere behind him, zeroed in on some red-hot oxy vamp armor, and blew up. Fragments of metal and plastic were thrown fifty feet into the air where they cartwheeled and fell slowly towards the ground.

Lando braked for a pile of debris, took a turn down a side street, and accelerated away.

The pilot finished her report. Tawson forced himself to remain calm as he looked at the twisted image of himself reflected in her visor. All right. The fugitives had unearthed a scooter somewhere and broken through the oxy vamp cordon. Bad, but not disastrous. That's what backup plans were for.

Tawson turned towards the rest of the pilots. He was proud of how calm he sounded. "Okay . . . round one goes to the rimmers. But scooter or no scooter, they will still have to come here. Let's get down to street level and provide them with a warm reception."

Lando's heart beat like a triphammer. They were close, very close, and would encounter the corpos any minute now.

There! In the doorway up ahead, a space-suited figure with a blast rifle aimed in his direction.

Lando fired a missile just as a beam of pure energy sliced past his head. The world grew darker as his visor polarized.

The corpos disappeared in a flash of white light. More figures appeared farther down the street. Lando pushed the red button again and swore when nothing happened. A red light blinked on and off on the control panel.

"Damn!" Out of missiles.

A matrix of crisscrossing energy beams converged around him and started to close in. There were five corpos, and their lack of infantry training showed in the way that they grouped together, all firing in Lando's direction.

The smuggler gritted his teeth and headed straight for them. Blue light slashed by his side, scorched his armor, and cut a groove along Wendy's left thigh.

Lando fired the reverse thrusters, saw it was too late, and closed his eyes.

The scooter hit the wall about fifty feet in front of the corpos but didn't crash.

The planet's light gravity, combined with the vehicle's antigrav units and forward momentum, sent it skittering up along a vertical wall. Lando looked, felt the scooter start to fall, and fired the forward thrusters in response. The scooter angled down towards the street.

Wendy saw a corpo fall, saw one of them bring a hand blaster up, and saw it burp blue light. The beam hit the side of the scooter an inch away from her left knee and burned its way out the other side.

Her response was unplanned, but lethal nonetheless. She squeezed the trigger.

Tawson saw his beam hit the scooter, saw it pass all the way through, and was busy congratulating himself when the sudden vacuum turned his body inside out.

Lando felt the controls go dead in his hands as Tawson's energy beam sliced through the fuel lines. The scooter's nose hit duracrete, bounced off, and was pushed upwards by the still-functioning antigrav units. The vehicle wobbled left and right and found its equilibrium. Momentum carried it forward.

Lando fired the reverse thrusters. Nothing. There was a pile of junk up ahead. "Wendy! Jump! I can't control it."

Wendy understood immediately. There wasn't enough oxygen for a fire, but fuel was streaming out the holes in the vehicle's side and spraying across her legs. She wasn't tall enough to simply stand up and let the scooter run out from under her, so she did the next best thing. She jumped straight upwards.

That strategy worked. Wendy jumped higher than expected and fell slowly. She landed standing up.

Lando did what Wendy couldn't, and stood up, allowing the scooter to run out from under him.

The vehicle hit the pile of rubble a few feet later, bounced off, and wobbled away.

Lando spun around, his blast rifle searching for targets, but found none. With Tawson down, and things going badly, the remaining corpos had faded into the rubble. These weren't the easy pickings that they'd been promised, and besides, a bonus doesn't mean a helluva lot when you're sucking vacuum instead of air.

Lando backed away, and Wendy did likewise, until part of a collapsed building provided them with cover.

Things went easily after that. They jogged a couple of blocks, arrived in the small red-light district adjacent to the spaceport, and saw the sign "Lucky Lou Enterprises, Ship Storage, Maintenance, and Repair."

A couple of pressure-suited locals stared as they approached but made no attempt to interfere.

The lock opened to Lando's touch and he breathed a sigh of relief as the outer door cycled closed.

They were in space a scant four hours after that, accelerating towards a nav beacon, preparing for a hyperspace jump.

It was a moment that might've been celebrated, that might've brought them closer together, but it didn't happen. Both sat slumped in their seats, staring at the stars, seeing them in completely different ways.

15

Lars Schmidt was extremely tired, so tired that his vision had started to blur, and he had trouble with even the simplest tasks. He'd been driving south for a long time now, probably days, but it felt like weeks.

It had been fairly easy going at first. Across the pan, down through a series of valleys, and out onto a vast arid plain. Flat, almost featureless country, but easy to drive through.

Schmidt called his truck "Honey," as in "come on, Honey, you can make it," and she had literally hummed across the plain with only one of her three drive axles engaged, and a huge plume of dust to mark her passing. Those were the good days, when he'd been fresh, and the driving had been easy.

But that was a long time ago, before the badlands, and before the endless hell that followed. Schmidt peered out through the half arc of dust-free windshield, fighting the wheel, gritting his teeth as Honey waddled her way up and out of another gully. The hundredth? The thousandth? The millionth? There was no way to tell.

Schmidt's mind had a tendency to wander, he knew that, but it seemed strange to take one section of a nearly lifeless planet and call it "the badlands." After all, the rest of the planet was nearly as "bad," and might've been classified as badlands somewhere else.

As a geologist he knew the truth, that the badlands were nothing more than a region of small hills and deep gullies formed through erosion.

Every now and then thunderstorms swept over the area and dumped two or three inches of rain onto the land all at once. The rain ran down off the hillsides, collected in the gullies, and gushed through the canyons in the form of flash floods. Tons and tons of dirt were washed away in the process. The result was a tortured hell of ups and downs.

Honey roared, all three drive axles engaged, as she dragged herself up and out of the gully and onto the top of a low hill. Schmidt stepped on the brakes, checked his scanners for danger, and killed both the engines. The temp indicators were bright red. Honey needed a rest and so did he.

He opened the door and climbed down from the truck. Dust puffed up and away from his boots. Right at that moment the sun came out from behind a cloud and bathed the land in gold.

The geologist turned and looked out over the equatorial zone. It would be worse, much worse than the badlands, but he felt refreshed nonetheless. He was close now, maybe ten or fifteen miles from the cave, and only hours from some much needed sleep.

The E-zone was flatter than the badlands, but broken just the same, and covered with thousands upon thousands of overlapping impact craters.

Some of the craters were relatively new. They had crisp, clean edges, and were nearly untouched by the effects of wind and rain. The ground around them glittered with countless pieces of out-flung metal speckled with rust.

Other craters were ancient things, depressions left by meteors that had struck hundreds, or even thousands of years in the past. They were little more than dimples now, softened by erosion, and filled with water or soil.

Schmidt looked up and squinted into the sun. Angel's halo, or ring, was almost directly overhead, but too thin to see. Each year it dumped around 250 million tons worth of debris into the atmosphere.

That meant that something on the order of 850 tons of metal hit each square mile of the equatorial zone each day. Enough to turn the surface into a hell of jagged points and razor-sharp edges. Chunks of iron lay everywhere, some blackened by heat, others rusted with age, and the most recent so shiny that they glittered with reflected light.

Schmidt had done the math during previous trips into the zone. Once a century or so, each square mile would be hit by something the size of a ground car, traveling at twice the speed of sound, and exploding on impact. When that happened, pieces of red-hot rock shrapnel would be hurled in every direction.

And on the average day, each square mile would be hit by two or three basketball-sized chunks of metal, about twenty-five hundred golf-ball-sized pieces of debris, and something like two hundred and fifty thousand metal peas.

That meant the chances of being hit by something the size of a pea were pretty good. Say, once every ten days or so.

Schmidt's hand went to the right side of his head. A meteor had hit his protective helmet during his most recent trip into the E-zone and laid him out cold.

He caught a glint of light out of the corner of his eye. Too high to be metal on the ground. It was there and then gone. The weasel was still with him. Not satisfied with its satellite surveillance, Mega-Metals had sent a robotic spy to keep an eye on him. An eye that would have to be blinded in the very near future.

The geologist smiled grimly, climbed into the cab, and started the engines. He'd drive for two hours, three at the most, then stage his little act. It would be a pleasure to find the little bastard and kill it.

The power-assisted steering wheel jumped and jerked in Schmidt's hands as he guided Honey out of the badlands and into the E-zone.

Progress was slow, but faster than the first few times that he'd entered the area and started the long slow process of creating a computerized map. Now it was a matter of following that map via the transparent heads-up display that hovered in front of the windshield.

Schmidt grinned. It seemed silly somehow, this business of using science to destroy science, of canceling out more than three thousand years of achievement. Yet, for all the good that scientific knowledge had made possible, it had produced unspeakable evil as well.

Schmidt remembered what it looked like to see hell bombs march across the land, to see entire cities turned to radioactive glass, to kill and kill without end.

Schmidt saw Janice next to him, the section leader's chevrons gleaming on the side of her helmet, her head just starting to turn towards him when the bullet hit.

The image had haunted him for years. The head turning, the eyes alight with intelligence, the lips parted to speak. What would she have said? That she was tired? That war sucks? He'd never know.

The bullet had not been aimed. It was a random thing, one of thousands pumped like water from a metal hose, spraying the land with death.

The bullet hit Janice between the eyes, shattered her skull, and churned its way through her brain. In just a few seconds, the lethal chunk of metal had nullified a lifetime of accumulated knowledge, erased a quirky sense of humor, and killed the only person that he loved.

It was then that Schmidt had done what they'd trained him to do, had bathed himself in blood, and been rewarded with the empire's highest honor.

"Damn them, damn them, damn them!"

All of a sudden Schmidt realized that he'd been screaming. Tears were streaming down his cheeks, Honey was still on course, and the E-zone was all around him.

Schmidt bit his lower lip and drove. Janice, and the three hundred and fifty-two ghosts of D Company, 1st Battalion, 2nd Marines drove with him.

It was nearly dark by the time Schmidt pulled into the center of an ancient crater and killed Honey's engines. He was struck by the almost total silence. No birds, no insects, no barking dogs. Just silence.

There were meteors though, and most fell silently, streaks of light that quickly disappeared. But there were larger chunks too, about one every minute or so, which left trails of green and orange across the sky. They reminded Schmidt of the Empire Day fireworks he'd watched as a boy.

He caught a glint of reflected light over to the right. Good. His friend the weasel was getting careless. Settling in like a bird on its nest. Conserving precious energy.

Schmidt took his time, setting up the folding table out where it could be seen, fixing dinner and eating it while the sun set over the horizon. Then, following the same pattern he'd used each night so far, the scientist entered the truck.

His bunk beckoned, but he ignored it and went straight for the tool box.

For one brief moment Schmidt wished that he'd given in and brought the assault weapon or blast rifle along with him. He saw the hand sledge and picked it up.

The hammer felt heavy in his hand. It was something his nomadic ancestors would have understood. A simple shaft with a hunk of metal mounted on the end. The hammer could build as well as destroy. And what blast rifle could lay claim to that? To having driven a nail? To having built a house?

Yes, Schmidt decided, the hammer would be better than the weapons he'd left behind. Much better.

The geologist stuck the handle through a loop in his belt and felt the weight of it pull down on his pants. He sucked in his breath and tightened his belt.

The hatch was something new, a modification made just prior to departure, and a key part of the geologist's plan.

He pulled the door up and dropped through, confident that the weasel couldn't see him under the truck and wouldn't be able to distinguish the geologist's heat from that still radiating off the vehicle.

It had been years since Schmidt had low-crawled anywhere, but the training was still there, memprinted on his mind. The plan was simple. He'd use the rim of the crater for cover, crawl along it until he found a break, and wriggle through.

The weasel could fly pretty well but would be awkward on the ground. And, given the fact that it believed its quarry had quit for the night, the machine had most likely powered down. That meant it would be grounded, less alert than usual, and vulnerable.

Schmidt found a gap in the rim and wriggled through. The sledge was a weight pressing against the small of his back.

He paused and pulled a small black box from his shirt pocket. He turned the device on, swept it back and forth, and smiled when a tiny red eye appeared. Good. The little bastard was over to the right somewhere.

Schmidt returned the box to his pocket and started to crawl. The countless rocks and pieces of rusty metal made it slow going. Time and time again he felt sharp edges slice through his skin.

He ignored the pain. It was worth it to get the weasel. Of course the geologist had never seen a real weasel, or even a picture of one as far as he could recall. Where did weasels live anyway? New Britain? Terra? It didn't matter. Weasels were mean and sneaky, just like robo-spies, and that's all he needed to know.

Schmidt paused, checked the little black box, and crawled on. There was very little light. He was closer now, much closer, and his breath came in short, shallow gasps.

There, just ahead—what was that? A piece of shiny meteorite? Or what he was looking for?

Schmidt paused and was glad he did. The shiny thing sprouted a small antenna. It whirred about a foot upwards, stopped, and blossomed into a tiny dish. The dish turned towards the north and stopped.

The geologist held his breath waiting to see what would happen next. About thirty seconds passed. The dish whirred, was reabsorbed by the antenna, and the whole thing was withdrawn into the robo-spy's flat, disklike body.

Schmidt let his breath out in a long, slow exhalation. So, the weasel had reported to its masters. What could be better? Odds were that they wouldn't expect another report until the following day. The intervening hours would give Schmidt one helluva head start.

He crawled forward, moving ever so slowly. The robo-spy was slightly uphill from Honey and over to one side. That made the going tougher, but provided Schmidt with better cover.

The geologist felt sudden pain as a jagged piece of metal bit into his thigh. He paused, shifted his weight away from the source of pain, and continued. There was a sharp, cracking sound from off to the right. A meteor hit. A small one, but a meteor hit just the same. It occurred to him that he'd forgotten to wear the protective helmet.

The distance closed. Ten feet, eight, six, four. Schmidt watched the shiny disk, waiting for it to sense his presence and come suddenly to life. It was nearly three feet in diameter and occupied the center of a small-impact crater. The truck, and the light that Schmidt had left on, glowed off to the right.

He did a careful push-up. Nothing. He let his knees touch and leaned back. Nothing. He reached for the hammer. Nothing. He put his left hand down and shifted his weight. Nothing. He started to stand.

"Hold it right there!" The voice was loud and came from the disk. Schmidt heard an angry whine as the machine's drive mechanism came up to speed. He dashed forward and brought the hammer down against the very center of the robo-spy's housing. It rang like a gong.

The machine tried to lift. Schmidt used a boot to hold it down. "Stop that! I belong to Mega-Metals Incorporated. You have no right to destroy company property!"

Schmidt laughed. He put all of his anger, all of his hate, into the next blow. When the hammer hit he could feel the shock all the way up to his shoulder. The metal housing broke and he felt something crunch.

There was a whirring noise. Schmidt saw the antenna appear like a snake from its lair. The robo-spy was trying to send a message!

The hammer descended again, sheared the antenna off at the base, and dented the machine's already shattered fuselage.

"Stop that! I belong to Mega-Metals Incorporated. You have no . . ."

Schmidt struck again, and the computer-simulated voice came to a sudden stop. The geologist didn't. He hit the machine again and again until his forehead was beaded with sweat and the robo-spy was nothing more than crumpled metal.

Then, dizzy from exertion and fatigue, he pulled the black box out of his pocket and turned it on. There was no sign of the little red eye. The weasel was well and truly dead. Pop goes the weasel.

Schmidt stumbled down the slope and climbed into Honey's cab. He dropped the hammer on the passenger's seat and started the engines. They filled the night with a deep throaty rumble.

A meteor hit somewhere to the east. One of the big ones. There was a flash of light, followed by a roar of sound.

The geologist popped two stim tabs, put the truck in gear, and bounced up and out of the crater. Just two more hours, three at the most, and Honey would reach the cave. He'd done his part. The rest was up Lando.

16

Lando brought *The Tinker's Damn* out of hyperspace, checked the scanners for trouble, and headed straight for Angel. No tricks, no scams, a straight high-speed run.

The smuggler knew it was stupid, knew he should forget the whole thing, and knew he couldn't. What had started as a matter of pride had become something more. Lando believed in what The Chosen were trying to do.

Not in their religion, not in their self-imposed isolation, but in standing up for their rights. And if that meant eco-war, then so be it. He'd deliver the microscopic warriors and clear out.

It took ten minutes for the first com call to reach them. Having "seen" *The Tink* before, the company's computers had little difficulty identifying her again.

Lando smiled as Lorenzo Pal appeared. The corpo still had a small bandage on the side of his head. "Well, look who's here. The slime ball himself."

Pal didn't reply. He couldn't. The words he spoke had been uttered ten minutes before. "You're in a world of trouble, Lando. Assault with the intent to commit murder, violation of flight protocols, and illegal flight from prosecution. Give it up. I'll see that you get a fair trial."

Lando didn't bother with an answer.

The smuggler touched a key and the screen snapped to black.

Wendy looked from the comset to Lando. "What will they do?"

Lando shrugged. "They'll attempt to intercept us in space, and failing that, to stop us on the ground. *The Tink's* more than a match for Pal's shuttles and tugs."

Wendy frowned. "I don't want any more killing, Pik."

Lando raised an eyebrow. "Oh really? Well, it just so happens that Mega-Metals doesn't play by the same set of philosophical rules that you do. And guess what? Neither do I. If they fire at me, then I'll fire at them."

Wendy was silent for a moment. She searched Lando's face for something that wasn't there. There was regret in her voice. "I'm sorry, Pik."

Lando knew what Wendy meant. She was sorry that it hadn't worked out, sorry that they were such different people, sorry that the universe worked the way it did.

He smiled and put his hand on hers. "I'm sorry, too."

Nothing more was said. Nothing had to be.

It took the better part of a standard day to reach Angel. Plenty of time for Mega-Metals to prepare, and plenty of time for Lando to sweat. Lorenzo Pal would have some sort of reception ready, but what? It didn't take long to find out.

The shuttles and tugs came out in a V formation, tugs first, shuttles second. Angel was huge behind them, a luminescent presence, her halo shining silver.

The Mega-Metal ships burped coherent light and fired their missiles. None of them could take The Tink one-on-one, so Pal hoped that their massed firepower would compensate for a lack of individual size and strength.

Lando held his fire, not out of deference to Wendy's wishes, but because there was no point in doing otherwise. Why kill if you don't have too? The smuggler headed straight into the enemy fire. Computers searched for openings, man-made lightning slashed through vacuum, and missiles accelerated outwards. The Tink's force field shrugged them off.

Wendy gripped her armrests, watching the other ships grow larger, waiting for Lando to fire. Then, just when she thought a head-on conflict was inevitable, Lando turned the ship to starboard, and dived towards Angel's ring.

Unused to fleet maneuvers, and unwilling to follow The Tink into the ring while bunched up, the corpos scattered. Shuttles and tugs zoomed in every direction as Lorenzo Pal screamed abuse at them over the radio.

There was little time for Wendy and Lando to celebrate their victory. The Tink was inside the ring now. Proximity alarms screamed, lights flashed, and Lando had his hands full as he conned the ship between mountains of floating rock.

It was an almost magic place. In spite of the fact that more than 100,000 years had passed, the chunks of rock and metal were still shiny. Light flashed this way and that, bounced off countless surfaces, and forced the ship's sensors to dampen down.

The larger objects tumbled along in majestic slow-motion. Some were huddled together like friends on a walk, while others drifted miles apart locked in their solitary orbits. They were glitteringly beautiful and very frightening all at the same time.

There was smaller stuff too, all the way down to tiny little things that sparkled like pixie dust and flashed when they hit the force field.

Lando checked the scanners. The ship's tac comp worked overtime as it tried to track and evaluate hundreds of potential targets all at the same time. It indicated that two, or maybe three of the bogies were shuttles.

Lando swore softly. Some enterprising souls had followed him into the ring. A huge chunk of debris floated up ahead. It had a rough asymmetrical look. He banked left and went around it.

A shuttle slipped in behind them. Twin beams of blue light raced past *The Tink* to hit a twenty-ton chunk of rock. Most of the energy was reflected back into space. Shafts of coherent energy bounced in every direction. One hit a smaller piece of junk and turned it to vapor.

An apartment-house-sized chunk of rock-metal aggregate floated up ahead. Lando put the ship into a hard right-hand turn. Wendy felt the bottom of her stomach fall out.

A shuttle appeared as *The Tink* rounded the rock. Lando grinned in satisfaction. The other vessel filled his heads-up target display. It had just started to turn when Lando heard a solid tone and saw the flashing green light.

The smuggler touched a key and a pair of missiles raced away. *The Tink* jerked in response. Wendy turned her head. Flame blossomed and the shuttle disappeared.

Lando checked the scanners again, found that the second shuttle had been lost in the shuffle, and headed down towards the surface. It was time to find Lars Schmidt.

Lando made an adjustment to the comset, found the frequency he wanted, and waited. Fifteen seconds passed before he heard the signal. A long, steady tone followed by two shorts. It was a recording. How many days had the geologist been waiting? There was no way to know.

The smuggler touched some keys. The NAVCOMP tracked the tone to its source, compared the coordinates with those Schmidt had provided earlier, and signaled a match.

Thus reassured, Lando continued to make his way down through Angel's halo, careful to avoid the larger hunks of debris, leaving the ship's force field to handle the rest.

It took some time to make the journey down through the debris field and into the upper atmosphere. Lando became increasingly worried as the space junk thinned out. The juncture between space and sky would be the perfect place for an ambush. What if Pal had a whole flight of atmospheric fighters waiting for him? Wendy said there weren't any, but what if she was wrong?

The Tink was a good deal less maneuverable in planetary atmospheres than she was in space. A squadron of well-flown fighters could blow her out of the sky. And what if they followed him to the rendezvous? That would spell almost certain disaster.

But his worries were needless. The sky below Angel's halo was overcast but free of fighters. Lando took the ship down hard and fast. He knew he was all over the company's radar and wanted to drop off.

The ship shuddered and bucked down through the atmosphere, making Wendy's already queasy stomach feel even worse, and claiming all of Lando's attention.

The equatorial zone came up to meet them, a vast strip of cratered wasteland, stretching like a belt around the planet's waist. It glowed as light rippled over hundreds of water-filled craters and glittered off shiny metal.

Lando took the ship even lower until it was barely skimming over the land, rising slightly to top low-lying hills, or swinging left and right to avoid jagged peaks.

Then, as the NAVCOMP announced that the rendezvous point was coming up, Lando cut power, dropped the flaps, and fired the ship's repellors. *The Tink* hovered in midair.

It started to rain, and big fat drops of water turned to steam as they hit the ship's force field. Lando approved. Rain meant clouds, and clouds meant that the Mega-Metals' surveillance satellites would have a harder time spotting them.

Two short peaks blocked the way, their flanks heavily scarred by meteor impacts, and worn by the effects of erosion.

Orange smoke billowed up. Lars Schmidt stepped out from behind a rock and waved. Lando rocked the ship slightly in acknowledgment. The geologist backpedaled and motioned for Lando to follow.

The smuggler eased his ship over broken ground, danced around the side of a reddish-orange rock, and spotted a large black hole towards the base of the left-hand peak. The cave was just as the geologist had described it. Large enough to hide *The Tink* but not so large as to attract attention in and of itself.

Schmidt backed into the cave and Lando followed. Dust billowed up and away from *The Tink's* repellors. It was difficult to see things located to port or starboard.

The ground rose a bit, forced the ship to rise with it, and slanted down into the cave. Lando liked that. The slight lip would make it even harder to see inside. Schmidt had stumbled across the underground cavern during one of his many field trips.

The landing lights came on. Lando saw something up ahead. It was a big boxy shape that quickly resolved itself into a six-wheeled truck. It had a cab, a connective tube made of pleated duraplast, and a large trailer. The vehicle had a sizable collection of dents, scrapes, and scratches. Many of these were overlaid with pea-sized meteorite craters. A little reminder of life in the E-zone.

The smuggler turned *The Tink* so that the external cargo hatch was positioned as close to the truck's tailgate as possible. The landing jacks touched down with a gentle thump. Lando waited for the ship to sag. It didn't. Lucky Lou's robo-techs had located the problem and "fixed" it. Lando shook his head in amazement. Now he'd have to hire someone to unfix it.

Wendy released her harness and headed for the main lock. Lando autosequenced the shutdown procedures.

Schmidt was waiting when the hatch whirred open. He saw Wendy and smiled. She jumped to the ground and gave him a hug. The geologist was surprised but pleased. He hugged her back.

The two of them appeared on the port security monitor. Lando tried to ignore them but found that he couldn't. Seeing Wendy with someone else hurt a lot more than he thought it would.

Lorenzo Pal was furious and Corvo knew it. She tried to appear calm but found that hard to do.

What if Pal blamed the screw-up on her? What if he broke her down to pit-boss? Or put her back on the line? Corvo had enemies . . . enemies that she'd made following Pal's orders . . . and they'd love the chance to take a shot at her.

A lot of things could happen out on the job. Your power plant could brew-up for no apparent reason, a boulder could fall out of the sky, or you could simply disappear. They never had found Petey Wilson. There were rumors that he'd been shredded and sent to Terra in a shipment of ore. Corvo bit her lower lip and hoped Air Six would arrive soon. Maybe the boss would relax when he had something to do . . . like find the smuggler and kill him.

Of course that might be easier said than done. Lando had done pretty well so far. He'd greased one shuttle, outrun the rest, evaded the company's radar, and vanished into thin air. The spy sats were searching for him but hadn't found a trace. Angel's halo was absolutely packed with metallic particles and they made a wonderful shield against most forms of detection.

As for the settlements, well, Pal had security teams in place in case the smuggler showed up there. Security teams that reported an unusual amount of activity. It was as though the sod-busters knew something that the company didn't and were preparing to deal with it.

Pal figured that the smuggler had put his ship down somewhere in the E-zone and Corvo agreed.

First came the robo-spy. It should have reported in by now. Destroyed? And if so, by whom? Its last known position was very close to where the computers thought Lando had touched down.

And what about the radio signal that had originated from that same quadrant of the zone? A long and two shorts. The signal was on a little-used frequency and no one had noticed it until Lando forced them to turn the computers inside out.

But why? Why land in the middle of a Class A disaster area? To hide something, that's why. But what? What were The Chosen up to, anyway?

That's what Pal wanted to know and Corvo couldn't blame him. She had a feeling about this. A feeling that something big was about to happen but didn't know why. The whole thing was weird as hell.

Pal strode back and forth across the reception area with his face locked in a semipermanent frown.

"Where the hell is that lifter? It should've been here by now."

Corvo heard the roar of engines and the mighty *whup, whup, whup* of giant helicopter blades. She rushed to the window. "The lifter's here, boss . . . right on time."

Pal ignored Corvo's comment as he strode towards the door. "Can't anyone be on time? Make a note of the pilot's name. I'll dock her pay a hundred credits for every minute that she holds us up."

Corvo sighed. She knew the pilot and liked her. She'd ignore Pal's order on the chance that he'd forget to check up on it.

Corvo followed her boss outside. She was from Terra, and the helicopter reminded her of a dragonfly, its huge rotors beating like wings, pushing air against the ground below. Dust billowed up as a clutch of cables jerked down towards the crawler.

The crawler was large, big enough to rival a tank, and equipped with two crablike arms. The company used the crawler, and others like it, to recover surface metals from their half of the E-zone. And, if the truth were known, they took metals from the other half as well.

The machine was so heavily armored that it could withstand a hit from anything up to an egg-sized meteorite. It had been bright orange at one time, emphasizing the similarity to a crab, but hard use had worn a lot of the paint away and left large sections of the hull to rust.

A black number "8" had been stenciled on the crawler's side, to which its driver had added a circle of white, and an even larger circle of black. The hand-painted letters right below it read "Eight-Ball."

The fact that the name glowed with freshly applied paint

said something about the vehicle's driver. He was a small man, smaller than Pal, and stood on the vehicle's front deck.

His name was Sato, and he'd been pushing heavy metal for a long time, so long that he'd become a sort of father figure to many of the younger drivers. He had black hair streaked with white, weather-beaten skin, and quick brown eyes. He wore light armor, a billed cap, and wireless headset.

Sato squinted upwards, watching the cluster of cable-mounted hooks that bobbed and swayed just over his head.

Corvo saw the driver's lips move and knew that he was talking to the pilot, coaching the cable down, sweet-talking it into his hands.

Sato's actions were a testament to his trust in the pilot's skill. One little error, one wrong move, and the hooks would take his head off. The cable dropped and steadied.

Corvo watched Sato jump, grab one of the hooks, and pull it towards the front left-hand corner of his massive vehicle. There was a heavy-duty eye bolt mounted in that location, and the hook snapped into place as if it was designed to go there, which it definitely was. The rest went quickly.

Sato took a quick look around, motioned for Corvo and Pal to climb aboard, and dropped through an open hatch.

Pal had spent very little time on the company's heavy equipment, so he made use of the ladder welded to the crawler's side.

Corvo climbed the way tool-pushers do, using the tracks, drive wheels, and guide arms as steps. She arrived first and had a secure grip on a handhold before the helicopter took off.

She enjoyed the look of fear on Pal's face as the crawler swayed into the air. The corpo scrambled up the last few rungs of the ladder, stumbled as the deck tilted to port, and threw his arms around a metal support.

Corvo made a mental note to dock the helicopter pilot's pay, after all. Pal would remember all right. There was no doubt about that.

Lando did his best to hang on as Honey roared her way to the top of a ridge, teetered for a moment, and half slid down the other side. The trailer was fully loaded with cylinders and heavy as hell.

The plan was to haul them north to a point just south of

the main settlement, where a team of scientists were preparing various methods of dispersal, including some custom-designed aerosol bombs, robotic ground crawlers, and short-range missiles. Technology hard at work destroying itself. Lando thought it was ironic, but his companions didn't seem to agree.

Time was of the essence. If the corpos caught them on the ground, with the organisms still inside the cylinders, the war would be over before it even started.

Lando, riding in back, leaned forward to speak to Schmidt. He had to yell in order to be heard over the noise of the truck's engines. "How much longer?"

Schmidt kept his eyes up ahead. The E-zone looked like a battlefield of overlapping holes and craters. The rain had stopped and the sun was shining.

"Oh, eight or nine hours maybe. Honey's doing the best she can . . . but those cylinders are pretty darned heavy."

Wendy, seated next to Schmidt, didn't say anything but thought she knew what Lando was thinking. Yes, time was critical, but there was something more as well. The job was over and so was their relationship. The smuggler wanted to lift, head for parts unknown, recoup his losses. And Wendy had little doubt that Lando could fight his way off-planet if he chose to.

But something had caused him to stay and see it through. His sense of honor? Stubborn pride? Affection for her? It made little difference. Whatever the reason, he had stayed.

Wendy watched the two men out of the corner of her eye. Schmidt and Lando. Lars and Pik. Scientist and smuggler. So different, yet so alike. Both competent, both strong, both honest in their own ways.

She liked Lars, and found him physically attractive if somewhat boring. But he believed the way that she believed, saw the future the way that she saw it, and was willing to work towards it. That was worth more than mere excitement, wasn't it? Wendy assured herself that it was.

It was uncomfortably close inside the crawler. Even with the air conditioning running at full blast, the control room was still too warm.

Not only that, but a long line of tool pushers had sweated

through more than forty thousand hours inside the enclosed space, and the smell of their perspiration had found its way into every nook and cranny of the machine's interior.

The result was a rich funky smell that no amount of deodorant would ever erase. Fresh air came from the open hatch but wasn't enough.

Sato sat like a king within his cocoonlike command chair, eyes constantly flicking this way and that, watching the video-feed from the helicopter and his own vid cameras.

The tool pusher had twelve different screens to watch, and those, plus a multitude of colored indicator lights, lit the space with a greenish glow. Things looked different from three hundred feet in the air and Sato liked that.

Pal was a good deal less comfortable. The fold-down jump seat was located behind the command chair and over to one side. It was intended for emergencies and check-rides. Because of that the seat offered very little in the way of padding and absolutely no back support.

Pal wanted to commandeer Sato's chair but was afraid to do so. What he knew about operating crawlers could be laser-inscribed on the head of a pin. What if he made a mistake? Screwed something up? Sato would tell the others and they'd laugh at him. No, that would never do.

So, unable to get comfortable, and unable to do anything about it, Pal turned his thoughts to revenge. He'd make the Wendeen bitch pay like she'd never paid before. Just the thought of it caused a familiar stirring between his legs. The corpo smiled.

But if Pal was uncomfortable, then Corvo was even more so, since she'd been forced to stand half-bent over in the small alcove that provided access to the tiny head, and next to that, an even smaller galley.

But it was either that or an unprotected ride in the cargo bay which took up the rear part of the crawler, and Corvo knew better than to try that.

She imagined what it would be like to be sealed inside a cold metal box, unable to see or hear, helpless until someone decided to let you out. She shivered. Uncomfortable though it was, the control room was better than that.

The pilot's voice was loud in Sato's ears. He had routed all incoming transmissions through his headset. "Knowledge is power." He'd read that somewhere and it was true.

"Air Six to Eight-Ball. Are you awake?"

Sato grinned. "Of course I'm awake. I was sipping some wine and listening to Movari's Fifth."

The pilot made a rude noise. "You might be sipping some wine, especially if it's cheap, but you wouldn't recognize Movari's Fifth if it was memprinted on what's left of your brain. The LZ's coming up. Five to dirt."

"That's a roger, Air Six."

Sato stuck his hands inside the control gauntlets and flexed the middle finger of his right hand just so. His command chair whirred to the left. "Hang on, folks . . . we're five to ground."

Pal scowled. "It's about time."

Corvo smiled encouragingly. "Thanks for letting us know."

Sato nodded, sent both of them a mental "screw you," and turned back to his controls.

The ground came up fast. The helicopter pilot had chosen the center of an ancient crater as her landing point. It was flat and relatively clear of debris.

Sato experienced the tight-gut feeling that always went with a drop into the equatorial zone. Had the odds piled up against him? Would this be the trip when some nameless chunk of hot metal came screaming out of the sky to take his life? Was it his turn to punch out?

He wanted to stretch, to ease tight muscles, but couldn't remove his hands from the gloves. Instead, he recited the prayer his mother had taught him. His eyes scanned the screens, which gave him twelve different views of the outside world. All of them wobbled and drifted to the right as the pilot made a last-minute correction.

"Ten seconds to dirt." The pilot's voice was flat and unemotional. Sato knew it would stay that way no matter what. He yelled to the others.

"Ten seconds to touchdown . . . Hang on!"

The landing was gentle by normal standards but worse than Corvo had expected. The crawler hit hard, sending a solid shock up through her slightly flexed knees, and throwing her against a durasteel bulkhead. She swore accordingly.

Pal was a little better off, but not much, and said some unpleasant things about the pilot. He was still at it when Sato popped the top hatch and crawled outside.

The helicopter threw a thick, dark shadow across the crater and blasted the entire area with grit. Pal popped his head out of the hatch, caught a face full of wind-driven dirt, and disappeared.

Sato released the cable hooks one at a time. "Okay . . . hooks one, two, three, and four are released. Thanks for the ride, Air Six."

The words were barely out of Sato's mouth before the hooks swayed upwards. "That's a roger, Eight-Ball . . . Have a nice trip. Air Six out."

Sato doubted that was possible, but kept the thought to himself. He dropped through the hatch into the command chair, slipped his hands into the control gauntlets, and pointed with his right index finger. A holo-projected heads-up display appeared in front of his eyes as the crawler jerked into motion. There was a pretty good-sized hill up ahead. He'd head for the top and take a look around.

Pal was peering over the tool pusher's shoulder and asking stupid questions when the transmission came in.

"Air Six to Eight-Ball."

"I read you, Air Six. Go ahead."

"You've got company, Eight-Ball. A truck of some sort. Sod-busters from the look of them. About eight miles due south and closing."

"That's a rog, Air Six. Eight and closing. How bout a look-see?"

"Roger that, Eight-Ball. One look-see comin' up."

Pal stabbed Sato's shoulder with a stiffened finger. "What? What did they say?"

Sato didn't like the feel of Pal's finger. He shifted his weight to escape it. "There's a truck eight miles to the south. Not one of ours. Coming this way."

Pal brought a fist down on his open palm. "It's them! It has to be! But why? What's the truck for? Full speed ahead, Sato . . . The fun has just begun."

17

Progress was painfully slow. There was no such thing as a straight line. Honey twisted and turned as Schmidt guided her around water-filled impact craters, over miniature mountain ranges, and through a maze of broken rock.

Lando didn't like it. He didn't like the situation, the E-zone, or riding in the back. He was used to being in control, to making his own decisions, to sitting in the driver's seat.

Honey leaned sideways as Schmidt pushed her through a narrow corridor. The passageway had been created hundreds of years before when a good-sized meteorite had hit the top of a ridge, plowed its way through, and sprayed the landscape with chunks of hot metal.

Lando was forced to hang on tight as the corridor narrowed and Schmidt put the right set of wheels up onto the bank. There was a clanking sound as two of the cylinders rolled together. Another couple of degrees and Honey would roll over.

But the gorge opened up, the bank disappeared, and the wheels hit the ground with a bone-jarring thud. That's when Lando saw the flashing red light and heard the buzzer.

Wendy looked at Schmidt. He frowned. "Bad news, I'm afraid. We've got company."

Lando felt emptiness where his stomach should be. "How many?"

Schmidt touched some keys in quick succession. Additional data appeared on the right-hand side of his heads-up display. "One vehicle, a crawler from the looks of it, and . . ."

A large black shadow flashed across the truck. They heard the roar of the aircraft engines. Honey rocked under the blast of displaced air.

Wendy leaned forward to look up through the windshield. " . . . and one helicopter."

Lando peered out through a side window. The helicopter was headed north. "It's leaving the area . . . That seems strange."

"Listen . . ." Schmidt touched a key and they heard a woman's voice:

" . . . about does it, Eight-Ball. We're flying on fumes. See you back at the barn."

A male voice came on: "Copy that, Air Six. Eight-Ball out."

"It makes sense," Schmidt said thoughtfully. "It would take a lot of fuel to airlift a crawler."

"What kind of crawler?" Lando asked, half afraid of the answer.

"Huge things with a lot of armor," Wendy replied. "Remember our visit to Security Control? A crawler was parked outside."

Lando remembered all right. A big ugly machine with crablike arms.

"Can we outrun it?"

"We can try," Schmidt answered grimly. "We can try."

"What about weapons?" Lando asked. "What have you got?"

Schmidt looked at Wendy, and something passed between them. An unspoken bond that would forever shut Lando out. The smuggler saw it and knew what the scientist would say.

"Nothing outside of that slug gun you're wearing. But that doesn't matter much, since I wouldn't use them anyway."

Lando slumped back in his seat. Great, just great. There were killers on the loose and his companions were pacifists.

But the worst part was his complete and utter helplessness. There was very little he could do but sit down, shut up, and hope Schmidt found a way around the crawler.

Honey roared loudly as Schmidt guided her down and through a small stream. Then they went up and onto a rocky slope.

The attack came without warning. The crawler had been waiting, hull down beyond the rise, like a wolf spider in its den. Now it roared straight at them, pincer arms spread, trying to grab some part of the truck and drag it to a halt.

Schmidt swerved, and Honey shuddered, as the tip of a durasteel pincer pierced her left flank.

Lando pushed himself away as rusty metal punched through the truck's armor-plated side. It was just the tip of a pincer but large enough to make a hole the size of his head.

Schmidt swore, the engines roared, and metal screeched as Honey pulled away. The pincer tore a four-foot-long gash in the vehicle's side.

Lorenzo Pal blasted over the comset. His laughter had a wild, almost demented quality. "That's right sod-busters! Run for your lives! Here we come!"

Lando looked up at the external monitors. One was packed side to side and top to bottom with the ugly-looking crawler. "Watch out!"

A pincer lashed forward and hit the trailer. The truck lurched and the entire vehicle rang like a gong. Schmidt applied power and the crawler fell behind. The truck was a little bit faster than the crawler, especially on open ground. There was an unexpected breeze from the gash in Honey's side.

But Honey had barely reached forty miles an hour when she ran out of open ground. Schmidt stepped on the brakes and swore when the wheels hit a rock. The entire front end of the truck bounced up and off the ground.

Honey hit hard. Wendy was thrown against her harness, and the tanks hit the front of the trailer.

Lando looked at the monitors and saw the crawler grow larger. Damn! If there was only something he could do.

"That way!" Wendy pointed towards the right. It was a narrow passageway, too narrow for the crawler to follow. The geologist nodded and turned the wheel in that direction.

The crawler was closer now. Lando saw its right-hand pincer flash forward. There was the screech of metal on metal as the crawler sank durasteel fingers into the top right-hand corner of the trailer's frame.

The engines roared as Schmidt did his best to pull away. Drive wheels spun and threw up fountains of dirt.

Pal's maniacal laughter filled the cabin. "Go ahead! Run! We have plenty of time."

Metal groaned, something parted with a loud report, and the truck jerked forward. Unable to follow, the crawler dwindled in size.

The scientist pushed forward as quickly as he dared, unable to see beyond the next curve, praying there was a way out. What if the passageway led them into a dead end?

The walls were tight and stained with rust. A jagged piece of rusty iron stuck straight out from the right-hand wall. Schmidt swerved but there wasn't enough room to clear the obstruction. Metal grated on metal as Honey slid by.

Lando felt his heart sink. The ancient Chinese had a name for this. They called it "the death of a thousand cuts."

They needed to seize the initiative, find a way to fight back, but his companions weren't likely to take that course. No, he'd have to wait for an opportunity and act on his own.

Wendy gave a sigh of relief as the rocky defile opened up onto a shallow basin.

Lando saw movement to the left and yelled "Over to the left, Lars! Here they come!"

Schmidt opened the throttles. The truck labored at first, fought the weight of the cylinders, and jerked forward.

Lando held his breath as they raced for the other side of the basin. The corpos had been forced into a different canyon, but had made pretty good time and stood a good chance of intercepting them towards the middle of the flat.

Closer, closer, damn! The entire vehicle shook as the crawler sideswiped them. Schmidt fought for control. Something felt different, but he wasn't sure what it was. A tire? Something mechanical? Whatever it was made Honey hard to steer.

Lando leaned forward to tap him on the shoulder. "Slow down when we reach the other side. I want to bail out."

Wendy started to frown but forced the expression away. This wasn't his fight . . . and besides . . . who could blame him? The smuggler had kept his side of the bargain and then some.

The geologist must have felt the same way, because he hit the brakes as they bounced off the pan and into the broken area beyond.

Lando released his seat belt, opened the rear passenger door, and jumped. The truck was still in motion. The ground came up hard and fast. He stumbled, fell, and rolled over. Dust swirled up and around him. The ground shook as the crawler approached.

Sato moved his finger a hair to the right and felt the crawler do likewise. His voice was flat and emotionless. "One of them bailed out. Shall I stop for him or chase the truck?"

"Stay with the truck," Pal replied. "We'll take care of him a little bit later."

Lando had just gotten to his feet when the crawler roared past. He caught a glimpse of the huge eight-ball painted on its side and something else as well. Something that might work in his favor. The top hatch was slightly ajar. Not much, inches at most, but just enough. Enough to stick his arm inside and empty the slug gun.

If he could catch up, *if* he could climb aboard, *if* the hatch remained open. Lando started to run.

Schmidt found it increasingly hard to steer. Given that, and given the crawler's other advantages, there was only one chance left.

Maybe, just maybe, they could circle around and find a place to hide the trailer. Then, lighter and faster, they could lead the crawler away and hope for the best. It was a chance at least, and some chance was better than none.

Sato had grown weary of the chase. Pal enjoyed this cat and mouse stuff, but he didn't. The more time they spent in the zone, the better the chances of winding up dead. Sato balled both his fists and the Eight-Ball skidded to a halt.

Pal screamed in his ear. "What the hell do you think you're doing? Go after them!"

Sato didn't look around. His eyes were on the screens. "I'm getting tired of your bullshit, Pal. Shut up and sit down. If your brain ran half as fast as your mouth, you'd see something very interesting."

Pal was completely speechless. His jaw worked but nothing came out. He was just about to fire Sato on the spot, when Corvo pointed towards the screens.

"Look, boss! Look at the dust! Sato's right!"

Pal looked. The truck had disappeared off the flat, but a cone of dust was pointed down behind the rim of the ancient crater. The dust was like a finger pointing at its prey.

Pal smiled. "Thank you, Sato. When you're right, you're right. Let's wrap this thing up."

Sato nodded, directed a silent "up yours" in Pal's direction, and performed a routine sweep of the screens. Movement caught his eye. His eyes went to the stern vid camera and stopped. What the hell was that? It looked as if someone was chasing the crawler.

Lando's lungs felt as if they'd burst. His heart was pounding like mad. Dust spurted up where his boots hit the ground. Just a little bit further, just a little bit further, just a little bit further.

Who knew why the crawler stopped? Who cared? Just a little bit further . . . twelve feet . . . eight . . . the crawler loomed in front of him . . . heat rising in waves off its rear deck, engine rumbling softly.

Lando was almost there, leaning forward, waiting for his fingers to touch hot metal, when the crawler's engines roared to life. Black smoke engulfed him as the machine rolled away. It was gone seconds later.

The smuggler stopped, put his hands on his knees, and sucked oxygen into his lungs. It was minute, maybe two, before he looked up. He saw it instantly. The spiral of dust, the crawler heading off to intercept, and the certainty of the outcome. Lando wiped the dust off his face with the back of his sleeve and started to jog.

Wendy looked up at the screens. "I think we lost them."

Schmidt shrugged. "I hope you're right . . . but it's too early to be sure. Let's find a box canyon or something similar. We'll stash the trailer and use the tractor to lead them away.

Wendy nodded her agreement and searched the monitors for some sign of what they were looking for. The problem was that there were so many passageways, corridors, and canyons, it was difficult to choose.

Schmidt skirted the edge of the very same crater that they'd been forced to flee a few minutes earlier. Was that good or bad? He wasn't sure. If only . . .

The crawler came out of a side passage at ten or fifteen miles an hour. There was a terrible crash as it hit Honey's right flank. The truck was lifted up off the ground and held there while both of the pincers went to work. Metal screeched and groaned as durasteel fingers cut their way through Honey's armor plate.

Schmidt gunned the engines but nothing happened. A metal claw smashed its way through Wendy's door, missed her arm by a fraction of an inch, and opened wide. Wendy hit her harness release and the geologist jerked her towards him just as the pincer snapped closed.

The rest was instinct. Schmidt tried to open the door, swore when it refused to budge, and hit the window switch. The reinforced duraplast made a whining noise as it disappeared into the door frame.

Pal's voice came over the comset. "Wendy? Are you there? Would you like this to stop?"

The pincers opened, closed on a section of the control panel, and pulled. There was a horrible crunching sound as a fifty-pound chunk of metal and plastic was ripped away. Wendy could see into the engine compartment and feel the heat that flooded out.

"Wendy, you could stop this. You liked what I did to you. I know that you did. Tell me you liked it and I'll make them stop."

The pincers took another bite of dashboard, and Honey's engines went silent as if cut with a switch.

Schmidt wriggled out through the window, desperately afraid that the truck would fall on him, but determined to drag Wendy clear. He grabbed her wrists. Wendy looked up at him and started to speak.

Schmidt saw Janice, saw her head start to turn, and knew the bullet was coming. He screamed "No!" and pulled with all his might.

Pal's voice was calm, almost conversational. "I like your body. What a waste it would be if the pincer cut it in half. But business before pleasure . . ."

Lando slipped, fell, and hit his knee on a rock. It hurt like hell. Damn, damn, damn! A battle raged just beyond the edge of this crater on the perimeter of the next. He could see the dust and hear the noise. The smuggler got up and limped forward.

Wendy popped loose and Schmidt fell backwards, pulling her with him. She was barely clear when the truck teetered and came crashing down. The cylinders made a loud clanging sound as they broke free of their tie-downs and rolled around inside the trailer.

Schmidt helped Wendy to her feet and they backed away as the crawler tore Honey apart. The crawler peeled the truck like a Terran orange. It ripped the armor off first, cut the frame into sections, and laid the interior bare.

The cylinders shone in the sunlight. They were naked and completely vulnerable. Tears ran down Wendy's cheeks as a pincer gave one of the cylinders an experimental nudge.

Engines roared as the crawler backed away.

Schmidt grabbed Wendy by the arm, jerked her towards a slab of rock, and pulled her behind it. It stood only waist-high, but some protection was better than none.

Metal clanged as Sato brought the pincers together. They formed a wall of steel. The crawler belched black smoke as it lurched forward. There was a clang and Wendy winced as pincers collided with metal cylinders. The tanks rolled away from the impact, banged off of each other, and came to a stop. The crawler hit them again.

Schmidt touched Wendy's arm and pointed towards the left. There was a pit in the middle of the crater, like the circle at the center of a bull's-eye, and that's where the cylinders were headed. Wendy scrambled up onto the top surface of the rock to get a better look.

She saw a cliff, a fifty-foot drop, and a pool of stagnant water. She bit a knuckle as she watched the cylinders near the edge.

The crawler stopped. Pal stuck his head out of the hatch. He waved. His voice boomed over the external loudspeaker. "Hey, Wendy! Watch this!"

The crawler roared, metal clanged, and the cylinders rolled off the edge. They fell, hit the jagged rocks below, and fell again. There were three almost simultaneous splashes. Vapor misted the air. The tanks bobbed, floated for a moment, and disappeared. A series of bubbles floated up from below, burst, and gave off clouds of gas. Languid waves rolled out to lap against the sides of the crater.

Wendy gave a long, shuddering sigh. The cylinders were gone. The dream was over. She jumped down off the rock. Schmidt did likewise.

The crawler backed away from the edge. It turned their way and stopped. Pal stood on top of the machine. About forty feet separated him from Wendy. He looked down at her.

"Well, I don't know what you had in the cylinders . . . but it's history now."

A blaster materialized in the corpo's hands. He aimed it at Schmidt. "Wendy and I want to be alone . . . so take a hike."

Schmidt's hands opened and closed. They were powerful hands, used to hard physical labor. To hell with nonviolence. The geologist had a sudden desire to wrap his fingers around Pal's neck. He started forward.

"Lars, no!"

The beam of bright blue light and the crack of a slug gun came almost together. A puddle of rock appeared next to Schmidt's right foot. It started to cool.

Pal looked surprised, staggered, and looked around. Lando fired again and the corpo flew backwards off the crawler. He hit the ground with a distinct thump.

Engines roared as the crawler turned. Smoke puffed away from Lando's arm as a pair of mini-missiles raced down to hit the right-hand track. The explosion was surprisingly loud. A link parted and the crawler came to a stop.

A scrap of white cloth appeared, followed by Corvo's arm. Sato cut the engines and pulled his hands out of the gauntlets.

Metal made a pinging sound as it started to cool.

Wendy looked at Lando. She knew that it was wrong, but she was grateful for what he'd done. A meteor, a big one, chose that particular moment to cross the sky and explode somewhere in the distance.

Lando took charge of Sato and Corvo while Wendy walked over to the cliff. There wasn't so much as a ripple to show where the cylinders had gone in. It was over. In spite of all their planning, all their work, the whole thing was over. The company had won.

Schmidt appeared by her side. The geologist stood there for a full minute. Then he started to laugh. It began as a chuckle, segued into a full-fledged laugh, and exploded into gales of uncontrolled mirth. The geologist clutched his sides as tears rolled down his cheeks and into his beard.

Wendy wanted to smile, but did her best to resist. It didn't seem appropriate. "What's so funny?"

Schmidt pointed down towards the pit. "The cylinders . . . they broke open as they fell. . . . Look around you. Metal everywhere. Food. Leaching down into the water. Soup. The tanks fell into a big bowl of soup!"

Unable to say more, the scientist laughed again.

Wendy looked from Schmidt to the pit. Metal? Soup? What did Lars mean?

Then it hit her. Of course! The bacteria ate metal! They would thrive in the metal-rich water below! The microorganisms would flourish and multiply. They would follow the equatorial zone around the planet. Then, bit by bit, the bacteria would move north and south along the veins of rich ore until they had spread far and wide.

It was perfect! Much better than any delivery system that the scientists could have devised! Schmidt and Wendy were still laughing when Lando made his way down to stand beside them.

They told him the joke and he laughed too. He looked down into the sludge. The army had landed and the war had begun.

18

The next few weeks passed quickly.

Annette Corvo proved to be a good deal more reasonable than Lorenzo Pal had ever been. Rather than punish the colonists, she wrote a report that blamed everything on her boss, and sent it to Terra. The suits started to arrive a week and a half later. They were on the same ship that brought The Chosen's legal team.

Lando spent most of his time ducking "thank you" dinners and finalizing the arrangements by which The Chosen were supposed to pay him. A rather unlikely possibility, but what the heck, a guy could hope.

The Chosen's lawyers asked Lando to make taped depositions for use in the legal battle that was sure to follow. Both the colonists and Mega-Metals had violated countless Imperial laws. The case would keep a dozen attorneys busy for years to come.

The company had already lost the first round by requesting a planetary quarantine, a condition that made it impossible for the colonists to import any additional microorganisms but applied to the company as well.

Had Mega-Metals designed bacteria of their own, and brought them in quickly enough, they might have been able to neutralize the invading army before it had time to spread. The corporation's scientists told the executives that, but most of them were lawyers, and refused to listen.

But even though the elders had won the first battle, they were almost sure to lose the war. When the last motion had been filed, and the last appeal had run its course, Mega-Metals would emerge victorious. The company had *lots* of money, *lots* of lawyers, and *lots* of influence.

But as Lando's father liked to say, "There's winning, and then there's winning. Be sure you know which is which."

Time was on the side of the colonists. The legal process could take as long as twenty-five or thirty years. More than enough time for "Dr. Bob's magnificent metal munchers" to colonize the planet, eat the company out of house and home, and block any possibility of commercial mining.

So what if the company won the lawsuit? What good is a judgment against a bankrupt organization? And who would buy half of a worthless planet?

No, the elders looked forward to losing, especially since the Imperial government had agreed to step in. Some rather bored looking marines had landed and were keeping a close eye on both sides. The company wouldn't dare pull anything underhanded with a company of marines looking over its shoulder.

Yes, things had gone pretty well for the settlers, but not for Lando. He felt sorry for himself. It was Wendy's fault. He'd been perfectly happy until she came along. First she'd given him something, then she'd taken it away, and now it hurt.

Lando had considered hanging it up. He could ask Wendy to marry him, he could build a house, he could scrape a living out of the soil.

But it didn't fit. Deep down, the smuggler couldn't stand the thought of living on an increasingly isolated planet, staring at the soil instead of the stars, doing something he didn't enjoy. No, he'd lift and do it soon.

And not just for emotional reasons. Tests had shown that the bacteria were still confined to the E-zone. But for how long? The government would impose a two-way quarantine one of these days, and ground whatever ships were dirtside at that particular moment. *The Tink* would be stranded on the planet, food for the metal-eating bugs, a monument to the past. It was another reason to lift.

Lando kept the goodbyes as brief as possible. The moment with Wendy was the worst of all. It took place next to *The Tink's* starboard landing jack. A light breeze swept down off the mountains, rippled through the crops on Elder's Flat, and teased her hair. She looked very solemn.

"Goodbye, Pik. I'll miss you."

Lando nodded. Something caught in his throat. "Goodbye, Wendy. I'll miss you too. Take care of yourself."

A tear ran down Wendy's cheek. She wiped it away with the back of her hand. "Me? Take care of myself? What could happen to me? You're the one who runs around smuggling illicit cargos, fighting for lost causes, and rescuing damsels in distress."

Lando traced the tear with his thumb. "And what happened to 'happily ever after'?"

Wendy shrugged and forced a smile. "'Happy' means different things to different people. Your kind of happy is out there among the stars. My kind is here on the ground."

Lando bent and kissed her lightly on the lips. He smiled. "Goodbye, Wendy."

Her eyes searched his face, as if trying to memorize each nook and cranny, storing it against future need. "Goodbye, Pik."

Lando turned then, waved to a small knot of well-wishers, and walked towards his ship. He didn't look back.

The next few weeks passed quickly. Lando made his way from Angel to New Britain, where he hired an appraiser and asked her to put a value on *The Tinker's Damn.*

She did, and although the number she quoted was a good deal less than what the smuggler had hoped for, he went to look at Nister Needles anyway.

By selling *The Tink,* and using almost all of his remaining money, the smuggler might be able to buy one of the sleek little speedsters.

Lando paid off the autocab, climbed out, and made his way through the standard security scanners and onto the apron. It was hot. He could feel the sun on the back of his neck and smell the heady mix of lubricants and fuel that hung just above the ground.

Out beyond the apron, row upon row of neatly parked ships marched away towards New Britain's rather imposing passenger terminal. It had multiple layers and looked a lot like a wedding cake. It shimmered in the distance like some sort of high-tech mirage.

Lando rounded the corner of a hangar and stopped to admire the ships arrayed before him. They were beautiful vessels, as slim and sharp as their name implied, and built for speed. Nothing could touch them, either in a planetary atmosphere or out in space. Even the navy used Nister Needles as couriers and fast patrol boats.

A heavily laden freighter roared as powerful repellors lifted it up and off its stumpy landing jacks. Lando turned to watch as the ship lumbered past, performed a slow-motion pirouette, and headed out towards a lift zone.

He turned back towards the speedsters just in time to see a spiffy-looking sales rep exit one of the ships, turn on a thousand-gigawatt smile, and march forward with hand extended. The sales rep's initial words were lost in the sound of the freighter's takeoff, but Lando could guess what they were.

"Hello, glad to meet you, blah, blah, blah." Lando sighed. He wanted to buy a ship, or at least discuss the possibility of buying a ship, but didn't look forward to the process.

It took more than two days of on and off bargaining to cut the deal. By the time it was over, Lando had little more than a brand new Nister Needle, some money for fuel, and the shirt on his back.

It was hard to part with *The Tink*. She was the first ship he'd ever owned, and had seen him through some tight scrapes. She looked old and forlorn sitting between a couple of clapped-out shuttles.

Lando knew it was silly, knew she was little more than steel and plastic, but couldn't resist walking over to say goodbye. He patted her port landing jack.

"Goodbye, old girl. I'm going to miss you. Take care of yourself."

The ship made no answer, of course, but Lando felt a slight lump in his throat as he walked away. For the second time in as many weeks the smuggler had parted company with something or somebody he loved.

The moment caused Lando to think of Ithro and home. It would be nice to see his father, show off the new ship, and recharge his emotional batteries. He couldn't really afford to make the trip, but what the hell, he'd keep the visit short.

Lando and the ship that he called *Wendy* lifted four hours later.

It took a small hyperspace jump and the better part of a week to reach Lando's home system. Ithro was the fourth planet in from the sun, and rather close to the nav beacon, but the smuggler angled in and away from it.

Jethro, the system's third planet, was wild, woolly, and close to lawless. The perfect place for smugglers, bounty hunters, mercenaries, and other members of the underworld to relax, spend their money, and figure out how to make some more.

As such, Jethro qualified as one of Zack Lando's favorite haunts. The old man didn't spend much time on Ithro anymore, not since the death of his wife, and his son's coming of age.

It had been eight years since the Imperial navy had raided Jethro, cleaned the place up, and left. Eight years during which things had quickly slipped back into the same old patterns. But the citizens of Jethro remembered the raid, and knew that another could come at any time, so they kept a close eye on incoming ships.

But while there were none of the formalities common to more civilized planets, Lando knew he was under surveillance, and was careful to follow certain unwritten rules of conduct.

He identified himself on a certain frequency. Then he deactivated the ship's weapons systems, killed the force field, and made one orbit of the planet. Plenty of time for Jethro's spy sats and sensor stations to check him out.

The com call was loud and abrupt. A male voice said, "Come on, Pik, and get your butt down here. The ole man's waitin' ta buy ya a beer."

Lando smiled. "That's a roger, Jethro. I'm on my way."

Jethro rose to greet him, a big brown ball, striated with wisps of white. Though blessed with close to Earth normal gravity, the planet had a poisonous atmosphere, and lots of volcanic activity.

The ship bucked a bit as it came down through different layers of Jethro's atmosphere, then smoothed out just above the surface. Lando kept the ship at about fifteen thousand feet. There was no point in crowding the volcanic mountains that dotted the planet's surface.

The ship's NAVCOMP recognized the settlement long before Lando did, beeped softly, and flooded his control screen with data.

Lando noted the wind direction, the recommended approach vector, and pushed the speedster down into a bowl-shaped depression. The long curve of a razor-sharp ridge passed beneath the ship as walls of volcanic rock rose to surround him.

Below, filling the bottom of the valley from side to side, there was a large greenish lake. It seethed and bubbled as noxious gases worked their way up to the surface to become part of the already poisoned atmosphere.

On the far side of the lake, halfway up a mountainside and growing larger with each passing second, was the habitat known as Forbo's Flat. It sat on a ledge carved from the side of a dormant volcano and wasn't much to look at. There were some scabrous-looking domes, a cluster of globular fuel tanks, and a sturdy-looking com mast. A ship took off, rocked its stubby wings, and blasted upwards.

The settlement was surrounded by piles of its own garbage. Lando watched a beetle-shaped crawler push a wave of refuse along in front of it. The machine stopped at the edge of the cliff and garbage fell like a skirt towards the lake below.

Wendy came in low, flared gracefully, and settled towards blast-scarred rock.

Lando saw a glint of reflected light from the other side of the valley and knew that a weapons emplacement was tracking his progress. Although the locals might be somewhat casual about matters of protocol, they weren't stupid. Just because someone *says* he's Pik Lando doesn't mean it's so.

A globe-shaped drone appeared in front of the ship. The words "Follow me" flashed on and off across the front of the device, slightly distorted by the curvature of its hull. There was a gust of wind and the drone bobbed slightly before it floated away.

Lando fed power to the speedster's repellors and followed. The little ship was incredibly maneuverable, and what might have been a chore in some other ship was transformed into pure pleasure.

The surface of the dome shimmered behind the protective force field. A pair of doors parted, and Lando guided *Wendy* into a rather spacious airlock.

The lock was capable of handling much larger ships and represented something of a luxury on a planet like Jethro. But, as Lando knew from previous experience, the landing fees would more than cover the cost involved.

The word "Wait" circled around the drone's middle and the smuggler obeyed. A glance at his stern monitor showed the doors had started to close.

Minutes passed while an assortment of noxious gases were pumped out of the lock and a breathable atmosphere was pumped in.

Then, when the drone again flashed "Follow me," and the inner doors slid open, Lando danced the ship forward.

The hangar was a large, well-lit place, already three-quarters full, and bustling with activity. A wild variety of people, maintenance bots, and automated equipment crisscrossed the lube-stained floor, coming, going, or just milling around.

A few of the humans, pilots mostly, turned to watch the speedster pass. A somewhat different reaction from the one that *The Tink* had elicited.

Lando smiled. It felt good to have something other people wanted.

He scanned the other ships. There were reentry-scarred shuttles, boxy-looking freighters, converted military craft, and some beat-up tugs. There was even a yacht or two, the property of successful smugglers or wealthy types looking for a good time.

Lando watched for his father's ship as the drone led him towards a distant parking space. There was no sign of her. The smuggler frowned. That seemed strange. Where was *Queenie*, anyway? His father rarely went anywhere without her. Lando shrugged. He'd know the answer soon enough.

He set the ship down with a barely felt thump. As he autosequenced the shutdown procedure the drone flashed "Have a nice day" across its midsection and floated off towards a new assignment.

Lando took a quick shower, slipped into a fresh set of clothes, and emerged from the ship feeling pretty good. It would be good to see his father again, and even better to show off his new ship, a tangible sign of his recent success.

So there was a spring in Lando's step as he made his way across the hangar towards the huge supergraphic that read

FORBO'S FLAT and pointed towards a pair of double doors. He whistled as he walked, nodded pleasantly to passersby, and savored the moment.

The world beyond the hangar was a dimly lit place, circular like the dome itself, and organized along rather basic lines. There were establishments that catered to basic biological needs like food, sleep, and sex, as well as other places that offered a wide variety of other products and services, such as cyber clinics, weapons boutiques, surgi-centers, and more.

The main passageway was packed with a multiplicity of humans, aliens, auto hawkers, beggars, pickpockets, and whores. Lando nodded, shook his head, or dodged them as the occasion demanded. He could remember walking this same corridor as a child, staring in open-eyed amazement at the color and activity, tripping over his own feet as he tried to take it all in.

Then, as now, his father had made a bar called the Smuggler's Rest, his unofficial headquarters. Lando saw the familiar sign up ahead, a blue holo proj that hovered in midair and colored the smoke that floated around it. Lando smiled in anticipation.

The front door was little more than a chain curtain. It rattled as he pushed it aside. The place was half full and many of those present were friends or cronies of his father's. Lando had known some of them since boyhood.

There was Trig Holman, one-time pilot and full-time stim junkie; Liza Santho, cargomaster and friend; Bido Balazar, mean as hell and twice as ugly; and plenty more. The razzing started right away.

"Hey! Look what the cat dragged in, it's Pik Lando!"

"Pik! Where'd you get that ship? Did some pimp leave it to you in his will?"

"Hey, Piko! Where's the ten you owe me? Bartender, set 'em up! Pik's buying the next round!"

Lando threw a hundred-credit note on the bar, wished he didn't have to, and gave a wave of acknowledgment. There was a roar of approval and the chrome-plated bartender started to pour the drinks.

Then Lando walked back towards the corner table, the same table where his father had cut a hundred deals, and he'd waited through endless hours of adult talk. He was there all right, a little older, a little grayer, but basically the same.

Zack Lando was somewhat shorter than his son, but built like a brick wall, and just as solid. Middle age had been good to him. Gray frosted his hair, wrinkles added character, and his teeth were bone-white. They showed through his smile. He stood and moved forward.

The two men hugged and hugged again. Zack put his hands on Lando's shoulders. "Here, let me take a look at you, son. Damn but you look good! Sit down. I'll buy you a beer."

Lando grinned. "Good. The C-note I threw on the bar was the last one I had."

Zack laughed and slapped his son's shoulder. "A little tight, eh? Well, no problem. The old man's got plenty. But what about that ship? Nisters don't come cheap."

Lando nodded soberly. "You can say that again. *Wendy* took *The Tink* and everything else besides."

Zack nodded understandingly. "I'll bet. Still, I know what *The Tink* was worth, and you must have run a pretty good scam to make up the difference."

Lando felt a flush of pride. That was about as close as his father ever came to giving a compliment. Lando was careful to downplay his reaction. He shrugged.

"I had some pretty strange clients and lost as much as I made."

Zack raised an eyebrow. "I sense a story worth telling. Here comes the beer. Wet your whistle and then tell me about it."

Lando did, starting on HiHo, and taking it all the way through the battle in Angel's E-zone.

"So," his father finished for him, "you took the profit, put it together with *The Tink*, and bought a Nister Needle."

He nodded approvingly. "Speed is a smuggler's best friend. You can forget all the fancy weapons systems and leather upholstery. It's speed that'll save your ass every time."

Lando had heard it all a thousand times before, but nodded dutifully. "That's right, Dad, and there's nothing faster than a Nister Needle."

Zack took a sip of beer and leaned back in his chair. "So, you've got a new ship but no spending money."

Lando nodded. "That's about the size of it. I thought I'd drop in, say hello, and look for a cargo."

Zack looked thoughtful. "Well, son, it just so happens that I'm right in the middle of a major scam and could use a little help. Interested?"

Lando frowned. "I don't need a handout, Dad. Thanks, but no thanks."

Zack laughed. "Handout? Did I say anything about a handout? Who taught you to be so pigheaded, anyway?"

Lando smiled. "It wasn't Mom, that's for sure."

The smile disappeared from Zack's face when he thought about his wife. "No, I guess it wasn't. Well, cut the crap and listen up. I need some help, and better you than a freelance gunner."

"Gunner? What for? How about 'speed is a smuggler's best friend,' and all that?"

Zack shrugged. "Every rule has its exception. This scam's different. Speed doesn't matter much. I don't *expect* trouble, but I don't trust the people involved, and it would be nice to have a backup."

Lando sipped his beer. There was an empty feeling in the pit of his stomach. There were two ways to make money in the smuggling business. You could take big chances and make big money, or take smaller chances and make smaller money. The second approach was generally the best. You lived longer and made more in the long run. Zack knew that. Hell, he had taught it to his son, but was now violating his own rule. Why?

Lando looked his father in the eyes. "This doesn't sound like you, Dad. It goes against everything you taught me. Why?"

Zack Lando opened his mouth, started to say something, and changed his mind. He laughed.

"You know what? I was just about to say something really stupid. Something along the lines of 'who are *you* to question *my* judgment?' But that would be stupid, since I was the one who taught you to question other people's motives in the first place. Well, the truth is that I'm taking a little more risk than usual."

Zack leaned forward across the table, his eyes full of excitement, his voice little more than a whisper. "This is the scam of a lifetime, son, the big one that makes all the others look like kid stuff, the score they'll remember a hundred years from now. Just think! Zack Lando scores big with his son at his side! Your mother would be proud!"

Lando nodded, and knew his father was wrong. His mother would've been scared and worried, anything but proud. She would have seen this for what it was.

Zack Lando hungered for something more than money, something harder to get, and something more lasting. He wanted smuggler immortality. A rep so big, so impressive, that he'd be known long after his death. A deity like Big Red, Arlow Sampson, or Istan Mugatha.

It had always been there, an almost worshipful respect for the best, and a desire to join their circle. But Zack was a conservative by nature, a man with a wife and son, a respected but second-echelon player.

Now Zack was making his move and Lando didn't like it. Everything was ass backwards. Sons were supposed to take chances, while fathers counseled caution.

Lando opened his mouth, and allowed it to close. One look in the older man's eyes told him it was hopeless. No amount of talk was going to change Zack's mind.

So Lando did the only thing he could do. He forced a smile, stuck out his hand, and said, "Okay, Dad. Count me in."

Exactly six days later Lando found himself standing on a white sandy beach watching a hovercraft speed away. Spray flew out and away from its duraplast skirts as it cleared the end of the reef and skittered into a turn. The roar of its engine dropped to a drone.

Lando turned towards his father. Like his son, Zack Lando was dressed in shorts and a T-shirt. The older man was sitting on a duffle bag and pretending to enjoy the sun.

The island was located near Ithro's equator and well within the sun belt. It was more than a thousand miles away from the spaceport where they had left *Wendy*, and hundreds of miles from the nearest habitation.

The hovercraft's skipper thought they were on a father-son outing, and had instructions to pick them up in eight days.

Lando gestured toward the pile of duffle bags and water-tight cases containing gear. "Okay, Dad. Give. What the hell are we doing on this island, and what's the camping gear for? You hate camping and always have."

Zack Lando did his best to look mysterious. Throughout the journey from Jethro, and the subsequent trip across Ithro's largest continent, he'd refused to provide his son with any real information. There was no real reason for this secrecy beyond the pleasure it gave Zack, and both of them knew it.

"All in good time, son, all in good time."

Zack made a show of wiping his brow. "Warm, isn't it? Let's take a dive. I hear there's some marvelous marine life around here."

Lando gave a sigh of exasperation and reached for his tanks. Fifteen minutes later the smuggler felt warm water slide across his skin as one world vanished and another appeared. The water was crystal clear and teeming with multicolored sea life.

Some was native to Ithro, like the school of two-heads off to his left, but the rest were specially designed Earth variants. Lando saw coral, some parrotfish, and beyond them a shadow that might have been a shark.

His father was just ahead, swimming strongly, kicking with his fins. A trail of silvery bubbles sailed back and passed Lando's head. There was something strange about his father's actions, something deliberate about the way he swam, as if he were heading somewhere definite rather than simply looking around.

Wait a minute . . . What the hell was that? Lando saw a large dark object that might have been rock except for a rather symmetrical shape. It looked familiar, but how could that be? Lando kicked harder as his father headed straight towards whatever the thing was.

Then Lando placed it, and couldn't believe his eyes. It was *Queenie!* His father's ship, some fifty feet underwater! What in the world?

Zack Lando swam straight for the ship's lock, motioned for his son to wait, and palmed the lock. It opened immediately. A light came on. A brightly colored gem fish swam out.

Lando followed his father into the lock. The outer door closed, the water level dropped, and their heads popped clear. Zack lifted his mask and Lando did likewise. The older man laughed. "You should see your expression!"

Lando shook his head in amazement. "This takes the cake, Dad. . . . I'd heard that the navy had submersible ships . . .

but I didn't know that *Queenie* qualified."

"And she didn't," Zack answered, gesturing toward the rest of the lock. "Not until I spent a half mil to convert her."

"A half mil?" Lando asked. "You put half a mil on a single scam? What is it? A cargo for some water world?"

Zack looked smug. "Nope. The cargo is for Ithro."

The last of the water gurgled down multiple drains. Lando looked confused, and was. "For Ithro? Then why are we hiding? Shouldn't we get the cargo first?"

Zack grinned. He stood and shrugged his tanks off.

"Nope. The cargo's aboard and has been for two months. That's the beauty of it. I have five million Imperials worth of Nerlinium Crystals sitting in the hold and no one the wiser."

Like everyone else in the empire, Lando knew that Nerlinium Crystals were the almost magic component that made faster-than-light travel a reality, and that a planet known as Molaria was their only known source.

And, like most of the other Imperial planets, Ithro had placed an extremely high duty on the crystals. So by buying them at the source, and smuggling them dirtside, a smuggler could make a rather tidy profit. No small task with Ithro's well-armed customs ships trying to catch you.

Lando shrugged his tanks off and heard them clang against the bulkhead as he stood up. "So, how did you trick the patrols?"

Zack palmed a switch. The inner hatch irised open. "I *didn't* trick the patrols. Not in the usual sense, at least. They're too damned good for that. I came in hard and heavy, fired a bunch of ECM stuff in every direction, and bulled my way past the weapons platforms. Great Sol, but you should've seen it! Missiles accelerating towards me, energy beams slicing this way and that, and *Queenie* dropping like a rock!"

Lando followed his father out of the lock. "So how did you escape?"

Zack laughed. "I didn't! I blew up about hundred miles from here. There was a big fire ball, wreckage all over the place, and no ship. Conclusion: target destroyed."

Lando shook his head in admiration. It was a beautiful scam. Right up there with the biggies. No wonder his father was proud.

Zack had dropped a specially designed bomb just above the

water. The device exploded, spread wreckage all around, and concealed *Queenie's* splashdown. Then, while the customs types scrambled to get to the scene, *Queenie* had scuttled along the bottom to her present hiding place, more than a hundred miles from the point of entry.

The two men left wet footprints down the shiny corridor. All around them could be heard the comforting murmur of air coming through ventilation ducts, the hum of fans, and the routine beeps that signaled an automated systems check.

Lando sniffed the air and smiled. *Queenie* smelled like home. He could detect the faint odor of his father's spicy gumbo, the lingering scent of an industrial-strength disinfectant, and something else that he remembered but couldn't quite identify.

Lando had done a lot of growing up inside *Queenie's* hull, and she evoked lots of memories. He'd hit his head on the junction box over to the right, helped his mother bend the color-coded conduit up ahead, been in charge of the big first aid kit that was clipped to the starboard bulkhead. A bit later he'd check to make sure it was properly stocked.

They passed through the lounge and the galley, and entered the control area. It was twice the size of *The Tink's* and nicely laid out. The main screen was filled with a beautiful scene of crystal-clear water, slowly moving fish, and gently swaying plants. It had a soothing effect, and Lando could have watched it for hours. He dropped into the co-pilot's chair and leaned back.

Zack ran a check on all of the ship's systems, nodded his head in satisfaction, and turned to his son. "So? What do you think?"

Lando smiled. "It's a great scam, Dad. One of the very best. You've got the goods, you've got them in place, and nobody knows. So what are you waiting for? And where do I come in? Or is this your way of giving me a handout?"

Zack grimaced. "I'll take the last question first. No, this is not a handout, I need your help. A cargo is one thing, but a well-heeled customer is another, and I found one through a third party. The deal was sealed just before you arrived on Jethro."

Lando shrugged. "Great. So what's the problem?"

Zack smiled slowly. "Do you remember a man named Dox Morlan?"

Lando frowned. "Some kind of official? Commerce Department or something like that?"

Zack nodded. "Try head of customs."

Lando's eyebrows shot up. "He's the customer?"

His father nodded soberly. "He's the one."

Lando thought about it. There had been rumors about Dox Morlan for a long time. Whispers of corruption, of dirty deeds, but nothing solid. So, was this what it seemed to be? A corrupt official using his position to make some extra money? Or just the reverse? An honest official out to nab a smuggler?

The delivery would be extremely dangerous. If Morlan was corrupt, then he could use his government resources to steal Zack's cargo. If he was honest, then the whole thing was a setup.

Lando's throat felt dry. He swallowed. "It stinks, Dad. What was it that you always said? 'Money doesn't mean much when you're dead'? Well, it's time to take some of your own advice."

Zack rubbed his jaw. "I've thought about it, son, believe me I have, and part of me wants to cut and run. But another part wants to see the whole thing through. This is the big one, son, the one that will make my rep, and fund my old age. If I give up and pass it by, I'll spend the rest of my life looking back over my shoulder."

There was a long silence as the two men looked at each other. One secure within the possibilities of youth, the other scared to let opportunities pass, afraid they wouldn't come again.

Lando was the first to speak. "So you're betting that Morlan is corrupt, and more than that, willing to do a straight deal."

Zack nodded. "My contacts tell me that he's as bent as a Zerk Monkey's tail. Not only that, but I've spoken with people who did deals with him, and were extremely pleased."

"Five million credit deals?"

Zack shrugged defensively. "No, but that doesn't mean anything."

"No," Lando admitted. "I suppose it doesn't."

"So you'll give me a hand?"

Lando forced a smile. "Sure, Dad. I'll give you a hand."

Zack beamed and jumped out of his chair. "I'll make us some lunch." His bare feet made a slapping noise as he headed for the galley.

Lando looked up at the main screen. A school of brightly colored fish exploded in every direction. A long torpedo-shaped body swept by, its dorsals cutting the water like knives, its long curving teeth visible behind thin lips. The smuggler shivered and turned away.

19

It was evening and the stars twinkled in the sky. A migratory bird, one of those genetically engineered for Ithro, gave its characteristic call. It was a long, lonely sound, made even more so by the fact that there were no females present to hear it, and wouldn't be for another five hundred miles.

There was activity deep underwater. The sea started to boil. Steam rose in a sudden rush. The bird blinked and shifted its weight from one leg to another. Fatigue fought the urge to take flight.

Fear won and the bird flapped away as a delta-shaped hunk of black metal broke the surface and hovered on roaring repulsors. Water ran off the thing's back in sheets, four pillars of steam pushed it upwards, and the air vibrated to its power.

Lando looked at his father with renewed respect. He'd never seen anyone attempt an underwater liftoff before, and Zack made it appear easy.

The older man checked his readouts, found everything to his liking, and switched to main drive. *Queenie* skimmed across the water, picked up speed, and lifted towards the sky.

Finally, when the ship was cruising at two hundred feet or so, they leveled out. The last thing Zack wanted to do was show up on radar.

"How far is it?"

Zack Lando eyed his scanners for any sign of company, found none, and spoke without turning his head. "The island is about two hundred miles due south. We'll be there in half an hour or so."

Lando felt the weight in his stomach grow even heavier. Every nerve in his body told him to give it up, to go somewhere else, to run for safety. He searched his father's face. If the other man had similar feelings, there was no sign of it in his expression. Determination, yes. Excitement, yes. But fear? No.

Lando forced his doubts down and back. The decision-making process was over. This was the time to prepare for whatever lay ahead. He brought *Queenie's* weapons systems on-line, ran them through an auto-check, and found everything to his liking. Energy cannon, missiles, and torpedos. All were ready to go.

Lando placed the weapons systems on STANDBY, checked to make sure that the co-pilot's position was off-line, and switched his controls to the simulation mode. An indicator light came on and the word "simulation" blinked green in front of him.

He opened a small storage compartment, removed a bundle of slippery black cloth, and shook it out. The fabric took the shape of a hood. There were no cutouts for mouth or eyes.

Lando slipped it over his head. The inside of the hood smelled like warm plastic and reminded him of years gone by. He'd spent hundreds, maybe thousands, of hours inside the simulation hood, dealing with everything from hyperspace jumps to galley fires.

An exact duplicate of *Queenie's* control systems and screens appeared in front of him. He turned his head to the left and a simulacrum called Instructor Jack nodded to him. He was holo-star handsome and extremely smug. Lando ignored the computerized image. Instructor Jack and he had never gotten along.

A menu of possibilities appeared. Lando used the button located on the top surface of his left-hand control stick to choose BATTLE, SIMULATED GROUND.

Another menu appeared. COMMAND, OR WEAPONS ONLY?

Lando chose WEAPONS ONLY. Simulated data and video flooded his screens. The smuggler saw a rocky landscape with twin moons rising to the east. Wait a minute, what was that? A hint of movement to the right? Maybe, but there was no confirmation on IR, so . . .

The world turned to flame. Instructor Jack screamed orders. A hundred dark forms rushed forward. Their energy weapons spat coherent light, missiles leaped away from their shoulders, and mortar rounds threw geysers of dirt into the air.

Lando found that the old skills were still there, that the simulator could still scare the hell out of him, and that Instructor Jack was still a pain in the ass.

When Lando pulled the hood off ten minutes later, he was soaked with sweat. His father glanced his way. There was tension around his eyes. "Welcome back. Ten to dirt. Stand by on weapons."

Lando did as he was told. All weapons were ready. Time slowed. Each second was a minute long. Zack watched the scanners. Sweat popped out on his forehead. He wiped it away.

A line of white breakers appeared and slid beneath them. *Queenie* dropped lower now, skimming above sandy desert, slowing as she neared the LZ.

A radio beacon beeped, and dots in the shape of a cross appeared in front of them. Zack killed the ship's forward speed, switched to repellors, and spoke from the corner of his mouth. "Watch the bastards, son. . . . One wrong move and hose 'em down."

Lando swallowed hard and felt bile at the back of his throat. He'd never seen his father this scared. Not the time on Dulo's moon, not when they lost the NAVCOMP halfway to Jethro, and not when the half-crazy merc attacked him with a force blade. It worried Lando to know that the man he'd always relied on, always looked up to, felt the same emotions that he did.

The red dots flattened and grew farther apart as the ship lowered itself onto the sand. It shifted under the landing jacks and held. Zack triggered a spot. It lit up the area in front of *Queenie's* lock. The red dots disappeared.

A male voice came over the speakers. "Hi there. Thanks for dropping in. Pop the cargo hatch and let's get this show on the road."

Zack spoke into a wireless headset as he released his harness. "Not so fast, my friend. Show me five big ones or the hatch stays closed."

"No problem," the voice replied. "I've got them right here. Cash certificates good anywhere in the empire. Come and get 'em."

There was something about the voice, something about the glib way the man talked, that set Lando's nerves on edge. "Stay in the ship, Dad . . . I don't like the way this guy sounds."

Zack Lando shook his head and touched the mute-switch on his headset. "We came for the money, remember? Now, watch the sensors, pop the rear hatch when I give the signal, and cook anything that looks weird."

Lando nodded as his father spoke. "That's a roger. I'm coming out."

Zack left the control room, and Lando turned his full attention to the sensors. IR showed a rather sizable blotch off to the right, just the right shape and size for a truck, and some smaller blobs that corresponded to people. Two of them to be exact.

The smuggler relaxed a little. The desert was as flat as a pancake. One vehicle, two people, and nowhere to hide. Things were looking up.

He kept a close watch on the sensors as Zack stepped out of lock, moved towards the ghostly blobs, and stopped. He had something in his hand. A suitcase of some sort.

"I'll be damned . . . Dox Morlan . . . so the rumors are true."

Lando could hear the other man's reply, thanks to his father's mike.

"They certainly are," Morlan replied cheerfully, "and in a month or two you'll be able to scream it from the rooftops. In the meantime, however, I won't mention your name if you don't mention mine."

Lando heard his father laugh. "Fair enough . . . now, where's the money?"

"Right here." Lando saw something hazy pass between the two figures. "Why don't you count it while my friend and I move the crystals out of your hold?"

"Seems fair," Zack replied evenly. *"Queenie . . . open the hold."*

Lando touched a key. The cargo hatch swung open and some indicator lights came on. Zack had addressed himself to the ship by prior agreement. The less Morlan knew about his opposition, the better.

Lando activated one of the hold's vid cameras. He saw that four trunk-sized cases had been secured to the deck. Two men appeared and headed straight for them.

One was short, stocky, and heavily armed. His head jerked this way and that like a bird on the watch for predators. He bent over a trunk, released a catch, and lifted the lid. Morlan? No, too twitchy.

The other man was taller, darkly good-looking, and visibly cheerful. He waved towards the monitor as if aware that Lando was watching, and undisturbed by it. Yes, this was Morlan. Lando was sure of it.

The smuggler felt a chill run down his spine as the men closed the trunk and moved it towards the hatch. Something was wrong. Very wrong.

Maybe Morlan did have plans to take his ill-gotten gains and flee for parts unknown, but why so casual about his identity? What if Zack were caught, or sold video of Morlan to the news nets, or a hundred other possibilities? No, it didn't add up. Morlan was too smart to make himself vulnerable.

Lando turned his full attention to the scanners. Normal, normal, normal. Everything looked so Sol damned normal. But it couldn't be. There had to be something unusual, something to give him a hint, something to tip Morlan's hand.

But try as he might, Lando found nothing at all. How about the truck? Was it loaded with mercs? Or concealing a missile launcher? Lando had just started to consider those possibilities when the transaction came to an end. The smuggler glanced at the security camera and found the hold was empty. He saw three blobs clustered around the back end of the truck.

"Well," Morlan said easily. "How's the count?"

"Five million," Zack Lando replied. "Right on the nose."

Morlan laughed. "That's good, because it's my money and I plan to spend every credit of it."

Everything happened at once. Zack Lando grabbed the case full of money and started to run. A third man popped up out of a hole in the sand and fired a shoulder-launched missile. It sailed into *Queenie's* cargo bay and blew up. An entire chorus of buzzers and Klaxons went off. Lights flashed red.

Lando gritted his teeth and concentrated on the heads-up display. He swiveled crosshairs to the left, heard a beep, and squeezed the trigger. Blue light passed through the short man and melted the sand beyond.

Lando looked at the IR screen. A blob was nearing the ship.

It fell as a line of white hit it from behind. The entire ship shook as something exploded.

Lando yelled for his father to get up, and swept the sand with blue fire. Morlan saw the beam coming and ran. It hit his feet first and ate him from below.

The man with the launcher fired again. He couldn't miss. This missile punched its way through a soft inner bulkhead and destroyed the drive room. A series of small explosions rocked the ship from side to side.

A prerecorded voice flooded the control room. It said, "Abandon ship, abandon ship, abandon ship," over and over again. The voice belonged to Lando's mother and he started to cry.

The man with the launcher stood straight up. The launcher felt warm against his cheek. Something winked blue. He ceased to exist.

Lando flipped a cover up, hit the button it had concealed, and heard the thump of a small explosion. He reached down to the left of his seat, found the handle, and gave it a twist. The emergency escape hatch fell open exactly the way it was supposed to.

The smuggler released his harness, stood up, and stepped through. It was a twelve-foot drop to the sand below. He got to his feet and started to run. He was a hundred and fifty feet away when *Queenie* blew up. The force of the blast knocked him off his feet.

He lay there for what seemed like hours but was a matter of only seconds. There was sand in his mouth and it stuck to his face where the tears had been. He spit it out and got to feet.

Dad . . . he had to find Dad . . . see if he was alive. He stumbled back towards the still-burning wreckage, finding Morlan's body first, and then his father's.

Zack was facedown near a pile of burning debris, a hole through his back, the case full of money only inches from his fingertips.

Lando kicked it out from under the wreckage and saw that it was charred. Another kick opened the lid. The five mil was a smoking mess.

The smuggler laughed, tried to stop, and found that he couldn't. Not until the laughter had turned to tears, and run their course.

Time passed and he staggered to his feet. By some miracle the truck stood untouched. There was a shovel clipped to its side. Lando took it and dug a grave for his father right next to the corpse of his beloved ship. The sand slid over and around his father as if welcoming him home.

On his way to the truck he saw the money case, stopped, and turned it upside down. A chunk of melted and half-melted plastic fell out and hit the sand. But wait! The bottommost layer of bills was untouched. Thirty or forty thousand, enough to get him off-planet, and far, far away. Lando peeled certificates away from the bottom of the case. His father's still-empty suitcase lay a few feet away. He grabbed it, stuffed the money inside, and looked around.

It would take them time to ID the bodies, get a make on *Queenie*, and backtrack from there. But the outfitter would talk, the Nister Needle would be found, and the whole thing would come together. Not the way it was, but the way it seemed to be.

Lando could see the headlines now: SMUGGLER MURDERS CUSTOMS OFFICIAL! It would be all over the place. They'd put a price on his head and dump his description into membanks all over the empire. Bounty hunters would add the particulars to the others they had memprinted inside their heads and the hunt would begin.

Lando looked up into the night sky. He saw hundreds, thousands, of stars. Each offered a place to hide. Maybe, just maybe, he'd find his way out of this mess. He turned his back on the past and headed for the truck.